It's a
Waverly Life

It's a Waverly Life

New Decade. New Job. New Shenanigans.

MARIA MURNANE

PUBLISHED BY

amazonencore

Printed in the United States of America.

Published by AmazonEncore
P.O. Box 400818
Las Vegas, NV 89140

ISBN-13: 9781612181493
ISBN-10: 161218149X

This book is dedicated to anyone who is still trying to figure it all out. (If you succeed, please give me a call.)

And to the munchkins who make life so much fun: Brookie, Jordo, Ryan (Bud), Lauren, Bellesters, and Jake. I love being your Auntie Ria.

Prologue

Time was quickly running out. What was I going to say? How could I explain last night? I squeezed the steering wheel and tried to think of something that would make sense to him. And to me.

I'm really sorry, Jake. I don't know what happened.

Jake, I'm so glad you came to see me, and I...I apologize for the way I reacted last night.

I suck, Jake.

His words snapped me out of my thoughts.

"Waverly, wasn't that the exit?"

I looked up and saw the airport signs in my rearview mirror. *Frick.*

"Oh gosh, I'm so sorry, Jake. You're okay on time, right?"

"Yeah, I'm fine. Are *you* fine?" He put his hand on my arm, and I swooned a little bit. God, he was attractive. And smart. And so nice to me, always. Even when I got nervous and acted like a lunatic.

"Yeah, sure, I'm good, just spaced out for a minute." I hoped he couldn't tell how rattled I was. What was wrong with me?

I took the next exit and looped around, and before I knew it we were pulling up to the terminal.

I still had no idea what to say.

I stopped the car in front of American Airlines and popped the trunk. "Are you sure you don't want me to come inside?" I looked at him and forced a smile. "I'm more than happy to."

He shook his head. "Two minutes after I get in there I'll be going through security, so it doesn't make a whole lot of sense."

I laughed. "Nothing I do these days seems to make a whole lot of sense." We both knew I was referring to more than just accompanying him into the airport.

He smiled and opened the passenger door without responding.

Good lord, I truly do suck.

I got out of the car. He set his bag on the sidewalk and shut the trunk.

This is your last chance, Waverly.

I swallowed. "Thanks for coming."

"It was my pleasure. Thanks for inviting me." He leaned down to hug me, then whispered into my ear. "It was great to see you, Waverly." His scent was intoxicating.

I held him tight, willing myself to explain—something, anything!—about my erratic behavior and the mixed messages I knew I was sending.

I took a deep breath.

Say something to let him know you care.

Nothing came out.

After a few moments of awkward silence, he let go of me and stood up straight. I gazed into his blue eyes and felt that pull I'd never felt before…even with Aaron.

I quickly looked at the ground.

He's amazing, Waverly. Stop being so scared!

"It was nice seeing you too," I finally whispered, keeping my eyes down, but I wasn't sure he heard me.

He brushed a strand of hair away from my forehead. His touch was warm and soft, just like I'd dreamed it would be last night. "Well, I guess I'd better get going."

"Okay, have a great flight home," I said softly.

Ugh.

"I'll call you, okay?"

I nodded and forced another smile. "You'd better."

I wanted him to know what was going through my head. I wanted him to know that I already missed him, that I didn't want our first weekend together to end like this.

My heart was aching, but my stupid brain overruled it.

I said nothing and got back in the car.

Please don't let this be over.

Chapter One

Two days to go.

It was only Wednesday, but I was already having trouble sleeping. For weeks I'd been counting down the days, just like little kids do with Christmas Eve, only sweeter. But also scarier, because Santa Claus can't break your heart.

I put on my black wool coat and headed out into the chilly November night to meet my friends a few blocks away at Dino's Pizza. On my way from my white Victorian apartment building, nestled on tree-lined Sacramento between Fillmore and Steiner, in Pacific Heights, the quaint San Francisco neighborhood I'd lived in for years, I admired the festive holiday decorations adorning the houses and shops. I smiled and thought for the millionth time how lucky I was to live in such a beautiful part of the world.

Dino's was decked out in white lights and filled with the aroma of hot, freshly made pizza dough. Andie and McKenna weren't there yet, so I sat at a table in the back and picked up the menu to ponder my options. Despite the fact that I'd eaten at Dino's approximately ten thousand times, not to mention the countless nights I'd ordered for delivery, I studied the menu every single time I went in there. I have no explanation for this behavior since I always ordered the same thing, but what can I say? I find comfort in tradition.

"Hey, lady, you waiting for us?"

As my friends approached the table, I rose to give them each a quick hug, standing on my tiptoes to reach the six-foot McKenna, then hunching over to embrace the five-foot-two Andie. As they settled into the chairs around me, Andie flagged the waiter and ordered three frosted mugs and a cold pitcher of Bud Light. It was one of our favorite Dino's rituals, perhaps even *the* favorite.

"It's good to see you, Wave." McKenna put her hand on my arm. "It seems like forever."

"That's what happens when you get married and move across the city. Darn that cute husband of yours, snatching you from us," I said.

"Oh please. Nob Hill is barely a mile away from here. It's just a fifteen-minute walk."

Andie poured us each a beer. "That's fifteen minutes too many. You know how I feel about exercise."

"You two are ridiculous," McKenna said.

"True, but it was more fun when you lived around the corner. It's not the same without you here," I said.

She reached over and squeezed my hand. "I know."

"What about *you*?" Andie said to me. "Jake lives in Atlanta. That might as well be a million miles away from here. If you leave, I'll be the only one left."

I coughed. "*Hello?* We just started dating. Long distance, I might add."

"So? He's a major hottie. If he asked you to move to Atlanta, would you go?"

I took a sip of my beer.

"Well?"

"I'm sorry, did you say something?"

Andie gave me a look. "Waverly…"

"What?"

"Jake *is* pretty cute," McKenna said.

"Yeah…he is." I could feel myself smile as I pictured his blue eyes.

"So Friday's the big trip?" McKenna said.

"It is indeed."

"Excellent. How long are you going to be there?"

"Three days."

"This will be the first time you've seen him in person since my wedding, right?"

I nodded and took a sip of my beer.

"Are you super excited?" Andie pushed her short blonde hair behind her ears and playfully bumped me with her knee.

I bit my lip and thought of our awkward goodbye at the airport. "Actually, I think I'm more nervous than excited."

"Why would you be nervous? You guys have such great chemistry," Andie said.

"I think that's *exactly* why I'm nervous."

"Understandable," McKenna said.

Andie patted the table with her hands. "Please. You shouldn't be thinking about nerves, my dear. You should be thinking about how much action you're going to get in those seventy-two hours."

"Andie!"

"Andie…" McKenna said.

"Well? Aren't I right?"

I blushed. "Maybe. We'll see."

"Wait a minute, back up." Andie moved a virtual stick shift into reverse. "What do you mean, *we'll see*. Haven't you slept with him yet?"

I shook my head.

"Really? Why not?"

"Have you ever noticed that you ask a lot of personal questions?"

She rolled her eyes. "Please, this is nothing. Now spill."

"Well, we've only spent the night together once, after Mackie's wedding." I swallowed and looked at my hands.

"And?" she said.

"And?" McKenna said.

"And…well, the thing is…" I kept staring at my hands.

"The thing is *what*?" they said simultaneously.

"Nothing happened," I said softly, looking up.

They said nothing.

"We had this amazing chemistry that had been building up ever since I met him at that trade show last year, but when we were finally in a position to act on it, I…I sort of…choked."

They both raised their eyebrows, sensing I had more to say.

"I'm not sure what happened, but once we were alone in the hotel room, I got really scared…and I froze."

"Ouch," Andie said.

"It was pretty bad…I barely even kissed him. He was really nice about it…but I think…I think I hurt his feelings."

McKenna squeezed my shoulder. "Oh sweetie, I'm sure he understands."

"I hope so."

"Why do you think you got so scared?" Andie asked.

"Honestly," my voice cracked a little bit as it turned into a whisper, "I think it was because I really…like him."

McKenna smiled. "But that's a good thing, Wave. It's been so long since you've really liked *anyone*."

"I know it has, but I'm having a hard time with it. I mean, even on the phone, I get flustered…and sometimes I think I end up coming across a bit…standoffish."

Andie sipped her beer. "That's totally understandable, given what you've been through."

"Having real feelings for someone again is much harder than I expected. I didn't think it would be so hard," I said.

"Have you told Jake about Aaron?" McKenna asked.

I scratched my neck. "He knows the basics. But I didn't go into the details."

"Then I'm sure he understands. I mean, he has a history too, right? We all do."

"I think he gets it. I mean, I hope he does…but…" My voice trailed off.

"But what?" Andie said.

"But what he doesn't know…is how afraid I am to let myself really fall for him. That if I do, he'll leave me like Aaron did."

McKenna shook her head. "You can't think that way."

I tried to smile and could feel a few tears welling up in my eyes. "I know I'm being ridiculous—Jake is *not* Aaron. But I'm finding it really hard to open up to him because I keep imagining the day when he tells me he doesn't want me anymore, then goes and marries someone else."

"McKenna's right. You can't think like that," Andie said.

"I just don't want to be…vulnerable again," I said softly. "Being vulnerable makes me feel…*weak*."

McKenna shook her head again. "Waverly, caring about someone does *not* mean you're weak. That's ridiculous."

I looked at her. "But if I let myself care about him, he can hurt me. And I don't think I can take being hurt again."

"So you're just going to go through life not caring about *anyone*?" she said. "*That's* your master plan?"

"I care about you two," I said.

McKenna sighed. "Okay, I know this may sound harsh, but that may be the dumbest thing you've ever said. Do you realize how dumb you sound right now?"

Andie laughed and looked at her. "Wow, that *was* sort of harsh. That totally sounded like something I would say, not you."

McKenna laughed too and narrowed her eyes at me. "Do you see what you've done to me? Do you see?"

"Just for the record, my exact words probably would have been, 'Suck it up and open the kimono,'" Andie said. "Just for the record."

"So noted," McKenna said.

I frowned at them. "Okay, fine, I'm being ridiculous. I admit it. It's just that I finally got to a place where I was happy being single, and BOOM, now my life is all complicated again." I spread my fingers in front of me.

Andie refilled our beers. "Look at it this way. If your life *weren't* complicated, it would be pretty boring. And that would make *you* pretty boring."

"Thanks for the pep talk. I think."

She turned to McKenna. "Hey, speaking of hooking up at your wedding, did I ever tell you I made out with one of Hunter's groomsmen?"

McKenna smiled. "Excellent. Which one?"

Andie shrugged. "God knows. It was an open bar. And get this—toward the end of the night, when it was clear I was going to end up with him, it dawned on me that I was wearing Spanx under my bridesmaid dress. Spanx, and only Spanx."

"Nothing else?" I said.

"Nothing else."

"Yikes. So what did you do?"

"I went to the ladies' room, took them off, and hid them in my pashmina."

"No way." McKenna laughed and covered her mouth with her hand.

"Way. I figured it was better to let him to think I'd gone commando than to let him see me in an enormous pair of flesh-colored spandex underwear. So from now on, if there is even a *remote* chance of hooking up, I will be wearing a thong underneath my Spanx."

"Thanks for that visual," I said.

"You're very welcome. So back to you and this weekend. Now *I* would sleep with a babe like Jake in a heartbeat, but you've got to do what's right for you."

"Thanks. I'll try to remember that."

"I'm sure you'll have a great time," McKenna said. "Just make it crystal clear that you're attracted to him. Guys need reassurance in that area, even more than we do."

Andie nodded. "This is true. Even hotties like Jake."

I crossed my arms. "At this point, I'm just hoping to get through the weekend without any embarrassing Waverly moments. Now that I'm thirty, I'm determined to reduce the number of those in my life."

"Good luck with that," Andie said. "Watch you trip on the sidewalk the *moment* we walk out of this place."

Chapter Two

"So you'll send it over by five?" Ivy said.

I took a sip of hazelnut coffee and adjusted the wireless earpiece to my phone. "Yep. I'm almost done, just putting on the final touches. I hope Larry likes it." It was around two o'clock the next afternoon, and I was sitting at my desk in my home office, editing my column.

"I'm sure he will. I know you've only written a couple of pieces so far, but they've been a big hit around here." Ivy was an editorial assistant at the *San Francisco Sun* daily newspaper.

"Really?"

"Oh yes. They've made us laugh amid all the depressing news we have to cover."

I smiled. "I'm so glad to hear that. I love writing them."

"Get any good e-mails this week?"

"Oh yes, a virtual mountain of bad date stories. One woman down in San Jose wrote that a guy took her to Chuck E. Cheese's... on a first date."

"You're kidding."

"Nope, and he'd told her he was taking her somewhere special, so she was wearing a cute dress and heels."

"No way."

"She said when he pulled into the *strip mall*, she thought he was stopping to ask for directions."

Ivy laughed. "Unbelievable."

"Exactly. I will never understand people."

In a fortunate turn of events, I'd recently been hired as a weekly columnist for the *Sun*. It all started after I'd quit my job in sports PR and launched a line of "just because" greeting cards for women called "Honey Notes." To my surprise, the cards took off, even landing in *People* magazine. When the features editor at the *Sun* called and offered me a position as a humorous relationship advice columnist, I thought it would be a fun diversion as I figured out my next career move. Who knows—maybe I'd even *learn* something. I had one high school boyfriend, one broken engagement, and about a billion bad dates to my name. I hardly felt qualified to be doling out advice, but then again, I guess I did have quite a bit of experience in the dating arena at this point.

I said goodbye to Ivy, then poured myself a fresh cup of coffee and scrolled through some new e-mails. By the time I finished reading the last one, from a freaked-out guy who had just discovered that a woman he'd been dating for two weeks had changed her Facebook profile to say *in a relationship* AND changed her picture to one of her with him, I was dabbing tears with a tissue, laughing and cringing. Was I really getting paid to read these crazy stories? Who *were* these people?

I continued tinkering with my column for a while, then decided a chocolate break was in order. I grabbed a fleece and headed out the door to stroll around the block for some fresh air…and to buy a fat chocolate chip cookie at Peet's Coffee & Tea on the corner of Sacramento and Fillmore, a regular destination of mine conveniently located a mere half block away.

On my way home, I stopped to check my mailbox in the lobby of my building. My back was to the staircase when I heard an unfamiliar voice.

"Well, hello there, I was wondering when I'd meet you."

An older man with pitch black skin, dark-framed glasses, and white hair smiled down at me from about ten stairs up. He was wearing a gray fedora, a white-and-green checkered dress shirt, and dark green pants held up by a pair of black suspenders, a newspaper tucked under one arm. I'd never seen him before.

"Hi." I put the remainder of my cookie back in the bag and slid it into my pocket.

He slowly descended the remaining stairs, using the railing to steady himself. When he reached the bottom he took off his hat, then approached me and extended his hand. "Allow me to introduce myself. I'm Red Springfield, new to apartment 2A. I'm from Springfield, Missouri, and no, there's no relation." He laughed, displaying a row of bright white teeth. I wondered what kind of toothpaste he used.

I took his hand. "I'm Waverly Bryson. It's nice to meet you, Mr. Springfield."

"Please, call me Red. Everyone calls me Red."

"Well, okay then, Red. You can call me Waverly. Everyone calls me Waverly."

He smiled and slightly bowed his head. "It's a pleasure to make your acquaintance, Miss Waverly. I saw your name on the mailbox and have been looking forward to meeting you. That's a lovely name you have there."

I laughed. "Lovely? That's a new one, but thanks. What brings you to San Francisco?"

"Family." He didn't elaborate, so I didn't ask.

"When did you move in?"

"Last month."

"Really? Last month?" It amazed me how I hardly ever saw my neighbors. After nearly nine years in the building, I still felt like I was the only person there who ever did laundry.

"Yes, my dear, nearly four weeks now." He pulled an envelope from his pocket and handed it to me. "Curious that I should meet you today, because I just received this letter in my mailbox. I was on my way down to give it to you, in fact."

"A letter for me?" I never got letters. "Is it junk mail?"

He chuckled. "I didn't open it, my dear."

I glanced at the envelope, addressed to me in bright red ink. I didn't recognize the handwriting, and there was no return address. Maybe it was from Jake? *Who writes letters anymore?*

"Thanks, Mr. Springfield." I was drawn to his brown eyes, which looked friendly and familiar, almost as if I'd seen them somewhere before.

"Please, call me Red."

"Oops, I mean thanks, Red."

He smiled. "My pleasure, Miss Waverly. It's time for my crossword now." He patted the newspaper under his arm. "I hope to bump into you again soon." He put his fedora back on, tipped his head slightly, and headed out the door.

Back in my apartment, I opened the envelope and pulled out a single piece of paper. One word was written in red, in the same neat handwriting:

Be

Be?

Be what?

I squinted at the paper. It had to be from a reader of my column, but who? I tried not to think about the fact that whoever had sent it knew where I lived. Sort of creepy, but I guess that comes with the territory when you put your name out there in public.

I tucked the letter into a drawer in my office, then sat down, finished my cookie, and e-mailed my column off to Ivy. I leaned back in my chair and glanced over at my calendar.

Just a few more hours until I see him.

* * *

That night I couldn't sleep. My flight to Atlanta was at eight, which meant I had to get up at five if I wanted to take a shower. I watched the clock beside my bed. *One fourteen.* I never slept well before an early flight, the fear of oversleeping always weaving its way into anxiety-riddled dreams. Add to that the anxiety of seeing Jake again, and I might as well have gotten out of bed and started running laps.

I closed my eyes and tried to focus on the weekend ahead.

Jake McIntyre.

I'd met him at a tradeshow party about a year earlier, back when I was still working at KA Marketing. My fiancé Aaron had called off our wedding only a year before that, and Jake was the first person I'd felt a true connection with since the whole debacle. He was a physical therapist for the Atlanta Hawks, himself a former Duke basketball player. We ran into each other a few times in the months that followed at various work-related events around the country, and though I was usually too tongue-tied around him to speak coherently, he didn't seem deterred by my awkwardness. Even though I'd only seen him intermittently, there was an undeniable chemistry there. Although at first I was convinced I was the only one feeling it, I was wrong (lucky for me). Our flirtatious banter evolved over time, and after yet another unexpected encounter, this time on a warm night in New York, he finally kissed me. For that brief moment, I think I forgot my own name.

That was two weeks before McKenna's wedding. My fear of getting hurt waned briefly in the afterglow of the kiss, so I rolled the dice and invited him to fly out to California and be my date. Everything that day and into the evening went perfectly—until I froze and screwed it up. And now my romantic pessimism was making an unfortunate comeback. *Ugh.*

My mind wandered to our contact since that awkward good-bye. Our interaction had gradually turned playful again, and he'd finally invited me to visit for what I was hoping would be a complete do-over. I was so grateful for a second chance, because I could feel in my bones that he was worth caring for. *Really* worth caring for.

After a while I opened my eyes and checked the clock on my nightstand.

Two twenty-three.

Ouch.

Thank God for coffee.

* * *

Eleven hours later I was in the restroom at the Atlanta airport, standing in front of the mirror and trying—unsuccessfully—to camouflage the puffy dark circles under my eyes.

"Maybe I could wear sunglasses all weekend?" I said to my reflection.

"Excuse me?" A plump, gray-haired woman at the adjacent sink gave me a confused glance.

"Sorry, just talking to myself." I grimaced as I dug through my makeup kit. "I didn't sleep very much last night, and now I'm paying for it."

"Sugar, you look lovely," she said with a smile on her way out.

I love Southern hospitality.

I pulled my long, dark hair out of my low ponytail and brushed it, then put on some sheer plum lipstick. Maybe that would distract attention from the puff? I stood up straight, smoothed my hands over my jeans, and took a deep breath.

Keep it together.

I checked to make sure I had nothing stuck in my teeth, then grabbed the handle of my carry-on and headed out the door.

* * *

I saw him before he saw me. He was leaning against the passenger door of a dark green Tahoe, scrolling through messages on his phone. His sunglasses were perched on top of his thick, wavy brown hair. He wore a khaki canvas jacket over a lightweight blue V-neck sweater and white collared shirt.

So cute.

"Hey there, stranger," I said.

He looked up and broke into a grin. "Hey you, come here." He opened his arms, and I trotted over to hug him. His blue eyes were as gorgeous as I remembered.

"Mmm, you smell good," he whispered into my hair. "Really good."

"So do you," I whispered back and lifted my head to kiss him. Good thing his arms were around me, because when our lips touched I think my knees buckled a bit. Now *that* would have been embarrassing.

The ice was broken. Thank God.

"Welcome to Atlanta." He grabbed my bag and opened the back hatch of his car. "I'm sorry it's so cold here."

I laughed. "Cold? It's got to be sixty degrees out. That's like a heat wave in San Francisco, remember?"

He opened the passenger door for me. "Ah, yes, how could I forget? Wasn't the cold weather in San Francisco the topic of our first conversation?"

"Indeed it was. That, followed by a discussion of why men around the globe continue to wear jean shorts."

When we got in the car, he reached over and lightly caressed my cheek. "I'm glad you're here."

I smiled. "Me too." His touch was gentle and warm, and suddenly I was even more nervous than I thought I'd be. *Don't freak out on him again.*

We drove from the airport into the late afternoon sun, first chatting about my flight, then his latest developments at work, then the Hawks game the following evening. I wasn't much of a basketball fan, but he had courtside seats for us. He'd be with the team during warm-ups and halftime and timeouts, but unless someone got hurt, he'd be able to sit with me the rest of the time. How could I not enjoy *that?*

"What's going on with the Honey Notes? Are they still flying off the shelves?"

I shook my head. "They're *on* the shelves, but not exactly flying off them anymore. Still, enough to pay the bills for now."

"How do you feel about that?"

"I think I need to come up with something new, but I don't know what it is yet."

"Do you have any ideas?"

I nodded. "I've been thinking about the idea of new ideas."

He laughed. "What?"

I cleared my throat. "I guess you could say I'm in the idea stage. There's just not much on the stage yet. So how about you? Seen any crazy ankle sprains lately?"

He laughed. "Are you changing the subject on me?"

"You catch on fast, Mr. McIntyre." I grinned at him.

He briefly removed his hands from the steering wheel. "Okay, okay, I'll back off the Honey questions. What about the newspaper column? How's that going?" We were driving by yet another identical strip mall. I made a mental note to count the number of T.G.I. Friday's I saw during the weekend.

I smoothed my hair with my hand. "I don't see a Pulitzer Prize in my future, but so far, Honey on Your Mind has been a lot of fun. It's amazing what people write to me, Jake. I mean, they share some nutty stories."

"Yeah? Like what?"

I spread my hands wide in front of me. "Like *everything.* Some of them hold nothing back in their e-mails. It's like they're the same people who post what they ate for breakfast on Facebook. I mean, who CARES what you ate for breakfast? WE DON'T CARE."

"Honestly, I think you should learn to enjoy knowing what people had for breakfast."

I looked at him. "What?"

"I made a tasty omelet today, red peppers and jack cheese, some nice onions in there. Even posted a photo of it online."

I rolled my eyes. "Please, like you even have a Facebook account. You barely use e-mail."

"Well maybe I'll just have to get one. And that reminds me, I need to tweet about that omelet when we get to my place."

I pointed at him. "Don't go there, Mr. McIntyre. No tweeting, or you can turn around right now and take me back to the airport. I'm serious."

"No can do, Miss Bryson. I've got you all to myself until Sunday, and I don't plan to let you go a minute earlier."

I could feel myself blushing. "You don't?"

"I don't."

I smiled and looked out the window. We were passing the eighteenth strip mall, the eighteenth T.G.I. Friday's. I stole a peek at Jake and thought about the weekend ahead. *Thank God it's Friday,* I thought.

* * *

Fifteen minutes later, we pulled up to a tidy, white Tudor-style house in a quaint part of Atlanta Jake told me was called Virginia Highlands. The house had brown shutters and a real mailbox on the sidewalk. He got out of the car to grab my bag, and for a moment I stayed in the passenger seat, studying the house. I'd known he lived a few miles outside of downtown, but I was unexpectedly struck by the difference in our living arrangements. He was a full-fledged homeowner. I was a perennial renter. He had a driveway, a garage, a front yard, *and* a backyard. I shared a coin-operated washer and dryer with the strangers in my building.

Although I was only three years younger than he was, I suddenly felt like he was a whole lot older.

Jake McIntyre was already an adult. Waverly Bryson was still trying to become one.

"Hey, you there?" He tapped on the passenger window and opened the door, snapping me out of my thoughts.

I blinked. "Sorry, I spaced for a minute. I love your house, Jake. It's really pretty."

"It's not fancy, but it's perfect for me. I'll give you the grand tour when we get inside."

We crossed the stone walkway to the front door, which he held open for me to pass through. I stepped inside the foyer and took a look around. The house wasn't huge, but the ceilings were very high, so it made everything look bigger. The walls were a pale beige with crisp white crown moldings, and the handsome oak furniture reminded me of a Restoration Hardware store. The place smelled a bit like Pine-Sol—I wondered if it had just been cleaned.

I loved it.

Jake walked into the living room and set my bag down on the dark hardwood floor. He took his coat off and tossed it on the couch, then began to turn in circles, pointing to the various rooms around him.

"Living room, kitchen, dining room, bedroom, bedroom, office, garage, backyard. There you go, the grand tour of Chez McIntyre." He took a little bow.

"Well done. How much do I owe you for that?"

"Come over here, and I'll tell you."

I slowly stepped toward him, and he put his arms around me. "I'm glad you're here, Waverly."

"Me too," I said softly, lifting my head.

I closed my eyes as he leaned down to kiss me. I could feel my face flush the moment our lips touched, and the floor underneath me went a little wobbly again. I breathed in the scent of his skin and kissed him back, melting into his warm lips.

When we finally broke apart, I stood back and exhaled.

"That was quite a welcome."

He pushed a loose strand of hair behind my ear and gently kissed the top of my head. "Are you hungry? Did you eat lunch on the plane?"

"Yes to hungry, no to lunch. Shame on those airlines for not feeding us high-calorie, highly processed food anymore. I did buy a high-calorie, highly processed poppy seed muffin at the airport for breakfast though. It was yummy."

"There's a little Italian place not too far from here that I've been wanting to check out. You game?"

"Sir, I'm game for anything." I pretended to swing a bat.

He scratched his eyebrow. "Did you just pretend to swing a bat?"

"Apparently I did."

"I'm guessing you've had a lot of coffee today?"

"Indeed I have. I think maybe it's time to switch to wine."

He picked up my bag. "I can help with that. Let me put this in the guest bedroom and pour you a glass. I need to make a few work calls before we head out. Do you want to take a shower or anything?"

I put my hands on my hips. "Are you saying I look dirty?"

"I'm not answering that."

"Oh my God, you totally think I look dirty!"

He laughed and disappeared into a bedroom, then quickly reappeared and walked past me. "You're crazy. Red or white?"

I followed him into the kitchen. "I swear I took a shower this morning. Damn recycled airplane air. And red please."

He opened a bottle of merlot and poured me a glass, then handed it to me and put a hand on my head. "Make yourself at home, okay? I'll be back in about ten minutes."

I pointed at him and walked toward the guest room to change. "Okay, but I'm not taking another shower."

* * *

"What do you think of Atlanta so far?" Jake asked as he refilled my wine goblet with pinot noir. Classical music played lightly in the background of the quiet, dimly lit restaurant.

I took a sip and set the glass down. "So far it's great, but to be honest, I'm a little disappointed that you chose this place for dinner." I gazed at a beautiful painting of Venice on the wall.

"You don't like it?" He seemed surprised.

"Well, the food was really good, but...the ambiance is so... charming and warm...and so...well...romantic."

He laughed. "And you have a problem with that *why*?"

I played with my earring. "It's just that, well, after driving by so many strip malls on the way from the airport, I sort of had my heart set on T.G.I. Friday's. That's all."

"Did you just say *T.G.I. Friday's*?"

I laughed. "Kidding."

"I figured."

"Being back in Atlanta makes me think of Shane. Have you seen him and Kristina lately?" Shane, a star player for the New York Knicks, had been Jake's roommate at Duke and was also a former client of mine.

He shook his head. "We don't play the Knicks until February. I'm sure we'll grab dinner or something when he's down here for that though. We usually do."

"Too bad you aren't playing them tomorrow night. That would have been perfect."

"True, but..."

"But what?"

"But then we'd spend the evening with Shane, talking about college basketball and the good ol' days, plus how you and he used to work together on that shoe campaign. And that would mean I wouldn't be having dinner *alone* with you."

I blushed. "Oh."

"I'll catch him in February. So tell me more about this column you're writing. You're having fun with it?"

"I am. I'm not exactly sure what I'm doing yet, but I'm definitely having fun doing it, whatever *it* is."

"That's the spirit."

I took a sip of my wine. "I mean, it's supposed to be an advice column, but most of the people who e-mail me don't even ask a question, Jake. They just send me these insane stories. Want to hear one?"

"Sure."

I put my glass down and closed my eyes for a moment, then opened them and leaned toward him. "Okay, okay, I've got a good one for you." I lowered my voice.

"Why do I feel like I'm about to hear something illegal?"

I laughed. "Please. So listen to this. This guy's wife pocket-dialed him when her phone fell out of her purse."

"Scandalous."

"Ha. So get this—her phone fell out of her purse because her purse *fell off the bed*...when she was hooking up with another guy."

Jake laughed. "So he heard?"

I nodded. "He heard."

"That's brutal. Yet hilarious. Got any other good ones?"

"I've got tons."

"Well?"

I leaned toward him again. "One of my favorites just came in the other day. A woman in Belmont wrote to say she'd been dating a guy for five months…and just found out he lives in his car."

"He lives in his *car*?"

"He lives in his car."

"How did she not notice?"

I shrugged. "Apparently he told her his roommate was studying for the bar, so they could never go to his place."

"And she bought that for *five months*?"

I laughed. "Apparently she is pretty dumb."

"No kidding."

"So what about you? Got any crazy dating stories you'd care to share?"

He scratched his eyebrow. "Crazy? Hmm…I don't know if I'd say crazy. Maybe a little odd, though."

"Like what?"

"Like this one woman I went out with a couple times. On our second date we went out to Lake Lanier, so she was wearing a bikini."

I nodded.

"And I noticed that she had her name tattooed on her back."

My eyes got big. "She did not."

"She did."

"Her *own name*?"

He laughed. "And it was pretty big, too."

"Like how big?'

"Big." He held his hands about a foot apart. "It went all the way across her back: *Tiffany*."

"Oh my God. What is wrong with people?"

"I don't know," he said, still laughing.

"So did you go out with her again?"

"Oh no, that was the end of that."

"Thank God. Otherwise, I'd have to wonder about you."

"Wonder about *me*? I'm just hoping *you* don't reveal some crazy side this weekend."

I smiled and tilted my head to one side. "But don't you already think I'm a little crazy?"

"True, but you're good crazy. I like good crazy."

I pointed at him. "You be nice."

* * *

After dinner we took a stroll around Jake's neighborhood. It was a chilly night, but his warm arm around me more than made up for the nip in the air.

"Thanks for dinner." I leaned my head against his shoulder. "That was delicious."

"Better than T.G.I. Friday's?"

"Definitely, although I *am* a big fan of their chocolate peanut butter pie."

As soon as I said that, I stopped walking. "Oh my God, that reminds me, I have a joke for you."

"A joke about the chocolate peanut butter pie at T.G.I. Friday's?"

"Sort of."

"Okay then, let's hear it."

I held out both my hands in front of me. "Okay, so there are these two peanuts walking down a dark street."

He nodded.

"And one of them is assaulted."

He raised his eyebrows.

"You know, *assaulted, a salted*?"

He smiled but didn't laugh.

"Isn't that funny? I think it's hilarious."

He smiled again but still didn't laugh.

"You're laughing on the inside. I know you are."

"I think I'm laughing *at* you, not *with* you." He put his arm around me and squeezed, then steered me back toward his house.

"I hope your street isn't super dark. I wouldn't want us to be *a salted*, you know."

* * *

The closer we got to his house, the more nervous I got. *Don't flip out.*

We walked in silence to the front door, which once again he held open for me. He helped me with my coat, then removed his own and hung both on the rack in the foyer.

"You have really good manners. Has anyone ever told you that?"

He smiled. "A few people."

"Thanks again for dinner. I had a really nice time."

"It was my pleasure."

We stood in silence for a moment. Then he took a step toward me, and I could feel myself starting to sweat. When he reached me, he put his hands on my face and leaned down to kiss me softly on the lips. Once again, I was entranced by his scent. I kissed him back, and he moved his hands to my lower back.

Then, very slowly, he stepped toward his bedroom, pulling me with him.

"Come with me," he said softly.

I followed him to his room, and ten seconds later our shoes were off, along with his sweater and shirt. He took my hand and led me toward the bed. When we reached the edge, he cupped my face with his hands, then gently brushed his lips against mine. His kiss was soft and warm, and this time I could feel its effects not just in my legs, but all the way through to my toes.

Still kissing me, he moved his hands from my cheeks downward, his fingers softly dancing over my shoulders and arms until they reached my waist. He paused for a moment, then slid both hands under my shirt. His warm touch made me catch my breath.

"You okay?" he said, softly kissing my neck.

"Mm." This time, I was more than okay.

He kept one hand on my stomach and moved the other briefly upward to tug on the lace of my bra. He kissed me on the lips and quietly pulled my shirt over my head and tossed it to one side, pulling away from me only enough to let the fabric slide between us. He cupped my face again and deepened our kiss, his tongue intertwining with mine. I could feel my heart beat faster, wondering what he'd do next.

"Still good?" he whispered.

"Still good," I whispered back.

He slid one hand behind me to unhook my bra, then let that hand rest on the small of my back while moving the other in front to touch my breasts, all without breaking our kiss. I caught my breath again, and his body responded and pushed against me. His mouth covering mine, he slowly guided me backward against the bed. I could feel my feet coming off the ground, but he was supporting the weight of my body with his strong arms, so I didn't feel like I was falling. Before I knew it, I was lying on my back.

He perched himself above me on his elbows, breathing heavily when we finally came up for air.

"Nice moves, did you learn those at basketball camp?"

He laughed and kissed my neck. "You're beautiful."

"So are you."

"Are you sure you're okay with this?"

I smiled.

"You sure?"

"I'm sure. And Jake?"

"Yeah?"

"You might want to move my suitcase from the guest bed-room."

He laughed and kissed my neck again, then slowly moved one hand to the button of my jeans.

* * *

When I woke up the next morning, for about three seconds I forgot where I was. I opened my eyes and studied the unfamiliar ceiling.

Why am I on the wrong side of the bed?

Then I remembered.

I'm in Atlanta.

With Jake.

I turned my head to the right. He was lying on his back beside me, his bare chest gently rising and falling with each breath.

I sighed and smiled.

Even asleep, he's gorgeous. And he doesn't even snore.

I wondered how long I could stare at him without crossing the line between cute and creepy. After a few minutes I figured I was getting close, so I decided to get up and make coffee. I carefully slipped out of bed and tiptoed toward the guestroom. When I reached the door I glanced back at him for a moment, then set off to find my suitcase—and the pajamas I hadn't yet worn.

Jake's kitchen was airy and bright, with stainless steel appliances that looked brand new. I found the coffee in the freezer, then opened the cabinets as quietly as I could in search of the filters. As I filled the pot with water, I glanced out the window to the backyard. Gold and red leaves swirled in the air around a big oak tree. It looked cold outside.

Waiting for the coffee to brew, I wandered into the living room and plopped down on the couch, surprised that I was awake so early given the time difference. *Adrenaline*, I thought as I sorted through a basket full of magazines. I found the latest issue of *Newsweek* and was about to open it when the picture frames on the mantel caught my eye. I put down the magazine and stood up.

The photos included one of Jake's parents, one of his young nieces, and one of him and his siblings. There was also one of Jake giving a toast at what looked like his brother's wedding, as well as one of Jake on the basketball court in a Duke uniform. I picked that one up and smiled at it. *So handsome, even back then.*

At the end of the mantel was a group shot that looked like it had been taken fairly recently, in Hawaii or some other tropical paradise. It was the whole McIntyre clan, all sun-kissed and radiant.

"What a good-looking family," I said under my breath.

Then I noticed something, and I got a sick feeling in my stomach.

A woman standing next to Jake had her hand on his arm. And from the way she was touching him, I was pretty sure she wasn't his sister. Or his sister-in-law. Or his cousin. Or anyone else he wouldn't kiss.

I leaned closer and wondered who she was. She was tall and brunette and pretty. Together they looked like the prom king and queen.

I bit my lip and remembered seeing Jake with a date at my former boss's wedding nearly a year earlier. I hadn't gotten a close look at her, but she was tall and brunette and, at least from a distance, pretty. Very pretty.

Was this the same girl? Why was she in a framed picture on his mantel? Did that mean she was still…in the picture?

"Hey you, I wondered where you went." The sound of Jake's voice made me jump.

I turned around. He was standing outside his bedroom door wearing a pair of pajama pants and no shirt, his hair a bit disheveled.

"I didn't want to wake you, so I made coffee." I pointed to the kitchen. "I hope you don't mind." I also hoped the stress in my voice wasn't too obvious, but there was no way around the fact that I was anxious.

He walked toward me. "Did you make it strong? I need you on your toes today."

I admired the definition in his chest and abdomen and thought about the night we'd just spent together. "You do?"

"I do."

"And why is that?"

He put his arm around me and steered me into the kitchen. "Because Atlanta has a lot to offer, Miss Bryson."

"I guess we'll see about that," I said.

* * *

"Do you miss sports PR? We've never really talked about that." Jake poured me a fresh cup of coffee, which I immediately doctored up with cream and sugar. "Shane says you were really good at your job."

I stirred the spoon slowly. "Yes and no. I definitely miss the people, or at least some of them, but I certainly don't miss the stress of dealing with high-maintenance clients, even the male ones. I didn't realize *men* could be divas until I worked with professional athletes."

He laughed. "I hear you there. What about being the boss? Do you miss that?"

I smiled and shook my head. "I was never the boss, Jake. KA Marketing is a huge company."

"But you were a senior account director, right? So you were *someone's* boss."

"Okay, true."

"Do you miss anything about it?"

I cupped the steaming mug with both hands and held it under my chin. "I used to think I'd miss the prestige of the high-profile campaigns, but it turns out I don't."

He scratched his eyebrow. "Yeah, I know something about that. Working with celebrity athletes isn't always as glamorous as it sounds."

"Exactly. It was fun for a while, but there's got to be more to life than helping rich people get richer. I just felt like it was time to do something different."

"Something more fulfilling?"

I nodded.

"Like the Honey Notes?"

I nodded again. "I know I can't live off them forever, but I also think there's something more that I could do with the idea *behind* them, if that makes sense. I feel like something's there, but I just don't know what it is yet."

"Something tells me you'll figure it out."

"You think?"

"I think."

"Thanks. At least *one* thing I've figured out is that I'm not so worried about how things look anymore. Now I'm more concerned with how they feel. I know that sounds a little new age-y, but I guess this is the new Waverly."

"And how do they feel now that you're in Atlanta?" He reached across the kitchen table and took my hand. The quick change of subject surprised me, and for a moment I couldn't bring myself to make eye contact with him.

Tell him how you feel, Waverly.

I wanted to, but suddenly all I could think about was the woman in the photo.

I feel vulnerable, I wanted to say. *I feel like I'm not as together as you think I am. I feel scared that if I let you in, you're going to break my heart like Aaron did.*

I wanted to open up. I really did.

But I choked and poured ice water on the moment.

"Things feel *chilly* in here, Mr. McIntyre." I pulled my hand away and playfully rumpled his hair, then stood up and wrapped my arms around myself. "I'm going to get a sweater."

Chapter Three

"Tell us everything. Leave nothing out." Andie spread her hands on the deli table between us.

"I can't tell you *everything*. Gory details are your style, not mine."

McKenna put a hand on Andie's shoulder and nodded. "It's called a filter."

Andie shrugged. "Fine, fine, just give us the highlights. Did you sleep with him?"

"Yes."

"And was it good?"

I picked up a forkful of Caesar salad. "Yes."

"How good?"

I smiled.

Andie pumped her fist, then gave McKenna a high-five. "I knew it! He's too good-looking for it not to be good."

I filled them in on the basics of the weekend, glossing over the steamy parts that were burned into my memory. Saturday before the Hawks game Jake had taken me to see the Botanical Gardens and Piedmont Park, and we'd spent most of Sunday wandering hand in hand around the Little Five Points neighborhood before my flight home. I was fascinated by Little Five Points, a funky section of town filled with indie cafés and artsy boutiques that made me feel even less hip than I normally did. My favorite part was a popular burger place called the Vortex Bar and Grill. The entrance is literally a giant skull, and the restaurant's slogan is "Because it's not too late to start wasting your life." We even came across a couple tattoo parlors along the way. (Jake suggested I get my name inked across the back of my neck.)

McKenna took a sip of her Diet Coke. "So how did you leave it? When's the next chapter of this budding romance going to take place?"

Andie nodded. "Inquiring minds want to know."

I bit my lip. "I'm not sure. He has a crazy schedule with the NBA season in full swing, and I'm not exactly flush with cash these days to go flying all over the place. But when he kissed me goodbye, it definitely didn't feel like the end, for either of us. We just never quite defined the terms."

"You didn't talk about it?" McKenna said.

I shook my head. "Honestly now, I have no idea what to expect."

"Did he bring it up?" Andie said.

"I think he started to on Saturday morning, but I changed the subject."

McKenna looked up from her plate. "Why?"

I picked at my salad. "Because...I saw a picture of him with another girl."

They both raised their eyebrows.

"It was framed, on the mantel in his living room. And it was *recent.*"

"Not his sister?" Andie said.

"I don't think so."

"Cousin?" McKenna said.

"I doubt it. She had her hand on his arm."

"Hmm..." Andie said.

"Exactly."

"Hmm..." McKenna said.

"Andie already said that."

She laughed. "I know, just processing. You didn't ask who it was?"

"I was too scared of what the answer might be."

McKenna frowned. "Waverly, we've already talked about this. You can't let fear stop you from getting close to him."

"I know, I know. And we did talk about some personal stuff, so I'm making progress. I think that was just a minor setback in an otherwise great weekend."

"So he knows you really like him?" Andie said.

"I think so."

McKenna narrowed her eyes. "Did you *tell* him so?"

"I may not have used those exact words, but I'm pretty sure he knows. I mean, he *must* know, right?"

She shook her head. "You'd better make *really sure* he knows, Wave. I know you think of him as some sort of superhero, but he's not a mind reader. Guys never are, even the smart ones."

I picked up my phone to check the time. "Oh man, I've gotta run. I need to be at a meeting in fifteen minutes."

Andie waved a hand in the air. "No problem. You don't have to be here for us to keep talking about you. Scoot."

I stood up and gave them each a quick hug, then bolted out the door.

* * *

I was conflicted about my new life as a freelancer. On the one hand, visiting the *San Francisco Sun* reminded me of how trapped I had felt when I had a regular job. I hated getting up early, especially on Mondays, and I could never take a nap in the middle of the day (one of my secret all-time favorite activities). But Jake had been right to suspect that a small part of me missed my former agency. Wandering the busy floors of the *Sun* made me nostalgic for the structure of an office, the camaraderie of being part of a team, the pride in *leading* a team. Plus I hadn't realized how much I'd miss the simple daily interaction with other human beings. It had only been a few months, and I was already contemplating getting a cat just to have someone to talk to. Yikes. So I was grateful for the Wednesday afternoon staff meeting at the *Sun*. It wasn't entirely necessary for me to attend, given that my column had nothing to do with news, but I wanted to make a good impression, and no one seemed to mind when I showed up every now and then.

"Hey, Waverly, how's it going?" Ivy looked up as I approached her desk. "Got bored at home?"

I crossed my arms and leaned over the low wall of her cube. "Exactly. What's new?"

She patted a huge stack of forms on her desk. "You're looking at it. Boring, boring, and more boring. Have I told you how much I hate this job?"

"Many times. You really need to quit."

"I know, I know. I'm just waiting for the right time."

"Still dreaming about photography?"

"Always."

"Don't wait too long. Life is too short to stay in a job you don't enjoy. Believe me, I know."

She started chewing on her fingernail and looked a bit stressed, so I decided to lighten up the conversation. "Hey, I got some great e-mails this morning."

"Yeah? Maybe some are from my friends. Seems like they're all dating crazies these days." She took off her horn-rimmed glasses and let them dangle around her neck on a retro silver chain. "I mean *lu-na-tics*."

I laughed. "There are definitely a lot of psychos out there. But on both sides of the chromosome. It's not just guys."

She nodded. "Oh believe me, I've done my share of stalking. Thank God that part of my life is over. I think my next tattoo might have to be Casey's name, just so he feels too guilty to break up with me."

"For real?" I remembered Jake's tattoo story. The thought of anyone's name tattooed on any body part was just...*ick*.

She shrugged. "Maybe. You can never underestimate the power of permanent ink. So give me a good story. Does anyone ever ask you for actual *advice*?"

I laughed. "Sometimes. Okay, I've got a good one. This girl who lives in Russian Hill e-mailed me yesterday to complain about a blind date she'd been on over the weekend at Houston's. She ordered a hamburger, and the guy ordered just a salad."

Ivy narrowed her eyes. "Just a salad?"

"Just a salad. And when she asked if that was all he was going to eat, he said he was a vegetarian."

She pushed a few red curls away from her eyes. "Okay..."

"So the food comes, and the guy starts eating his salad. The girl picks up her hamburger, and as soon as she takes a bite, he makes a mooing sound."

"A what?"

"A mooing sound, you know, like a cow."

"You're joking."

"Not joking. So she looks at him, and he says something along the lines of *I'm sorry, but I can't stop thinking about how you're eating a dead animal.*"

"There's no way that really happened."

"She could be making it up, of course. You never know."

Ivy put her glasses back on. "Okay, that's it. I'm getting Casey's name tattooed on my hip after work tonight. I'm locking that man *down*."

"You ladies talking about me again?"

We both turned our heads as Nick Prodromou, the *Sun*'s IT guy, approached Ivy's cube.

"Hi, Nick, how's it going?" I said.

He yawned. "It's going. Where there are computers, there's always a need for the master." He was wearing a yellow shirt that said, "EVEN AWESOME NEEDS TO SLEEP."

I laughed. "Nice shirt."

"Isn't it amazing? I bought it at Walgreens on the way to work this morning."

"You bought it this morning?" Ivy said.

"Indeed I did. My bowling league was last night, so I didn't have anything to wear today. I couldn't just show up to work in my jumpsuit."

Ivy and I exchanged glances.

"Come again?" I said.

"You wear a jumpsuit?" Ivy said.

"I'm confused," I said.

"The whole bowling team wears them. They're amazing. Last night my roommate had friends in town, and they were staying in my room, so I hooked up with this new girl on the team so I'd have somewhere to crash. I didn't have time to go home before work this morning, so I stopped at Walgreens and tossed the shirt on over the jumpsuit."

I stared at him. "You hooked up with a girl on your bowling team just so you could have a place to *sleep*?"

"What's wrong with that?"

"Do you even like her?"

He shrugged. "Warm bed."

"*Warm bed?* That's your answer?"

"Very warm, actually. I had to open a window."

I laughed. "Don't you think she'd be upset if she found out the real reason you hooked up with her?"

"Perhaps, but I'm going to file that under *Not My Problem*."

I turned back to Ivy. "What were we just talking about?"

She reached for her phone. "I'm scheduling that appointment right now."

* * *

Later that night, there was a message on my phone from Jake, but it was too late in Atlanta to call him back. The time difference made it hard to connect, but I secretly liked that we couldn't talk all the time. I was surprised at how much I thought about him, how often I wondered what his opinion on something would be, how many times I felt like calling just to say *I miss you*. But despite my feelings, I just wasn't ready to be in touch on a daily basis. I needed to keep some emotional distance, so while I always returned his calls, I tried to avoid jumping to the phone every time I wanted to hear his voice.

Besides, the messages meant that I could listen to his voice… over and over.

"Hey there, it's Jake. Just calling to say hi and see how your week's going. We lost tonight, but it wasn't all bad, no injuries. After the game I was approached by an executive of one of the pro leagues down in South America about a project…might be some opportunity for me there…just something to think about. Anyhow…give me a shout when you can…I…miss the smell of your hair."

I closed my eyes and smiled. For this Waverly moment, his voice was enough.

Chapter Four

A week or so later, I was working on my column when the phone rang. It was Scott Ryan, a reporter from *The Today Show* who had long ago transitioned from media contact to dear friend.

"Scotty! How are you? It's been ages!"

"I'm good, my love, hanging in there. The winters here are even worse than I'd feared."

"Super cold?"

"You have no idea. I thought Dallas was cold. New York takes *cold* to a whole new dimension."

"How's Tad?"

"He's great, even bought me a down sleeping bag in the shape of a coat as an early Christmas present. He doesn't want me to freeze to death after I up and moved here just to be with him. He said he'd feel guilty."

I laughed and picked up my coffee mug. "I'm sure he'd feel more than *guilty.*"

"He'd better, he'd better. So listen, my love, I don't have much time to chat, but I wanted to ask if you'd be up for putting your pretty face on the show. We could really use you."

I put the mug down. "The show?"

"Yes, my dear, the show."

"*The Today Show?*"

"The one and only."

"But why?"

"We're doing a Valentine's Day feature on relationships, and they want to have an expert or two on hand. Given that you're an advice columnist now *and* have a successful line of greeting cards for women, I suggested you, and they agreed."

"For real?"

"Of course. I think you'd be great, plus it would be great exposure for your new gig at the *Sun*, not to mention your Honey Notes."

"But Scotty, I don't *really* know anything about relationships."

He laughed. "Come on now, Waverly, give yourself some credit. You were in *People* magazine just a few months ago. To a lot of people, that makes you a minor celebrity, regardless of your credentials."

"What would I have to do? What would they ask me?"

"It would be easy. Seriously, a piece of cake. You'd have to give a few words of wisdom, maybe tell a disastrous dating story or two, and snap, you're done."

"That would be it?"

"That would be it. Plus you'd get a free trip to New York. How can you pass up a chance to come visit *me*?"

I laughed. "You make it sound so easy."

"It will be, I promise. Now say yes so I can get back to work."

Why not?

"Okay. Let's do it!"

"Beautiful. I'll be in touch with the details after the holidays. I look forward to seeing your lovely face in February."

"Bye, Scotty." I hung up the phone.

I was already nervous, but kind of excited too.

For a moment I thought about calling Jake to tell him, but instead I dialed McKenna's number.

* * *

That Saturday, for a change of scenery and some relaxing girl time, McKenna, Andie, and I drove fifteen minutes north of San Francisco to have lunch in the quaint town of Mill Valley. It was a crisp, clear day with very little wind, and the water beneath the Golden Gate Bridge was unusually placid. After a yummy lunch of hot tomato soup and sourdough bread at Depot, we wandered over to LaCoppa Coffee in the center of town. Andie bought us all hot chocolates and sat down across from us at a large oak table.

"So you're really going on *The Today Show*?"

I blew on my hot chocolate. "Is that nuts, or what?"

"You'll be great," McKenna said. "The camera loves you."

"Thanks, Mackie. I just hope I don't say something stupid. Live TV is a lot of pressure, and we know how I can be under pressure."

"Yeah, you do tend to choke under the spotlight," Andie said. "Remember when you were the emcee at that charity fashion show in college?"

"You mean the one where I *fell off the stage*? Do you think I will *ever* forget that?"

"That was an awesome Waverly moment. One of my all-time favorites."

McKenna laughed. "I'd totally forgotten about that. I think I choked on whatever I was eating at the time. Didn't you break your wrist?"

I held it up. "Sometimes I can still tell when it's going to rain."

Andie clapped her hands together. "I love it."

"Of course you do. My embarrassing Waverly moments are to you what your crazy Andie stories are to me. Speaking of which, do you have any good ones we haven't heard yet?"

"Actually, I do. Wanna hear it?" Then she lowered her voice. "It's pretty gross."

McKenna and I leaned in and lowered our voices too. "Yes," we said in unison.

She pushed her hair behind her ears. "Okay, here goes. Last week I had a date with this guy I met at an engagement party. His name is Will, and I cannot emphasize enough how good-looking he is."

"So how did you end up on a date with him?"

"Waverly!" McKenna hit my arm.

"Oops, sorry. I didn't mean it *that* way. You know what I meant, right, Andie?"

She shrugged. "No worries, I know I'm cute. So anyhow, after chatting with him at the party, he asked me out, and a few days later we went to an amazing dinner at Gary Danko. We shared a bottle of nice wine, had great conversation, great chemistry. I was totally into it."

"He took you to Gary Danko on a first date?" I raised my eyebrows.

"Affirmative."

"Wow, impressive."

"So?" McKenna said. "Then what happened?"

"After dinner he asked if I wanted to see his apartment in the Marina, and I said sure."

McKenna laughed. "Of course you did."

"Did you sleep with him?" I asked.

McKenna hit my arm again. "Catch up. Of course she did."

I rubbed my arm. "That hurt a little bit."

She looked back at Andie. "And?"

"And the sex was amazing—I mean *amazing*. Some of the best I've ever had."

"Excellent," McKenna said.

Andie took a sip of her hot chocolate. "It was awesome."

"So what happened then?" I asked.

She put her hot chocolate down. "So when it was over, we were both just lying there for a few minutes, trying to catch our breath."

"And?" McKenna said.

"We were totally basking in the afterglow."

"So…?" McKenna and I said in unison.

She put both her hands on the table. "And, unfortunately, ladies, that's where the magic ended."

We stared at her.

She leaned closer to us and lowered her voice again. "So once we finally caught our breath, we started cuddling and chatting…"

We kept staring.

"And then, literally two minutes later, I started to feel sick."

We said nothing.

"Like *stomach sick*, sick."

McKenna sat up straight. "Oh no."

"Oh yes. It was not good. And the problem was, he has a studio apartment, and the bathroom is like, pretty close to the bed."

"Oh no." I made a face.

"Oh yes. But I had no choice, I had to go in there."

She took another sip of her hot chocolate, and we waited.

She put her mug down on the table.

"Then I got diarrhea, and it was loud."

"OH MY GOD!" I covered my mouth with my hands.

"*So* loud. I'm sure he heard every squirt."

"NO WAY!" I yelled through both hands. I now had tears streaming down my face.

McKenna dabbed her own tears of laughter. "I can't believe it."

"Oh, believe it. I had to believe it myself for about three hours, which is how long it lasted."

"THREE HOURS?" I yelled again. "What did you eat?"

"God knows. And could you please keep it down? We're talking about diarrhea here."

"Has he called you since?" McKenna asked, still laughing.

Andie tilted her head to one side. "Would *you* call me after hearing that?"

McKenna scrunched up her face. "Ooooh, good point."

I finally calmed down enough to speak at a normal decibel, although I was still laughing. "I'm so sorry, Andie. That's really brutal."

"It's okay." She waved a hand in the air. "To be honest, it killed the romance for me as well. But I've moved on, because I'm a champion, and that's what champions do."

I moved to her side of the table and put my arm around her. "Andrea Barnett, I think we need to get you your own TV show."

"I would consider that."

Girlfriends are the best.

* * *

We left the café and strolled aimlessly around the cute downtown streets, window shopping and chatting more about the possibility of my having a monumental Waverly moment on *The Today Show*.

"What if I do something totally embarrassing? Do you know how many people watch *The Today Show*?"

"Yeah, but who *are* they?" Andie said. "I mean, do you know anyone who actually watches *The Today Show*? Doesn't everyone you know have a job?"

"This is true. Except for me, I guess."

"Please, stop complaining. You have a great job," McKenna said. "Just not a traditional one."

"Yeah, you're a *minor celebrity*. Isn't that what your TV friend Scotty called you?" Andie said.

I laughed. "You two are way too nice. I woke up at ten o'clock yesterday."

Andie nodded. "Just as a minor celebrity should. *Major* celebrities don't wake until after twelve. But seriously, who are the people who watch *The Today Show*? You know they're out there, but you don't know who they are."

I pointed at her. "That's how I feel about people who litter, or who don't wear seatbelts."

"Exactly. There you go."

As we headed back to the car, we passed a woman pushing a stroller. As soon as she was out of earshot, I turned to McKenna and Andie and lowered my voice.

"Did you guys *see* that?"

"What?" they both said.

"That lady who just passed us. Did you see that awful lace headband she had on her baby? Does she really think that looks *good*?"

"Baby headbands are child abuse," Andie said.

I held up my arms. "I don't understand what's going on with fashion these days. I went shopping last week and tried on what I thought was a long shirt to wear with jeans, but then I realized it was a dress. What is up with that? I mean, it barely covered my butt."

"That's the style right now," McKenna said.

"But why? I mean, literally, one tiny breeze comes along, and *HELLO, this is my butt*."

Andie shrugged. "Maybe you should start doing some lunges."

I looked at her. "You never stop, do you?"

McKenna laughed but didn't say anything.

I put my hand on my hip. "I mean, am I that old that I don't even know what's in style anymore? Is thirty really that old?"

"It's not about age, it's about attitude," Andie said. "But be careful. Once you stop paying attention, it's downhill *fast*. Next thing you know, you'll be wearing mom jeans."

"Hey now, I will *never* wear mom jeans. Do you hear me?"

"I'm just saying that maybe you should watch a little more MTV and a little less Lifetime."

I frowned. "But I love Lifetime."

"People who wear mom jeans watch Lifetime." She held her hand up to her stomach, then raised it way above her belly button.

"Ouch," I said.

She put her hands in a prayer position and bowed slightly. "My work is done here."

The three of us strolled in silence for a moment. Then McKenna, who had been unusually quiet all afternoon, stopped walking and turned to face us.

"I'll be wearing mom jeans soon."

"What?" Andie said.

McKenna smiled. "I mean…mom-to-be jeans."

"OH MY GOD!" I yelled at her. "You're pregnant!"

Her eyes welled up with tears. "Can you believe it?"

"OH MY GOD!" I yelled again. "You're going to be a mother! I'm going to be an auntie!"

We had a group hug for a moment, then I pulled away and looked at McKenna again. "If it's a girl, you're not going to make her wear a frilly headband, are you?"

She laughed. "Definitely not."

"Just checking." I bent down to pat her stomach. "Auntie Waverly's got your back, my little friend."

* * *

Later that evening, I stood in front of the bookcase along the back wall of my office. I reached up and ran my finger along the photo albums from high school and college.

I pulled down an album and returned to the living room, then sat cross-legged on the couch and opened it. In picture after picture, there she was: McKenna Taylor, my best friend since the first week in the dorms. As I turned the pages and laughed at bad outfit after bad outfit, awful haircut after terrible makeup job, she was by my side. I'd stood by hers at her wedding, when she became McKenna Taylor Kimball, and now she was going to become a mother.

Please don't leave San Francisco, I thought. I had so many friends who had done that in the past few years. Gotten married, had a baby, then moved to the suburbs to start the next chapter in their life. It was understandable, of course, but once they moved away, I rarely saw them. I didn't think I could handle it if McKenna left. She was more than a friend; she was a sister. And as an only child, that meant the world to me.

I knew change was a part of life, but I still hated it.

Chapter Five

After dinner the next evening, I curled up on the couch with a blanket and a bowl of chocolate chip ice cream to watch *The Fantasia Barrino Story*. It was on the Lifetime channel, of course, and I shed a few tears along the way. How can anyone not love watching sappy movies on Lifetime?

After Fantasia proved all the haters wrong and triumphed on *American Idol*, I picked up my phone and called Jake. It had been a few days since our last conversation, and I was excited to share the big news about McKenna and Hunter.

He answered on the second ring. "Hey you, it's good to hear your voice."

"Hey back." I smiled into the phone. "Is it too late to be calling?"

"Nah, it's good. Plus I'm in Utah right now, so it's only eleven o'clock here. We play the Jazz tomorrow night."

"That's right, I think you mentioned that. I can't keep track of your crazy schedule."

"There's always NBA dot com. It's really not that hard. And you seem to have a pretty busy schedule yourself these days."

I didn't say anything for a moment. Then I looked at the remote control sitting on my lap. *So busy.*

"Yeah, I guess so." *What is wrong with me?*

For another brief moment, there was silence. Then he spoke again.

"Did you have a good weekend?" I loved the natural ease of our banter, but our conversations about weekends could sometimes teeter on the brink of uncomfortable because we didn't address the fact that they might involve other people. I hadn't been dating anyone else, and I didn't really *think* he'd been dating anyone else, but I didn't know for sure. And for some reason, I didn't want to know, especially now that I'd seen that picture in his house. But despite my reservations, I couldn't get him out of my head.

"The weekend was pretty good." Then I told him about the call from Scotty and the Valentine's Day feature for *The Today Show*.

"Wow, first *People* magazine, and now this? Pretty soon you'll be on *Dancing with the Stars*."

"Please, you've seen me dance. You think America is ready for that?"

He laughed. "When are you flying to New York?"

"The day before the taping. I guess that means the day before Valentine's Day."

Suddenly, I didn't know what to say next. Is there anything more awkward than talking about Valentine's Day with a guy you've recently slept with for the first time?

I decided to change the subject.

"So hey, guess what else? McKenna's pregnant!" I said with way too much enthusiasm.

"Really? Already? That was fast." He sounded genuinely surprised.

Again, I didn't know what to say next. How quickly I'd managed to find something even *more* awkward to talk about with a guy I'd recently slept with for the first time.

"I know, but she and Hunter have been together forever, so they're ready. I think they pulled the goalie the night of the wedding."

He laughed. "Good for them. They'll make good parents."

"You think so?"

"I know so. I know I only saw them together once, but I could tell by the way they interacted with each other."

"Really?"

"Definitely. I pick up on that sort of thing pretty quickly. I guess it's the psych minor in me."

"You and your amateur psychoanalysis. It's always right on the money, though. Remember how you diagnosed my childhood angst the first time we met?"

He laughed. "I never claimed to be a professional. And everyone has childhood angst."

"Oh please, your family sounds perfect."

"Not always. Maybe you should come down to Florida to see what a McIntyre family holiday is like. That would give you the real picture."

I coughed and felt my cheeks get hot.

Did he just invite me to spend the holidays with his family?

I didn't respond.

I couldn't think of anything to say.

Nothing.

Say something, Waverly!

"So, um, how's your sister doing?" I asked.

He didn't reply immediately, although why would he after I'd changed the subject like that? Why was I acting so evasive? I wanted to say I would love to spend the holidays with him, that I would love to meet his family, but once again, my brain wasn't in sync with my big mouth.

"Natalie? She's good. She's not due until February, so her doctor gave her the green light to fly. Good thing, because my mom would throw a fit if the whole family weren't there, especially since my brother and his wife just had their twins."

"Seems like everyone is having babies these days," I blurted, suddenly regretting the comment. Why couldn't I stick to less awkward topics?

Again, he didn't respond for a moment. I pounded my forehead lightly with my fist. *You suck, Waverly.*

He broke the silence. "It'll be great having another kid in the mix. I love the older ones, but they can be little terrors. We're all hoping for a boy this time though. After four girls, it's time for some blue in the family. And I'm not just saying that because I went to Duke."

Another brief silence. *Snap out of it, Waverly.*

"You know, the Blue Devils?" he said.

I blinked. "I'm sorry, I spaced for a moment. Yes, Blue Devils, got it."

"So, I guess you're headed to Sacramento for Christmas?"

So much for that invitation.

I swallowed. "Yes, but just for a few hours. My dad has to work on Christmas Eve and Christmas night, so I'll drive to his place late Christmas morning to have lunch with him. Then I'll come back to San Francisco for dinner with McKenna and Hunter. Nothing too exciting. But then again, spending time with my dad isn't all that exciting." My mom died when I was just a baby, so Christmas was always just my Dad and me. The holiday tended to be quiet, relaxing, and for the most part joyful, yet a bit sad as well.

"Too much Scrabble for you?"

I laughed, feeling more like myself and less like an idiot, although at times I couldn't tell the difference. "Exactly. You can play only so much Scrabble before you have to use words to actually *talk* to each other, and that's not exactly my dad's strong suit. I've finally accepted it, though. I love him, but I definitely got my Chatty Cathy gene from my mom, or at least that's what my dad always says. According to him, she could talk the paint off a barn."

"I bet she was a pistol."

"Hey now, that's my dear departed mom you're talking about. Though I imagine you're probably correct, as always."

"Not always."

"I doubt that. You smart. Me not as smart."

He laughed. "Smartass. It's too bad that your dad has to work on Christmas, but it's good to hear that he's holding down a steady job after being a pro athlete. So many of the guys I work with didn't finish college, and it's not clear what they would do for a living if suddenly they couldn't play ball anymore."

"Hello? Don't you think they'd be busy figuring out how to spend their millions?"

He laughed again. "True. It's a different world now."

"Exactly. Unfortunately, even if my dad *had* made it to the big leagues, he played his baseball about thirty years too early to have that problem."

"But you're not bitter."

"Nah, who would want millions in a trust fund? That would totally suck. So hey, speaking of professional sports, tell me more about this South America thing you mentioned. Sounds exciting."

"It's Argentina. They've offered me a temporary stint in Buenos Aires. Apparently they need a physical therapist who's fluent in English because so many of the foreign players in the league don't speak Spanish."

"Jake *habla Español*?"

"*Un poco.*"

"*Muy bien.*"

"*Gracias.* I speak enough to get by."

I pulled my knees up to my chest. "Are you going to go?"

"I'm not sure. I had a great time when I visited Buenos Aires last summer, so it's tempting. But it wouldn't be for a couple months, which gives me some time to decide."

"You should totally go."

"I should?"

"Sure, why not?"

He didn't say anything.

I bit my lip. *Why did I say that?*

Still nothing.

"Maybe I'd even come visit you," I blurted. I tried to sound playful, hoping he couldn't tell how anxious I was.

"That's a long way away, Waverly." I wasn't sure if he meant distance or time, and suddenly I was full of doubt—*again.*

* * *

After I hung up the phone, I grabbed my coat and went for a walk, trying to process what had just happened. I thought about Jake constantly, yet every time he reached out to me, I pulled back in some way. Why was I so convinced he would hurt me? Did he even know how I felt about him?

I held my coat tight around me and walked down Fillmore Street toward Walgreens, suddenly craving chocolate. On the way I passed a new store that specialized in trendy baby clothes and furniture. I hadn't gone in there yet, but I assumed the entire inventory was overpriced, because everything in Pacific Heights is overpriced. Perhaps I could afford a cute outfit or two for baby Kimball, but probably not much else.

I stopped and peered into the dark window, thinking of the life growing inside McKenna, wondering what taking the next step in my own life would feel like, whatever that step was. Would knowing be more scary that not knowing? Was that what I was afraid of?

I peered into the darkness, but I couldn't see anything clearly.

Chapter Six

I had stayed up late on Christmas Eve watching TV, so I slept in on Christmas morning. Groggy and in need of holiday caffeine, I shuffled into the kitchen in my pajamas to put on a pot of coffee. Fresh mug in hand a few minutes later, I curled up on the couch to admire the pretty lights and decorations on my tree. It wasn't very big, but it was the perfect shape, and I loved it. Ever since I was a kid, I'd been obsessed with finding a flawlessly shaped Christmas tree, and after years of fruitless searching, I'd finally done it.

By ten thirty I was on the road. Traffic was light, and I tapped my fingers on the steering wheel and sang along to the Christmas carols on my way inland. I couldn't carry a tune to save my life, so I made a point of not singing under normal circumstances. But when the holidays rolled around, I merrily butchered my way through every catchy tune that came my way.

I pulled up to my dad's complex shortly after noon. He'd recently moved from a double-wide to a new place, and I was looking forward to seeing it. A one-bedroom apartment in Sacramento might not seem like luxury real estate to most people, but for my dad it was like being upgraded to first class.

I navigated through a maze of identical wood-shingled buildings until I found his unit in the back. I parked and climbed the stairs to the second floor, and just as I knocked I remembered the

Santa hats I'd brought in my purse. I pulled one out and quickly put it on before the door opened.

"Well hello there, Santa. Or should I call you Mrs. Claus?" he asked.

"Santa will do just fine. Merry Christmas, Dad. I brought you one, too." I pulled out the other hat for him. "*You* can be Mrs. Claus."

"Come on in, come on in." He put the hat on as I entered, then awkwardly patted my shoulder. That was the extent of our holiday embrace.

I quickly scanned the living room. It was nothing fancy, with plain brown carpet and little in the way of furniture, but it was clean, and, well, not a trailer, so I loved it. In the corner sat a small tree, even smaller than mine, neatly decorated with a single strand of white lights and just a few ornaments.

"I like your tree, Dad."

He smiled. "It's not much, but it's perfect for me. Let me show you around." I followed him down a narrow hall to peek in at the single sparsely decorated bedroom. On the way back to the living room I poked my head into the small but immaculate bathroom. Then he showed me the tidy little kitchen. It always impressed me how neat my dad was. Most men I knew were slobs. Then I thought about how neat Jake's house was too—and immediately felt a sting at the thought of him in Florida with his family, all the way across the country.

Through a screen door behind my dad I noticed a tiny deck overlooking a courtyard, which was filled with potted plants and flowers. Given how much he loved all things green, I was surprised he didn't grow his own Christmas tree.

"Can I get you something to drink? Lunch will be ready in about half an hour."

I shook my head. "No thanks. Well, actually, some water would be nice. I'm just going to wash my hands." On the way to the bathroom, I stopped to check out the framed photos in the hall. Most of them were of me as a kid. Me in a ballerina outfit. Me in a soccer uniform. Me in a leotard for gymnastics. Me holding a clarinet. Seems like I'd tried everything at least once, some things only once. I glanced back to my dad's Spartan living room. As a child it had never occurred to me how hard it must have been for him to fund the activities I'd treated so capriciously.

My eyes moved along the wall, then stopped at a photo of my parents on their wedding day. I'd always loved that photo. It had been ages since I'd seen it, because during the years my dad lived in the double-wide, he hadn't hung anything on the walls. They were both so happy, smiling widely for the camera. Eager to see what life had in store for them, for his baseball career, for their future.

Not knowing that cancer would soon take it all away.

Then I spotted another picture I hadn't seen since I was younger. It was of my dad and the rest of the AAA team for the San Jose Giants, smiling broadly at the prospect of the bright future ahead of them. I'd spent hours studying that photo as a little kid, wondering what would become of them all.

I looked back toward the living room again. My dad was sitting quietly in a chair, watching the Lakers game on TV.

Suddenly I wanted to hug him.

But I knew I wouldn't, because I never did.

* * *

"So you're enjoying the restaurant?"

He nodded. "I really am. Who would have thought? I may apply for an assistant manager position soon."

"That's great, Dad, really great."

We were sitting at his small dining room table, eating roasted turkey and mashed potatoes and watching the basketball game. Both of us still wore our Santa hats.

"Dad?"

He kept his eyes on the TV. "Yeah, baby?"

"Do you know what happened to the guys from your baseball team?"

"The Giants?"

"Yeah, from the picture on the wall. Do you still keep in touch with any of them?"

He shrugged, still looking at the TV. "One of the guys still writes now and then. He was the one who got me into Scrabble, actually."

I raised my eyebrows. "*That's* how you got into Scrabble?" Minor league baseball hardly seemed like a place to play Scrabble.

"Yep. And we were the only ones with kids back then, so we hung out a lot on the road and looked out for each other, to keep out of trouble, you know?"

I nodded. There was so much about my dad I *didn't* know.

He shrugged again, still looking at the TV. "Anyhow besides him, it seems like no one really writes letters anymore."

I smiled at the innocence of his comment. He had a cell phone, but for the most part he ignored modern communication. Our worlds were eternally intertwined, yet they barely intersected.

"I brought you something." I stood up and reached for my purse on the couch, removing a small box. "Merry Christmas, Dad. I hope you like it."

He took the box and unwrapped it, then slowly removed the lid. Inside was a Swiss Army knife I'd had engraved with his name on it. *Paul J. Bryson.*

"Baby, I love it." He turned it over in his hand and ran his fingers over it. "It's beautiful."

"Since you can already fix anything and everything, I figured with this in your pocket you could *really* fix anything and everything." I, on the other hand, could barely pound a nail straight. I pointed at him. "It's not fair that I managed not to inherit a single one of your MacGyver genes. Not to mention your athletic genes, which apparently went into the hamper and never came out."

He laughed. "You got your mother's brains and her looks, now that's for sure. So don't you be complaining." He stepped toward the tree, then leaned down and picked up a small package. "I've got something for you too." He handed it to me.

"Thanks, Dad. I love the wrapping paper." The thin, flat box was meticulously enveloped in shiny red with a silver ribbon. It reminded me of the Santa hats we were wearing.

I opened the box.

Inside was a thirty-dollar gift certificate to Olive Garden.

He smiled. "Merry Christmas, Waverly."

I smiled back. "Thanks, Dad."

I was trying not to laugh, trying not to cry, and feeling horrible for wanting to do both.

Chapter Seven

"I like it, like it, like it." Larry Bergman, the red-cheeked features editor at the *Sun*, tapped his chubby fingertips on his desk. "It's just what we need to bump up readership for your column. The advertisers will love it, which means our publisher will love it too. This is a great way to start off the year."

"I hope so." It was the first week of January. Larry had just returned from his vacation, so I'd finally brought up the *Today Show* opportunity.

"The column is doing okay locally." He leaned back in his chair and folded his arms to rest across his globular belly. "But we need to attract a readership that goes beyond the Bay Area. And being on national television will certainly help with that."

"I hope so." I quickly realized I'd already said that. It was amazing how inarticulate I could be at times, given that I was being paid to use…words.

"Did they give you any details?"

"Not many, but Scott Ryan said it would be a pretty straight-forward panel, probably just two or three of us. He thought they'd probably ask me to share an example or two of typical e-mails I get from readers, then offer a piece of advice for Valentine's Day."

Larry unwrapped a big piece of green taffy and popped it into his mouth. "I like it. You'll need to grab people's attention, make them want to check out the column, give that panel some *oompf.*"

He made fists with his chubby little hands, which made him look like a Cabbage Patch Kid. I wanted to hug him.

I stood up. "Will do. I certainly have enough material to consider. I got an e-mail this morning from a woman who was accused of cheating after she didn't respond to *ten* text messages from a guy she'd been on like three dates with. He'd sent them over the course of two hours on a Saturday afternoon, when her cell phone was turned off because she was at a movie. I swear, Larry, people are *crazy.*"

He shooed me out the door. "I like it. Now go make us proud, Waverly."

I saluted. "I'm on it."

On my way out of the building, I ran into Nick in the lobby. He was carrying a brown paper bag from Noah's Bagels and had on a light blue T-shirt with COUGAR BAIT emblazoned across the front.

"Walgreens?"

"T.J. Maxx."

"Nice."

"You know it."

"Don't you ever get in trouble for wearing stuff like that to work?"

"Are you serious? This is a *newspaper,* Waverly."

"So?"

"*So,* it's a paper dinosaur in a digital world. In the middle of *Silicon Valley,* of all places. They've got much bigger problems to worry about than my choice of office attire."

"Really? I didn't realize."

He laughed. "Don't you read the papers? Oh, wait, that's right, *no one does.*"

"Is it that bad?"

He shrugged. "I just know it's not good. But they need me, because I'm the only one around this place who knows anything about technology."

I smiled. "So it's all about Nick?"

He headed for the elevator. "You know it is. And don't think I don't have *that* on a tee shirt too."

As the doors closed behind him, I wondered if he was right. Was the *Sun* doomed? Was my column doomed? I pulled my phone out of my purse. This could be important, and I wanted to talk to someone about it. Someone who cared about me and my future.

I stared at the phone in my hand.

I'm calling Jake.

I squeezed the phone.

I'm totally calling him. I'm not calling McKenna or Andie this time.

I took a deep breath and dialed his number, then exhaled and smiled.

I did it!

I'm moving this relationship forward. I'm opening the kimono.

It went straight to voicemail, no ring.

Ugh, his phone is turned off.

I thought about leaving a message, but I couldn't think of something witty to say, and I wanted to be witty. I wanted to be charming. I wanted to be something completely different than what I was feeling at the moment.

Before his voicemail got to the beep, I hung up and called McKenna instead.

I'll call him tomorrow, I thought.

I stood there for a few moments, then slowly turned toward the bus stop. On the way I passed my favorite homeless person in San Francisco, the guy who carries a sign that says "I bet you can't hit me with a quarter." I smiled at him, then hurled a quarter in his direction. In a city where on any given day you are one hundred times more likely to be asked for spare change than for your phone number, you've got to reward anyone with the ingenuity to stand out like that.

I mean it. I'll really call Jake tomorrow, I thought again.

* * *

When I got back to my apartment, I picked up the phone to call Scotty.

"Okay, it's official. I'm in. They said yes."

"That's great news, sweetheart." Scotty was the only man I knew who could call me pet names without sounding patronizing or lecherous. I could practically feel his pretty green eyes sparkling through the phone.

"My editor really liked the idea." I leaned back in my chair, which creaked a bit. I made a mental note to put some WD-40 on it. Then I chuckled silently because I knew I never would.

"Of course he did. Everyone loves *The Today Show.*"

"I just hope I don't blurt out something ridiculous. I have a tendency to do that when I get nervous."

"Oh pumpkin, please, you'll do great."

"Fingers crossed. I've been reading through my *favorites* e-mail folder this afternoon, you know, to prepare something good, something really entertaining."

"Perfect, that's what you need to do."

"But I've got to tell you, Scotty, this is harder than I thought it would be."

"Harder? Why?"

"Because I have so much material here that I'm finding it hard to choose what to go with."

He laughed. "That good? Or should I say, that bad?"

"*So* bad. Wanna hear some?"

"Oh yes. Lay it on me."

"Okay." I sat up straight and put my hand over the mouse. "I'll read you a few short ones. You ready?"

"Ready."

"Okay, here goes: 'Dear Waverly, what the hell is wrong with men? My boyfriend of three years just broke up with me over e-mail. E-MAIL. After THREE YEARS. He hopes we can be friends. I hope he contracts E-coli.'"

"Oh my," Scotty said.

"Oh yes. Here's another one: 'Dear Waverly, I just found out the guy I've been dating seriously for five months has an estranged wife (AKA HE IS MARRIED). He told me this while we were on vacation together in Hawaii. He also slipped in that he has two kids. Then he proposed. I proposed that he get his lying ass on a plane back to Oakland.'"

"Ouch."

"Yep. And check this one out: 'Dear Waverly, I just got a text message from my BOSS that said, "Thanks for the awesome dream last night." Btw, my boss is male and has a wife, and my name is Brian. WTF??'"

"Good lord."

"You said it."

"You think the last guy is referring to a senator, a congressman, or an evangelical TV pastor?"

I laughed. "That's not bad. I should have used it in my reply."

"You weren't kidding about the abundance of material."

"That, my friend, is the horror of being a single person in the San Francisco Bay Area."

"Not that you would know."

I sat up in my chair. "Hey now, I'm single."

"Sweetheart, you are so not single."

"Yes, I am."

He laughed. "No, you aren't."

"Yes, I am. We haven't had the talk, Scotty. So nothing is official. Jake is not my boyfriend. We're not exclusive. We don't even live in the same city."

He sighed. "Gorgeous, I'm not talking about labels or geography, I'm talking about your heart. Don't try to tell me it isn't one hundred percent taken."

I opened my mouth to tell him he was wrong, but then I realized something.

He was right.

* * *

It was nearly four o'clock the next morning when I woke up and realized something else.

I sat up in bed, half asleep, but aware that something was wrong.

Oh no.

I got out of bed and groggily stumbled into my office, moving aside my notebook, calculator, and phone to look for my calendar. I was the one of the last people alive to use a paper planner, but I loved writing things down with an actual pen. It kept me organized and on top of things.

Until then, apparently.

I flipped the pages back to November, then started counting forward from the last date I'd circled in red. My fingers tapped along the days, then stopped.

I bit my lip.

I'm late.

Chapter Eight

For three days, I ignored it. I also ignored everything else. I don't think I'd ever gone so long without talking to McKenna, although she may not have noticed given all the life changes she was dealing with. Andie was at a conference in San Diego. So I'd basically been holed up in my apartment, eating chocolate and hoping it wasn't true.

On day four, I checked the calendar again.

Ten days late.

I was never late.

This is not good.

Could I really be pregnant? I put my hand on my stomach to see if it was any bigger. Then I looked at my boobs. Still small. *Actually, that part would be pretty cool,* I thought for a moment. Then I smacked my forehead and told myself to get a grip.

It was time to find out.

I zipped up my fleece and grabbed my keys. Next stop, Walgreens. I just hoped I didn't run into Nick in the checkout line. Maybe he could buy me a shirt that said KNOCKED UP AND SINGLE.

As I walked down Fillmore Street, I wrapped my arms in front of me. Given the situation, I couldn't help but notice my bare left ring finger. Regardless of what Scotty had said about my heart, the truth was that I *was* single. There I was, on my way to buy a pregnancy test, alone. Jake was probably on a plane somewhere over Indiana or Illinois or Iowa at the moment, clueless. His ignorance was my fault, of course. I hadn't returned his last call, not sure what to tell him, or even how to tell him. What would he think? Would he be as freaked out as I was? Would this make him run for the hills?

After making my purchase, I headed back up the street to my apartment, staring at the sidewalk and holding the Walgreens bag so tightly that I thought the plastic might melt into my skin. I could feel the tears welling up in my eyes.

Please, God, I know I never go to church, but please, don't let me be pregnant.

"Well hello there, Miss Waverly."

The sound of his voice stopped me in my tracks.

Please, God, please also don't let this bag be see-through.

I raised my head and smiled.

"Hi, Red. How are you?"

He stopped walking, then took off his fedora and bowed his head slightly. As always, he had a newspaper tucked under his arm. "I'm wonderful, Miss Waverly, just on my way to volunteer at a soup kitchen."

"A soup kitchen? What do you do there?"

"Whatever they need me to do."

"How did you get involved with that sort of thing?"

"Oh, I've been helping out at soup kitchens for years now. It started when I struck up a conversation with a newly homeless man—in line at Starbucks of all places. He'd lost his job and had no family to fall back on."

I titled my head to one side. "If he was homeless, why was he spending his money on Starbucks coffee?"

Red smiled. "He wasn't, my dear. He was in line to request an application for employment."

I blushed, embarrassed at my assumption.

"It sounds simplistic, but sometimes even a smile can make a difference in someone else's life," Red said.

I nodded as I stood there, impressed not just by his kindness, but by his wisdom. I wondered how my life would have gone if my dad hadn't been there for me, however dysfunctional our relationship. At least we *had* a relationship. I knew he was always there if I needed him.

"You're a good person, Red."

He bowed his head. "Just doing my part, Miss Waverly. So how are *you*?"

Talk about a loaded question. "I'm good." I squeezed the Walgreens bag. *Ha.*

He narrowed his dark brown eyes. "You sure, my dear? You look a little...anxious."

I swallowed. "Just trying to work through some writer's block. Did I tell you I write a newspaper column?"

"You did indeed. You know I'm a word man myself." He patted his newspaper. "So you've got a tangle of thoughts bumping around in that pretty head of yours but don't know how to straighten them out?"

"Something like that."

He didn't speak for a moment, then slowly tapped two fingers to his temple. "You know, Miss Waverly, sometimes you just have to let things happen."

"Let things happen?"

"Exactly. Loosen your grip, and things will work themselves out. It's like my crossword here." He held up the newspaper. "I find if I'm patient enough, the answers eventually come to me."

"Do you think so?" Suddenly I felt like crying. Were we talking about my column? I certainly wasn't. I held onto the Walgreens bag.

"Have faith, Miss Waverly."

"Thanks, Red, I'll try."

Suddenly a breeze stirred around us, and I wrapped my arms around myself to stay warm.

"It's interesting, isn't it?" he said.

"What is?"

He turned his head, and my eyes followed to a storefront that was boarded up.

"You can look at this as someone's failed dream, or as the chance for a new dream to take flight. It's all in your perspective," he said softly.

I stared at the vacant building. I couldn't even remember what used to be there.

He took his fedora off again and pointed up the street with it. "Now get yourself back inside to get warm, my dear. I don't want you to catch cold."

"Okay, Red, thanks. It was…it was nice running into you."

He bowed his head again and smiled. "Always a pleasure, Miss Waverly."

* * *

When I got back to my apartment, I put the cotton balls away and set the pregnancy test on my kitchen counter.

Should I take it and then call Jake? Or should I call him and then take it?

I didn't know what to do, but one thing I did know was that I didn't want to be pregnant. Not yet, maybe not ever.

I thought about what Red had said.

Things will work themselves out.

I contemplated the box on the counter.

Red was right.

First I would tell Jake. Then I would take the test.

I pulled my phone out of my purse and called him, but it went straight to voicemail. This was no time to call McKenna or Andie first. I had to leave a message.

"Hey, Jake, it's me, Waverly. I think you're in...Phoenix? Salt Lake City? I swear I'm going on NBA dot com right now. Anyhow... I'm sorry to have been a little MIA lately, but...um, I'd like to talk to you about something. Please give me a call—thanks. Um...I hope the Hawks are winning, wherever you and they are. Bye."

I hung up the phone and cringed. I was the worse voicemail-leaver ever.

* * *

Jake called me back that night. When I saw his name on the caller ID, I thought of the unopened pregnancy test, still sitting on the counter. I took a deep breath and answered.

"Jake, hi."

"Hi." His voice sounded...off.

"I'm sorry I haven't called you back in a few days." I immediately felt like I was going to cry. "I've been a little stressed out. How are you?" I sat on the couch and curled my legs underneath me.

"Actually, I'm not so good. I have some bad news." He didn't sound angry, just...sad.

"Bad news?"

There was a moment of silence before he spoke again.

"Waverly..." His voice trailed off.

"Yes?"

"My...my sister lost her baby," he said quietly.

Oh my God.

I opened my mouth, but nothing came out.

Oh my God.

Finally I was able to speak. "Oh Jake, I'm so sorry. What happened?"

"She woke up in the middle of the night bleeding, a lot...so Tim called an ambulance..." His voice cracked a little bit. "And when they checked on the baby...there was no heartbeat."

"Oh my God...I...I don't know what to say. Is she okay?"

"She is now. She lost a lot of blood and is really weak, but she's going to be fine."

I didn't say anything.

"It was a boy."

I still didn't say anything.

"She told me they were going to name him Jake," he said softly. Suddenly I started to cry.

"I'm...so...sorry," I said, catching my breath and wiping tears from my face with my free hand. "I'm so...so...sorry."

"Thanks. I am too."

"When did it happen?"

"Three days ago."

Three days ago. And I didn't even know because I hadn't returned his last call...for three days.

"Oh Jake, I should have called you back earlier. I'm so sorry I didn't call you back."

"It's okay, really." Again, he didn't sound angry. Just sad, very sad. And tired.

"I really wish I could be there with you right now. I wish I could...give you a hug," I said softly.

"Thanks." Then he sort of laughed. "But then again, do you even know where I am right now?"

I winced. "Phoenix?"

"Nice try. Try Cleveland."

"I mean Cleveland?"

"That's better." He laughed...sort of.

"I'm so sorry, Jake. Really, I'm so sorry."

"Thanks, I appreciate it. So you said you wanted to talk to me about something?"

Oh no.

I wanted to tell him, but this was hardly the time. I couldn't do that to him.

"Um, it's nothing important compared to what you're going through right now. We can talk about it another time."

"You sure?"

"Definitely." I looked up at the ceiling. "And I...I was wondering if maybe...if maybe I could come see you sometime soon?"

"You want to come see me?"

Please, please say yes.

"I mean, I mean, if you want me to."

He didn't say anything for a moment, so I spoke again.

"I'd...I'd really like to see you." I'd thought those words a billion times, but I couldn't believe how hard it was for me to say them out loud.

"Waverly, you know I want to see you too," he finally said.

I exhaled, and I could feel myself smile.

"Okay, I—"

He interrupted me. "But...I need to focus on my family right now."

I felt like I'd been kicked in the stomach.

"Oh, of course...of course you do. Of course you do."

"I have nonstop travel with the team for the next couple weeks, and then I'm taking a leave and flying up to Boston at the end of the month. My mom's headed up there now, to help with the girls when Tim's at work, and I'm going up for a few weeks to help...to give my mom a break. Natalie's still really weak, and she's pretty torn up emotionally, too."

I nodded into the phone. "I can only imagine how hard this is for all of you. That's...that's really nice of you to go and help out."

"It's the least I can do."

I kept nodding into the phone but didn't say anything.

"Listen, I've got to try to get some sleep, okay? I've got a lot to do tomorrow," he said.

"Sure, of course, of course."

"I'll call you, okay?"

"Sure." I wiped a tear from my cheek.

"Okay, then, I'll talk to you later. Thanks for calling."

"Jake?"

"Yes?"

"I'm so sorry," I whispered.

"Me too."

I think we both knew we weren't talking about his sister anymore.

Chapter Nine

After a restless night, I woke to the sound of my phone ringing. I grabbed it, hoping it was Jake.

It was Andie.

"Hey," I said groggily. "Are you back? And why are you up?" It was barely nine o'clock. Andie never got up early on the weekends.

"I got back last night. Wanna grab brunch? I woke up early craving blueberry pancakes."

I yawned. "Okay, sounds good. Curbside Café at ten? I need to take a shower."

"Done. See you then."

I hung up the phone and lay back on my pillow, closing my eyes and reliving the previous night's conversation with Jake. After a few minutes I threw the covers off, then sat up and swung my legs onto the area rug laid over the hardwood floor. My legs felt heavy and weak, just like my heart. I stretched my arms over my head and yawned again. Maybe a shower would help.

* * *

"I have news," Andie said just seconds after I sat down across from her.

I looked up from the menu and raised my eyebrows. "News? Do tell."

As soon as she caught my eye, she could tell something was wrong. "Hey, are you okay? You don't look very good."

I sighed. "That's because I'm not very good."

"What's up?" She reached across the table and put her hand on my arm. Andie wasn't touchy feely like McKenna, so I knew I must look like crap.

I tried to smile. "I'll tell you my news after you tell me yours, okay?"

"You sure?"

"Definitely. Your stories always cheer me up."

"Okay, deal. So are you ready?"

"Let's hear it."

She grinned. "I met a guy."

"Really? Where?"

"At the conference. It was crazy."

"I'm sure it was. Details please."

After ordering, Andie turned to face me and spread her hands on the table, her eyes open wide.

"Okay, so the third day we were there, a bunch of us from my firm were at dinner when my coworker Alyssa suggested we do a round of shots and head out to a karaoke bar."

"Shots and karaoke? This story can only go downhill."

She laughed. "I know, I know. So we all did a tequila shot, right there at the dinner table. Then we went to a random karaoke bar, where we ended up mixing with a big group of other people from the conference. There were so many of us that we basically took over the place."

"Nice."

"Everyone totally sucked at karaoke. I mean *sucked*. Of course I was laughing at how bad they all were—you know how much I love to make fun of people."

I nodded. "It's one of your best qualities."

"Then this guy standing next to me called me out for mocking everyone, and dared me to go up there with him and do better."

The waiter served us our coffee. I turned mine into a milkshake with cream and sugar. "Okay, keep going."

She pushed her hair behind her ears. "So we got up on stage and sang 'Islands in the Stream.'"

"'Islands in the Stream'? As in Dolly Parton and Kenny Rogers?"

"We were awful, Waverly. *So* awful."

"How could you *not* be awful? I mean, 'Islands in the Stream'? Yikes."

"It was hilarious, but so much fun. Afterward, we went back to the bar and started chatting. And before I knew it, it was two in the morning, and the bar was closing."

"Awesome. So you hooked up with him?"

She shook her head. "If you can believe it, we said goodbye, and I went back to my hotel to sleep for like four hours. The next day at the conference was a bitch, by the way."

"I know that feeling."

"But it was so *weird*, Waverly, I mean, I really clicked with this guy. I think I would have hooked up with him if I hadn't. Does that make sense?"

I laughed. "That's so twisted, but I know exactly what you mean."

"So anyhow, the next day I ran into him at the conference, and we ended up having dinner that night."

"Nice."

She added sugar to her coffee and stirred it. "We went to this cute place in the Gaslamp Quarter, had an outrageously unhealthy dinner, and chatted about...*everything*. He's really interesting. And it was almost like hanging out with you and McKenna, that's how comfortable I was with him. Then after dinner, we strolled around and made fun of all the muscle people."

"Muscle people?"

"Have you ever been to the Gaslamp Quarter in San Diego? If so, you'd totally understand."

"A lot of big hair? Overly tan people, men in tank tops, women wearing banana clips? That sort of thing?"

She snapped her fingers. "*Exactly.* For such a small area, it's got to be one of the top selling markets in the world for acrylic nails. I loved it."

"I'll put that on my list of places to visit."

She lowered her voice. "I think I like him, Waverly. Like *like* him, like him."

I smiled. "Are you going to see him again? Where does he live?"

"He's from Nebraska, but he lives here. Isn't that awesome?"

"No way. He lives *in* San Francisco? Or just near here?"

"*In* San Francisco."

"Wow. What are the chances?"

"I know, can you believe it?"

I leaned back in the booth. "That's really great that he lives here, Andie. Because trying to get a relationship off the ground long distance is...brutal."

"Oh no. What happened with Jake?"

I sighed. *I might as well just come out with it.*

"Well, let's just say that Mackie might not be the only one wearing mom-to-be jeans around here."

"WHAT?!"

I leaned across the booth and put my hand on her mouth. "Shhh, you're screaming."

She lowered her voice. "Holy frick, Waverly, you're pregnant?"

"No, no, I don't know for sure, I'm just...late."

"How late?"

"Um…Eleven days?"

"Oh Jesus."

"I know."

"Are you normally late?"

"Never."

"Did you guys use protection?"

"Yes."

"Have you taken a pregnancy test?"

"I bought one yesterday, but it's still sitting in my apartment."

"Did you tell Jake?"

I picked up a paper napkin and started tearing it into pieces. "I was going to last night."

"And?"

"I called him, but before I could say anything he told me that his sister, who was like eight months pregnant, had just lost her baby."

Her eyes got big. "No way."

I kept tearing the napkin. "He was so upset, so I just…I just couldn't bring myself to say anything."

"Holy hell."

"I know."

"What are you going to do?"

I put my elbows on the table, then put my face in my hands. "I don't know."

"The first thing you need to do is take that test. You have to find out."

I looked up at her, red-eyed. "But—"

She threw some money on the table and stood up, grabbing my arm. "But nothing. C'mon, let's go. You're taking that test right now."

"Do I have to?"

"Yes, you have to. And if it's positive, you have to tell Jake right away. If that man is going to be your baby daddy, he has a right to know."

"Did you just say *baby daddy*?"

"MTV, remember? Now let's go."

I left the mountain of napkin bits on the table.

* * *

"Well?" Andie said loudly through the door.

"Give me a minute. I'm peeing on the stick."

"I can't take the suspense. I can't believe you and Mackie might be knocked up at the same time."

"You and me both." I zipped up my jeans and looked at the stick, which was now sitting on the sink. "Talk to me, stick," I said softly. "Tell me what to do if I'm pregnant."

"Are you talking to the stick?"

"Do I have to answer that?"

"You're insane. Now get out here."

I opened the bathroom door, stick in hand. Together Andie and I walked into the kitchen, and I set it on the counter.

"How long do we have to wait?" she asked.

I handed her the box, which said FIVE-MINUTE PREGNANCY TEST in huge letters on it. "That would be five minutes, Einstein."

"Hey now, you're barely pregnant and already all hormonal and mean. They have medication for that, you know."

I snatched the box back from her. "Very funny."

For the next few minutes we waited in silence, standing close to each other and hovering over the stick on the counter.

"For some reason watching this thing is making me think of those birds that fly into windows," I suddenly said.

"What?"

"Haven't you ever seen one of those little birds that doesn't realize there's a window there, so they try to fly right into your living room, and then *WHAM*, they hit the window and fall onto the ground and just lie there, and then you go outside and sort of stand over them for a minute, not knowing if they're going to get up and fly away or not?"

"Are you insane? What are you talking about?"

I shrugged. "I'm just saying that that's what this reminds me of. Sort of."

"I really wonder about you sometimes."

"Thank you for that. I totally needed to hear that right now."

Suddenly she hit me on the shoulder. "I think it's done."

I picked the stick up and stared at it. "It's blue. What does that mean? Am I having a boy?"

She grabbed the box and read the back.

"Blue...blue means...."

"Well?"

She looked at me.

"Well?"

She smiled. "Not pregnant. Blue is definitely not pregnant."

I reached for the box. "Are you sure?"

"Read for yourself."

I did, and she was right.

Suddenly I felt lighter. I sat down at the kitchen table and exhaled deeply.

I gazed at the table, saying nothing.

"I bet you get your period today," she said.

I looked up. "You do?"

"Yep. Now that the stress is gone, it'll come. Stress can really mess you up."

Now *that* was an understatement.

Chapter Ten

A couple of weeks later, I entered the *Sun* building for the weekly staff meeting, officially without child. Andie had been right, and all was back to normal in the nether lands. I hadn't heard from Jake though, and it was killing me. I'd e-mailed him once to say hi, trying to be as casual as possible while still letting him know I cared. I didn't want to come across as desperate to talk to him, even though of course I sort of was.

He hadn't replied yet.

I waved at Larry through his open door. He was on the phone and waved back, but he didn't look as jolly as he normally did. Then I passed Ivy's empty cube. She was in Kansas visiting her parents. When I got to the conference table, I sat down and pulled out my notebook. I was ten minutes early.

"Hey, Waverly, how's it going?"

Nick was standing in the doorway wearing a brown V-neck sweater over a green shirt.

"No offensive shirt today?"

He held a finger up to his lips, then pulled up his sweater. Underneath his shirt said, "I WANT TO BE YOUR BABY DADDY."

"Oh good lord."

"Isn't it amazing? Even *I* know this is too much for the office, though. Thus the grandpa sweater."

I sighed and started drawing circles on my notepad.

"Hey, what's wrong? I thought you'd love it."

I ignored him. I didn't mean to be rude, but I just didn't want to talk to him about *that* shirt, not then.

"Waverly, are you okay?"

I hoped he couldn't tell that I was on the verge of tears. "I don't really want to talk about it," I said without looking up.

"Okay, just checking, just checking. Chicks, man, I swear you're all nuts."

"Hey now, I am *not* nuts." Although to be honest, at that moment I couldn't be sure I believed that myself.

"Okay, fine, fine, you're cool, I gotcha."

I finally made eye contact with him. "I'm sorry, Nick. It's not you. I just have a lot on my mind right now, and it's stressing me out."

"I completely understand. There's a foolproof solution for that, by the way."

I raised my eyebrows. "There is?"

"There is indeed."

"What is it?"

"Alcohol. It's God's medicine."

I laughed. "Nick, I think *you're* the one who's nuts here."

"See? Made you smile. But seriously, let's grab a drink after work. It'll make you feel better."

"I'm sorry, I can't tonight. I have to work on my column."

"What about tomorrow?"

I mentally scanned my calendar, which I was pretty sure was free. Andie was obsessed with Gaslamp Guy, so she was totally off the radar, and I hadn't connected with McKenna in the last few days. I'd told her about the pregnancy scare, however. I couldn't keep that from her.

"I think I could do that," I said.

"Cool. Have you been to the Northstar? It's right by my apartment."

"The one in North Beach? On Powell?"

"It's on Powell, but it's in Prodromou Gulch."

I squinted at him. "Prodromou Gulch? What's that?"

"It's a small but up-and-coming neighborhood nestled between Telegraph Hill and North Beach. There are some really cool bars over there."

"Wait a minute. Isn't your last nam …Prodromou?"

"Indeed it is."

"Then what the…?"

He put one hand on the doorjamb. "Think about it, Waverly. Every neighborhood got its name somehow, right? You've got the Marina, the Tenderloin, the Mission, Russian Hill, Nob Hill, and new ones are popping up all the time. I mean, now we've got the freaking *TenderNob*, for God's sake."

I tried not to laugh. "TenderNob? As in the area between the Tenderloin and Nob Hill?"

"My point exactly. If people can come up with the TenderNob, why can't I come up with Prodromou Gulch?"

"You *are* nuts. How exactly do you expect to get people to start calling it *Prodromou Gulch*?"

He pushed the sleeves of his sweater up to his elbows and lowered his voice. "That's where my genius comes in. I figured I'd place a few ads on Craigslist for apartments there. Maybe rate a few bars on Yelp, have my friends sprinkle a few comments on Facebook and Twitter. Plant some digital seeds, then step back and watch them grow."

"That's your genius plan?"

"Do you doubt me?"

I tilted my head to one side and thought about it. "That's actually pretty creative."

"Of course it is." He patted himself on the back. "Okay, I gotta run. I'll see you tomorrow."

A few minutes later the meeting started, but I couldn't focus on anything anyone was saying. I sat in silence and doodled aimlessly on my notepad, just like I used to do in high school. This time, however, instead of drawing hearts and sunsets, I wrote the same sentence over and over.

I miss you, Jake McIntyre.

* * *

That afternoon I had a call with Wyatt Clyndelle at Smithers Publishing, the company that managed the printing and distribution of my Honey Notes.

"Have you put any thought into new cards like we talked about?" Wyatt said. "Sales are steady, but some new cards would really help give the line some legs."

"I've definitely been thinking about that."

"That's great news. Anything you'd care to share?"

"Actually, let me rephrase that. I've been thinking about thinking about that."

He laughed. "What?"

"I know that sounds crazy, but I swear I have an idea brewing. It's just in the very early stages, so early that I'm not exactly sure what it is yet."

"Well, keep me posted. My ears are always open."

"Okay, will do."

I hung up and reached inside my desk drawer for a pad of sticky notes and a spiral-bound notebook. I wrote "HONEY BRAINSTORM" on a note and stuck it to the edge of my computer monitor. *Maybe that will help speed along the creative process.* Then I opened the notebook and began to jot down some thoughts, determined to bring life to the idea rolling around in the back of my head. After filling several pages, I reviewed what

I'd written and smiled. It needed work, but I liked where it was going.

My brain was getting tired, so I decided to shift gears and spend some time on my column. When I put the notebook and sticky notes back in the drawer, I noticed the envelope with the mysterious red handwriting. I pulled it out and took another look at the lone sheet of paper inside.

Be

"Be *what*?"

I put the letter away and opened my e-mail, eager to distract myself with stories of lives other than my own. After scrolling through the bunch, I picked three to include in that week's column:

Dear Waverly: Last night my boyfriend sat me down and told me he'd done a lot of thinking since graduating from business school. Apparently he wants to run his life like a Fortune 500 company, because he basically informed me that, while he does care for me, he doesn't see a future for me within the organization. He laid out his case like a hard-core business plan, and then he laid me off.

My reply: Honey, note to self: Don't date MBAs unless A) you knew them way before they went to business school, or B) they work for a nonprofit. No offense to any other MBAs reading this, but you're probably a little full of yourself.

Dear Waverly: Let's see if you can top this. I went to a "date my friend" party last night, where everyone had to bring someone of the opposite sex they love but don't LOVE. Built-in screening for cool people, right? So where was that filter when the girl I started talking to said she was studying colonoscopy, then added, with a freakish amount of energy, "I love the colon!" Okay then. I'm out.

My reply: *Honey, don't go knocking the potential for free medical care. I agree, however, that professing a passion for the large intestine is a bit odd. But something tells me that if she'd been smokin' hot, you'd have found her strangely attractive, as opposed to...just strange. Come on, you know I'm right...*

Dear Waverly: I live up in Tahoe, right in Tahoe City. I went on a first date with a guy the other night, and it was really fun. He even called the next morning and wanted to meet for lunch, but I told him I couldn't because my car was snowed in. Then he offered to come over and shovel my driveway for me. Flattered, I said, "You'd really do that for me?" And you know what his response was? He said, and he was NOT kidding, "Sure, why not? I could use the money."

My reply: *Honey, you totally should have let him do it. Then, after he'd toiled long and hard to free your car from the snow, you could have driven away with an air kiss and said you'd pay him back by letting him kiss your ass.*

I reviewed the column and laughed, already feeling better about my own romantic situation.

I was about to close the program when a new e-mail appeared in my inbox. As soon as I saw the sender's name, my mouth went dry. I clicked to open it:

To: *Waverly Bryson*
From: *Jake McIntyre*
Subject: *re: How are you doing?*

Hi Waverly, I'm sorry I haven't been in touch. It's been an emotional trip, and to be honest I didn't want to drag you into it. Just a hard time all around on the family. Nat's doing better now, though.

You must be getting geared up for the big appearance on The
Today Show. *I know you'll do great—you always do.*

Take care,
Jake

I read the e-mail over and over again, then leaned back in my
chair. I had no idea what it meant. It was hardly flirtatious, but it was
definitely kind. I had to remember what he was dealing with, right?

I hoped I wasn't grasping at straws.

After a few minutes, I sat back up and replied:

To: *Jake McIntyre*
From: *Waverly Bryson*
Subject: *re: How are you doing?*

Hi Jake, I'm glad to hear things are going okay. Don't worry
about not being in touch. I completely understand that you need to
deal with this right now. I'm thinking a lot about you though, and
your family too.

Things out here are going well, and yes, I'm definitely nervous for
my TV appearance next week. Here's hoping I don't trip on the way out
to the stage. But if I do, please don't post the video clip on Facebook.

Love,
Waverly

I hesitated for just a second, then hit *send.*

* * *

The next evening I took a cab over to the Northstar to meet
Nick for a drink. He was sitting at the bar when I arrived, and as

I approached he stood up and majestically swept his arm across the room, as if showing me a lovely dining set I could win on *The Price Is Right.*

"Welcome to Prodromou Gulch." He did a little curtsy.

I curtsied back. "Why, thank you. It's a pleasure to be in such an up-and-coming part of town, especially one that's your name-sake."

We sat down at the bar, and I leaned forward to check out the shirt he was wearing under an unbuttoned checkered flannel. It said, "I'M EVEN BETTER LOOKING IN PERSON."

I laughed. "How long have you been dressing like this?"

"A while. I like to keep things interesting."

"Well, you're certainly doing a good job." I patted his shoulder. "You're nothing if not interesting."

"Why, thanks. Now what can I get you to drink?"

We ordered a couple Blue Moons, and then he turned to me. "So did you hear about Larry?"

"Larry from the *Sun*?"

"The one and only."

"What happened to him?"

He gestured over his shoulder with his thumb. "Gone."

"What? Why?"

"Laid off."

"Really, but when? I was just there yesterday."

"A couple hours after you left. I *told* you there was trouble brewing." He pretended to churn a vat of butter.

"Oh my God." Suddenly I remembered the unhappy look on Larry's face when I'd seen him the day before. "You were totally right."

He took a drink of his beer and set it on the bar. "I'm always right. Haven't you realized that yet?"

"So what happens now?"

"I heard they're handing the department over to Eloise Zimmerman."

I raised my eyebrows.

"You've never heard of Eloise Zimmerman?"

"Who?"

"You've never even heard of her *hair*?"

"I work part-time, remember?"

"Okay, true. Eloise Zimmerman's been at the *Sun* since…like… a hundred years before we were born, and let's just say she's…"

He paused.

"She's what?"

"Whacked." He took another drink of his beer. "Yep, that about sums it up. She's whacked, and she has this matching crazy black beehive hairdo. It's totally old school. Amazing, actually."

"Wonderful. And she's my new editor?"

"For the time being, at least."

"Did anyone else get laid off?"

"I think about twenty percent of the company."

"Oh man. I wonder if I'm next?"

"Could be. I have no idea what they're paying you, though. And you don't get benefits or anything, so maybe you're safe."

I played with my earring. "Hmm, I'm basically working for minimum wage given how much time I spend on my column, so maybe you're right."

He held his beer up to mine. "Here's to being cheap."

I laughed and clinked my glass against his. "You should put *that* on a shirt."

We ordered two more beers, and before long we were a bit tipsy. Or at least I was.

"So Eloise Zimmerman really has a beehive?"

He nodded. "It's unbelievable. High and black, with some white stripes on the side." He lifted his hands about a foot over his head. "From the right angle, it could pass for a skunk."

"Wow."

"It's phenomenal. And I've heard that when she gets angry, she can yell pretty loud and shake her head, and sometimes she shakes it so hard that some strands come loose from the hive. That's when you *know* she's pissed."

"Lovely. I'm really looking forward to that."

"I haven't seen it, but I hear you could charge admission."

I lifted my glass to my lips. "Our librarian in high school had a beehive. But she was nice, and she never yelled. I bet raising your voice breaks some librarian code."

"I slept with the librarian when I was in high school."

I nearly spat out my beer. "What?"

"It was amazing. And she definitely raised her voice."

"You slept with the *librarian*? Who does that?"

He pointed to himself and grinned. "That would be this guy."

"You are unbelievable."

"It was a good time. Oh yeah it was."

"So was she right out of college or something?"

He shook his head. "Oh no, she was old."

"Please, she was probably like twenty-five. That just *seemed* old back then." I took another sip of my beer.

He shook his head again. "No, I mean she was *old*. She might be dead now."

This time I did spit out my beer.

"Oh my God, you're hilarious." I reached for a napkin to blot the beer off myself and the counter. "How are you not a stand-up comedian?"

He shrugged. "There's still time. Actually, I *have* been kicking around the idea of a TV show."

"A TV show?"

He nodded.

"A TV show about what?"

"Me, of course."

"A TV show about *you*?"

He nodded again.

"How so?"

"I was thinking it could be like a workshop, or perhaps a clinic. Whatever the format, it would teach people how to be like me."

"You want to make a TV show to teach people how to be like *you*?"

"Exactly. Not that anyone could ever *totally* be like me, of course. But it would be something aspiring awesome people could do. It would be like a boot camp for how to be awesome."

"You're unbelievable."

"Of course I am. I'm amazing. Now let's order some real drinks."

I waved my hands in front of me. "No thanks, I don't do so well with those."

He scoffed. "Please. We're ordering something amazing from that bartender right over there, although I've chatted with the dude before, and I know he prefers to be called a mixologist."

"A mixologist? What's that?"

"My point exactly. It's like trying to call a mechanic an *automobile surgeon*. Hello? Dude, you're a bartender."

I laughed. "You can order whatever you want. I just feel safer ordering beer or wine."

"Why? Mixed drinks are fun."

"I know, and that's exactly the point. But you can go really quickly from having like, one vodka Red Bull, to waking up and asking yourself, *What happened last night?* You know what I mean?"

He laughed. "Oh yes, I do, and that's the genius of it." Then he turned and ordered two vodka Red Bulls.

I stood up to use the restroom. "Okay, but I'm only having one."

* * *

Three drinks later, Nick and I were still sitting at the bar. I figured that was the safest position for me to be in because I knew I'd wobble if I tried to stand up.

He put his hand on my shoulder. "So, what's your deal? You show up at the office once a week and write about romance, yet you aren't married, and you don't appear to have a boyfriend. What's the story there?"

It was bound to happen. I was about to be exposed as the little guy behind the curtain in *The Wizard of Oz*.

"I almost got married once," I blurted, then quickly covered my mouth with my hand. Stupid mixologist.

"Really? I had no idea. When?"

"A little over two years ago."

"What happened?"

I picked up my drink. "Want to know the truth?"

He nodded. "Always."

"He called it off two weeks before the wedding."

Nick suddenly looked uncomfortable. "Oh man, I had no idea. I'm really sorry."

"It's okay. I'm over it now, finally. It took a long time, though."

"That really blows. Did he tell you why?"

I cleared my throat. "He said he wasn't in love with me."

"Oh man, that's brutal."

"Yeah, it wasn't fun."

"So what about now? Do you have a boyfriend?"

"No, not really." *Because I'm an idiot,* I thought.

"Do you want a boyfriend?"

I tried to smile. "Doesn't everyone want a boyfriend?"

"I certainly don't."

I pushed his shoulder. "So witty. So, so witty."

"So is there a guy in the picture now?"

"Yes...sort of...I mean...yes...I think so."

"What kind of answer is that?"

"Well, I'm pretty gun-shy given what happened to me before...and it's complicated because he doesn't live here, so I'm...and I'm...just trying to take it really slowly. I'm also hoping I don't blow it. Although I fear I may already have."

He laughed. "*Just hoping I don't blow it.* Now that would be a great aspiration to put in your *Sun* bio, since you're the resident relationship *expert* and all."

"Thanks for that, Nick. So what about you? Do you have a girlfriend?"

"Not currently."

"Do you want one?"

"Do I want a girlfriend? Sure. Do I want more than that? No."

"*More than that* as in a wife and kids?"

"Bingo."

I pushed a loose strand of hair behind my ear. "So you're not cut out for a life in the suburbs?"

He paused for a moment before answering. "Maybe someday in the future, but definitely not yet."

I completely understand.

"In fact, sometimes I have nightmares about picket fences... and little people," he said.

"Little people?"

"You know, *little people.*" He made quotation marks with his fingers. "Kids."

"Nick Prodromou, you're crazy. Although I've recently had a nightmare or two of my own about kids, so I guess I'm crazy too."

"Sometimes I wake up in a cold sweat. It's terrifying."

I laughed. "Seriously, you need to think about stand-up comedy. I'm not joking."

"So hey, speaking of your column, I have a question for you." He lowered his voice and leaned toward me.

"Talk to me." I lowered my voice too.

"I sort of have a dilemma in the romance area."

I raised my eyebrows. "You? I'm surprised."

He sat back up straight. "Why do you say that?"

I took a sip of my drink and set it down on the bar. "With the *baby daddy* T-shirts and bowling team stories and all, I just figured you weren't one for romance."

"Okay, I'm a little inebriated, but I have a confession to make." He leaned in close to me and put his hand on my knee. "You see, the thing is, I have a crush on this really cute girl from the office."

I felt my hands go cold. "You do?"

"Totally. And when I see her, I get so nervous that sometimes I end up coming off a little cocky."

"You? Cocky? Never."

"I know that might sound hard to believe, but it's true. And remember that this is just between you and me. And the mixologist. Damn talented, that man is. One more round of drinks and I may end up trying to pay our bill with a Starbucks gift card."

I opened my purse. "I think I have a library card in my wallet if that gets declined, although now that I think about it, you probably still have yours from high school."

"Well done. So back to my crush. Can I tell you who it is?"

I didn't reply, but he leaned closer toward me and put his mouth right next to my ear. I could feel his breath as I held mine.

He hesitated for a moment, and I wished I could keep him from speaking.

"It's Ivy," he said softly.

I sat up straight. "You have a thing for Ivy?"

"Big time."

"But doesn't she have a serious boyfriend?"

"Unfortunately so."

"Oh Nick, I'm sorry. Are you going to tell her?"

He looked at me like I was crazy.

"Are you crazy?"

"Well, why not?"

"How about because she *loves* the dude?"

I put my index finger on my chin. "You make a good point."

"That and the fact that I just told you I'm not ready for anything super serious yet. And you know how Ivy's totally itching to get married."

"Another excellent point." I tilted my head to one side. "Hmm…you think maybe she's your parallel universe girl?"

"My what?"

I shifted on the barstool and put my hands in front of me, palms facing each other with all ten fingers pointing up. "Your parallel universe girl. She's perfect for you in every way, except for the inconvenient fact that she happened to meet someone else first. So even though you and she totally click, it just can't happen this time around. But in a parallel universe, you'd be a great couple. Or amazing, as you would say."

"Hmm, maybe you're right."

"Maybe *you* should write to my column." I smiled and held my drink up.

"And maybe not. This information is hardly for public consumption, got it?"

I put my hand on his shoulder. "I have to say, you have really surprised me tonight. Nick Prodromou is a total softy. Who would have guessed?"

"Hey now, if you tell anyone, this little buddy-buddy thing we have going on here is *so* over."

I laughed and stood up, steadying myself with one hand on the bar. "Okay, okay, although to me you are now the tin man from *The Wizard of Oz*. And while I've really enjoyed visiting Prodromou Gulch, drunk Dorothy here really needs to get herself back to Kansas."

"Ivy's from Kansas," he said with a drunken smile. "Maybe you can bring her with you the next time you come to town."

* * *

The next morning I didn't wake up in Kansas, but I did have a Texas-size hangover. I sat up in bed and put my hands on my forehead. *Ugh.*

"Damn you, Nick. And damn that mixologist too."

I dragged myself into the kitchen and poured some ground coffee into the machine, laughing at myself and wondering how long it had been since I'd drunk so much on a school night. *At least I don't have to go to an office right now,* I thought. *And at least I didn't do anything stupid.* As I waited for the coffee to brew, I scrambled up a salty plate of eggs and cheese, then opened a cabinet and took out some Advil. After a moment I opened the cabinet again and pulled down a bottle of multivitamins, thinking maybe a mass infusion of nutrients would somehow help. It couldn't *hurt*, right?

I gulped the pills down and headed down to get the newspaper. I hoped no one would catch me in my robe and slippers in the nine seconds it took to run to the lobby and back.

Of course I was wrong.

"Why good morning, Miss Waverly."

I smoothed my hand over my hair and cursed silently. Red was walking down the stairs, dressed to the nines, as usual.

"Hi, Red, how's it going?"

"I can't complain, can't complain." He tipped his head slightly. "How about you?"

"I'm hangin' in there." *Hanging over there.*

"Did you get through your…writer's block?" The pause was slight, but noticeable.

"Yes, I did, thanks for asking."

He smiled. "I had a feeling you would work through it."

I took a step toward my apartment, then stopped.

"Red?"

"Yes?"

"Can I ask you something?"

"Why, sure you can."

"How…how are you always so sure about everything?"

He narrowed his eyes slightly, but didn't say anything.

"I mean…you seem so…I don't know…*optimistic* all the time. How do you do that?" I thought of all the e-mails I'd gotten from disillusioned readers, not to mention the uncertainty of my own situation. "Don't you ever get down about how life is going?"

He smiled again. "My dear, your life is happening all around you, every day. It's always going to be a puzzle, but the choice of where to put the pieces is yours, *always* yours."

I didn't say anything.

"Are you all right, Miss Waverly?"

"Yes, I'm fine. Thanks, Red. You're right. I think I really needed to hear that."

He tipped his head again. "Anytime, Miss Waverly."

Back in my apartment, I poured myself a cup of coffee, then sat down to eat my eggs and read the paper. When I got to the word jumble, I thought of what Red had just said.

The choice of where to put the pieces is yours.

Before I could continue that thought, I suddenly remembered something.

I put down my mug.

Holy crap, I'd spoken too soon. I *had* done something stupid the night before.

I got up and ran to my phone, then checked my "sent" text messages and winced.

There it was, sent at 2:12 in the morning:

Hi Jake...I miss youu so muck. Xoxo, Waberly.

I miss you so MUCK?

Waberly?

I put my hand on my forehead.

Nice e-Waverly moment, loser.

At least I hadn't mistyped *his* name.

I walked into my office, then opened my desk drawer and pulled out the mystery letter with the red ink.

Be

I thought again about what Red had just said.

Maybe I needed to just let things be?

I looked at my phone again.

Apparently that was easier said than done.

Chapter Eleven

I flew to New York a day early in a futile effort to get over the jet lag—and accompanying puffy face syndrome—before my early morning TV appearance. I was having dinner with Scotty the night before the show, which gave me nearly a full day to explore New York on my own. I also had plans to meet my friend Kristina Santana for coffee. She was married to Shane Kennedy, the NBA player who had once been my client.

"How are you? It's been ages!" Kristina stood up and gave me a big hug, then took a seat across from me on the plush green couch. I'd just come in from a chilly stroll through Central Park and was now defrosting in a cushy chair in the lobby of the equally cushy New York Athletic Club, an old-school establishment right on Central Park South.

"So tomorrow's the big day. Are you excited?"

"I'm nervous, but definitely excited."

She shooed my words away with her hand. "Please. You'll do great. Don't be nervous."

"Ha, that's easy for you to say. You skated on live TV in the Olympics. Compared to that, *The Today Show* is nothing. Hmm… actually, compared to that, *everything* is nothing."

"Not true. Med school was way harder than the Olympics."

I rolled my eyes. "Could you be any more perfect? Please tell me you have webbed feet or horrible cellulite or something. Throw me a bone here."

She smiled and took a sip of her tea. "I'm not worried about tomorrow. You'll do great. Just be sure to mention sex in there somewhere. Everyone loves that."

I blushed a little bit. "Thanks, I'll try to remember that."

"So how's life in San Francisco? I've been so busy at the hospital that I've lost touch with everyone and everything. Did you realize I'm not even on Facebook?"

"And thank God for that," I said, suddenly wondering what Jake had for breakfast that morning. I hadn't heard back from him after my drunken text message and had been too scared/proud/embarrassed to contact him again. "Life is interesting. Seems like there are a lot of babies in it right now."

She gave me a look, and I held my hand up. "Not *me*, but McKenna's pregnant."

"Really? Good for her."

"And for a week or so, I feared I was too, but I'm not, thank God. I actually took a pregnancy test, my first ever. Pretty scary."

"I've done that. It's definitely scary."

I nodded. "*Terrifying.* I was seriously freaked out for a few days there. So what about you, are you knocked up too?" A prim, blue-haired lady sitting at the couch next to us turned her head in horror, and I pulled my neck in like a turtle.

"Excuse me, ma'am. Won't happen again," I said.

Kristina laughed. "Do I look pregnant?"

I lowered my voice. "Of course not. You are still my beautiful Olympian-turned-pediatrician friend with flawless skin. I should really hate you."

"Thanks for not hating me. And *no*, I'm not pregnant. Shane's on the road way too much to go there right now. Someday we'll have kids, but not until after his basketball career is over, when he can really be there with them."

"I'm glad to hear you're waiting. I've had enough baby talk for a while."

"So what's going on with Jake? The last time I saw you, the two of you seemed to be getting along really well." Kristina and Shane had attended McKenna's wedding.

I smiled. "Yeah, we get along great."

She raised her eyebrows. "Apparently so, given that you had a pregnancy scare."

"This is true."

"I sense a *but*."

"Well…we get along great, we really do."

"Still sensing a *but*."

"But yes, it's hard with the distance. And you know about my trust issues, not to mention my all-around insecurity issues, so I'm trying to take it slow."

She sipped her tea. "How's that going?"

"The issues thing or the taking it slow thing?"

"Both."

"I'm doing my best to get over my issues. And I'm also doing my best to take it slow, just to let things happen at their own pace." Then I laughed a bit awkwardly. "Okay, I flat-out admit that I'm not doing a very good job at either, but I swear I'm trying my best."

She leaned over and squeezed my knee. "Hey, if you're trying your best to make it work, then that's all you can do."

"So I've been told."

"And if you're *not* trying your best…" She pointed to the door. "You know my thoughts on people who hedge their bets when it comes to relationships."

I laughed. "Oh yes, Miss Tough Love, I know. But I'm determined to try, because Jake is a really good guy."

"Believe me, I know. Shane adores him."

I do too, I thought.

* * *

The next morning I woke up while it was still dark, tired but also jittery with nerves. At Rockefeller Center, I took the elevator up, tapping my fingernails against the walls as I gave myself a silent pep talk. *Remember what Andie said,* I thought. *No one I actually know is watching this.*

When the elevator door opened, I was greeted by a no-nonsense twenty-something dressed in a smart black pantsuit and equally smart black-framed glasses. Her jet black hair was smoothed back into a low bun. She reminded me of a young Michelle Obama.

"Waverly Bryson?"

"That's me."

She held out a hand and smiled. "I'm Donna Pittman, assistant to the stage manager. Welcome to *The Today Show*."

I shook her hand, marveling at how put-together she was in the middle of the night, not to mention the dead of winter. *If I had that job, I'd probably show up for work in sweats,* I thought. Then I quickly realized that that is probably why I didn't have that job.

I followed Donna in silence down a long corridor, admiring the many framed pictures of former *Today* guests on the walls. She stopped in front of a closed door and put her hand on the doorknob.

"This is the green room. You can relax here until Tina comes to touch up your makeup. Then I'll come find you and take you to the soundstage. Sound good?"

For a moment I was tempted to salute, but for once my brain overruled my nervous system. I managed to eke out a nervous smile. "Sounds good, thanks."

She smiled back and opened the door, gesturing for me to enter. Inside I noticed a woman seated on one of the couches. Judging from her stiff helmet of blonde hair, I guessed she was a former beauty pageant contestant. Donna poked her head in the door before she left and introduced me.

"Waverly, this is Wendy Davenport. She'll be joining you on the segment. Please, help yourself to something to eat." Donna pointed to a fancy breakfast spread, then left us on our own.

"Hi, Wendy." I held out my hand and smiled. "It's nice to meet you."

Wendy glanced up from her magazine and half smiled. "Hello." She took my hand but didn't shake it. Instead her hand just lay there in mine, limp.

I did the best I could to salvage a handshake, then sat down on a couch across from her. *You'd think they'd teach handshakes in beauty pageant school,* I thought.

"Are you from New York?" I asked.

She shook her head and returned to the magazine.

Okay then.

I stood up to inspect the breakfast buffet. I had just poured myself a steaming cup of coffee when the door opened. I turned around to find a short woman with frizzy red hair smiling at me from the doorway.

"Waverly?"

I nodded, and she motioned at me with her finger. "I'm Tina. Come with me. Let's make you pretty."

"I like the sound of that." I grabbed a bagel and leaned down to grab my purse, then turned to Wendy to say goodbye.

She didn't look up from her magazine.

"Bye, Wendy," I said anyway.

* * *

About thirty minutes later, I was seated on a couch again, but this one was on the actual stage of *The Today Show*. It was far off to the right from where the anchors sat. According to Donna, we would be interviewed by a features reporter named Crystal Jennings. I was disappointed because I'd had a crush on Matt

Lauer since high school and thought we might have a moment. *Oh well.*

If it couldn't be Matt, I wished Scotty were the one doing the interview. At dinner the night before, he'd reiterated that the piece would be short and sweet. "It'll be a day at the beach," he'd said. "A walk in the park."

I shifted my gaze from Matt Lauer and Ann Curry to the rest of the studio, but I didn't recognize a soul. *I wish I watched The Today Show enough to know who Crystal Jennings is,* I thought with a laugh.

Wendy sat down next to me, again with the half smile. I moved over on the couch and tried to get comfortable, then checked the tiny microphone attached to my dress.

Donna appeared out of nowhere, adjusting her headset. "Are you two ready? Crystal will be out in a minute."

I cleared my throat. "I think so."

Wendy said nothing.

"You'll do great," Donna said.

"Thanks, Donna, I hope so."

Again, Wendy said nothing. *And she's going to be on TV?* I thought.

Donna turned on her heel and disappeared into a sea of cameras and lights, leaving me with Wordless Wendy. I'd given up trying to get her to speak, so I inspected my fingernails in awkward silence until Crystal approached us a few minutes later. We both stood up, and Wendy's face suddenly lit up like the sun.

"Crystal, darling, it's soooo lovely to see you," she said with an enormous smile. They hugged like long lost sorority sisters, and I raised my eyebrows.

"You look amazing. Did you get a new ring?" Crystal took Wendy's left hand in hers to admire the enormous rock perched on the fourth finger. It looked like an ice cube.

"Just a little Valentine's Day present," Wendy said with a wink.

Crystal turned to me. "Waverly, it's so lovely to meet you." She seemed genuinely friendly, so I relaxed a bit.

"It's nice to meet you, too." I smiled and extended my hand.

"So you two have met?"

Apparently sitting in total silence next to someone qualifies as *having met*, because Wendy and her huge crazy smile responded in the affirmative.

Crystal adjusted her microphone. "This should go really smoothly. A few quick questions for each of you, and we'll be done. We'll keep it lighthearted and fun."

"Sounds wonderful," Wendy said, again flashing the grin, which was beginning to freak me out.

"We'll start shortly. Just wait for my cue."

Suddenly my hands started sweating, and I felt a massive wave of panic course through me. I don't think I'd ever been so nervous. I took a deep breath and closed my eyes. I could only hope stage fright wouldn't render me completely frozen when the cameras turned on.

* * *

A few minutes later, a flash of bright lights filled the room. As Matt Lauer passed the figurative torch to Crystal, all I could think was that I hoped the nuclear glow wouldn't magnify every pore on my face.

After the introductions, Crystal turned to Wendy. "You're a married mother of three, correct?"

Wendy smiled widely. "I married my high school sweet-heart, and now we have two beautiful girls and a boy...and two adorable dogs and a cat. My husband and kids are celebrating Valentine's Day here in New York with me tonight, probably in Times Square. I'm sure it will be very romantic." She spoke with a Southern drawl I hadn't noticed earlier.

Crystal laughed, and I could hear additional laughter throughout the studio.

"Sounds like quite a family," Crystal said.

"Oh, they're wuunderful," Wendy said, patting her hair. "They absolutely make me who I am as a relationship expert. I love my family to pieces, and without them in my life, I wouldn't feel like I could genuinely offer advice to anyone."

I blinked. *Did she really just say that with me, the single, childless columnist, sitting right next to her?*

"Of course, of course," Crystal said. "Family is very important. Do many of your readers ask you about that? How to keep the magic going when you have a family?"

"Oh *yes*. So many of my readers are juggling marriage and children, and careers now too, which makes it hard to keep that spark alive. I always tell them it's critical to keep the channels of communication open. Long-lasting love is *all* about communication."

Interesting statement coming from someone who doesn't speak unless the cameras are on, I thought.

Suddenly Crystal turned her attention to me.

"Waverly, again, thanks so much for joining us this morning."

I smiled and tried to look her in the eye without getting more nervous than I already was. "I was happy to be invited."

"So what do *you* have planned for Valentine's Day?"

I froze for a moment. Why was she asking me that?

"I guess this is it." I put my palms up in front of me and forced a smile.

She laughed. "You're not married, correct?"

I nodded. "That's correct."

"Have you ever been married?"

"No, but my column focuses more on dating...as opposed to married life."

Wendy unexpectedly poured her syrupy voice onto the conversation. "But you *were* engaged once, isn't that right, Waverly?"

What?

I hoped she couldn't see the confusion in my face. Was I on trial? How did she know that? What was going on?

I tried to mask my distress with another smile. "Yes, that's true. I was engaged once." I looked out at the sea of cameras and wondered if Scotty was in the room. Why hadn't he warned me about this airbrushed nightmare?

"Really? So what happened there?" Crystal said.

I cleared my throat and sat up straight. I was determined not to crack. "Unfortunately, we just weren't right for each other. But the good thing is that we realized it before it was too late." I stole a glance at Wendy. *Take that, you fake Southern bitch.*

"What about now? Do you have a boyfriend?" Crystal said.

FRICK.

I'd prepared a great answer for *Are you seeing someone?* But somehow it never occurred to me that the question would be posed another way.

"A boyfriend? Um, not currently."

I heard Wendy shift in her seat next to me. I think she may even have chuckled under her breath.

But ask me if I'm seeing someone! I pleaded with my eyes. *Ask me if I'm seeing someone!*

Crystal turned to face the camera and smiled. "Okay then, we have two relationship columnists here, one happily married with three children and three pets, and one single. This should make for a fun conversation."

More laughter from the camera pit, and suddenly I wanted to drop to the ground and crawl away. I remembered those *Jesus Saves* pamphlets in the subway and thought maybe I should have taken one. I could use a little saving at the moment.

I did my best to keep smiling and nodding as Crystal asked Wendy several questions I didn't really hear. I didn't really hear Wendy's answers either. I spaced out so completely that I don't think I really heard anything until Crystal uttered my own name several moments later.

"So, Waverly, what about you?" Crystal said.

I blinked and hoped the blank look on my face would tell her to repeat the question.

She didn't miss a beat. "What's on the mind of single people out there? Is there a common theme you've been seeing?"

I put my index finger on my chin. "Besides bad dates? Because dating disasters are definitely a popular topic of complaint."

She laughed, as did the crew, and I felt myself loosening up. Despite the rocky introduction and my momentary space out, I had prepared well for the interview, and I knew I could do a good job.

"Dating disasters?" Crystal raised her eyebrows. "That certainly sounds interesting. Do you want to share one or two with us?"

Now we're talking.

I was about to recite a couple stellar ones from my dating treasure chest of horror, but before I could pull out anything, Wendy pulled the rug out from under me. She leaned toward Crystal and put her hand up.

"If you don't mind," she purred in her Southern drawl, "I'd loooove to hear about the last bad date *Waverly* went on."

I looked at her and hoped my mouth wasn't open. *What?*

She smiled. "I mean, it's been ages since I've been on a date with anyone besides my huuusband, so I'd luuuv to hear what it's like in the trenches from someone who's still there. Don't you agree, Crystal? You're happily married too. Aren't you curious?"

"Why, sure," Crystal said with a laugh. "Why not? Waverly, let's hear it. Got any good stories of your own for us?"

I dug my fingernails into the fabric of the couch.

Oh my God.

I hadn't been on a bad date in months. Except for my December trip to see Jake in Atlanta, I hadn't been on a date at all.

Crystal was eagerly waiting for me to reply, probably along with a good chunk of the TV audience. I'd already said I didn't have a boyfriend, so it was too late to mention Jake. And if I wasn't dating, what the hell was I doing writing a column about dating?

I'm so dead right now.

Then suddenly it came to me.

Lie.

Just tell some stories from before you started seeing Jake, a little voice in my head said.

Technically, that isn't lying, right? Just a chronological adjustment?

You can do it, the little voice said. *You are the queen of bad dates.*

I smiled and sat up a little straighter. I could do this. I could totally do this.

"Actually, I've had some pretty crazy dates lately."

"Really?" Crystal said. "Do share."

I took a deep breath, then I jumped in…reached back in time…and pulled some of my legendary dating disasters into the present.

First I told the story of the guy who took me to a lovely dinner up in Sausalito for our first date, with great conversation and chemistry, followed by a walk along the water and a stunning view of the San Francisco skyline. During the walk he held my hand and told me what a great time he'd had, and how much he was already looking forward to seeing me again. After that romantic declaration, he kissed me gently on the mouth, squeezed my hand, then calmly mentioned that—by the way—his last relationship was with a *man.* Then he asked if I was okay with that.

Next I explained how a coworker wanted to set me up on a blind date with his college roommate, so I agreed to meet the guy for a drink. He was nice enough, so one drink turned into two, which turned into dinner, over which the guy casually mentioned that he was...still married. *Oh, so you're separated?* I asked, to which he coughed and replied, *Not legally.* In other words, *I'm totally married.* Nice. Might want to punch that ticket before you get on the dating train, my friend. Might also want to punch my idiot friend who set us up, while you're at it.

I topped it off with a gem about a man McKenna's husband Hunter set me up with. He was an ER doctor who worked with Hunter on occasion at UCSF, and Hunter said he was friendly and single. That was pretty much all I knew going in, but at least he wasn't married. When I showed up at the bar, he was wearing a huge Yankees jacket, like the scary replica kind that is blue wool with white leather sleeves and all sorts of awful patches all over it. It also turned out that he lived in Fresno, which on a *good* day is a four-hour drive from San Francisco. He said he trekked all the way to UCSF twice a month because he loved blood and the "rush of working on gunshot victims." Oh, and he was fifty-one years old, with two ex-wives *and* two kids in college. I thanked Hunter for introducing me to Fresno Gramps, then promptly asked him not to set me up anymore.

When I finished speaking, Crystal's mouth was open, as I imagine was most of Middle America's. Wendy was a bit pale.

"Wow," Crystal said. "You've just made me appreciate my husband more than I did this morning. Thanks so much for sharing." Everyone in the camera pit laughed.

"My pleasure." I laughed too. It was frightening how much material I had to draw on from my own life. I was, indeed, the queen of bad dates.

It was a dubious title, but it was all mine.

Crystal smiled at the camera, then turned to face us. "So moving on, how about a word of Valentine's Day advice for our viewers? Wendy, have any tips for our married fans out there?"

Wendy smiled, then slowly crossed her hands over her heart and sighed. I wanted to kick her.

"To me, every day with my husband is Valentine's Day, and that's how I think every married person should live their life. So my word of advice today—and every day—is to say *I love you*, every single morning when you wake up, and every single evening before you lay your head on the pillow. Don't take a minute for granted, and be sooooo grateful that you're not going through life...alone."

Again, I hoped my mouth wasn't open. *Is she for real?*

"Thanks for that, Wendy," Crystal said. "And Waverly, what about you? Any parting words for our non-married viewers out there?"

"I guess...I guess I'd have to say, don't post anything about your Valentine's Day plans on Facebook."

"Don't post your Valentine's Day plans on Facebook?"

I nodded. "Yes, don't do it, because all you're going to do is annoy your single friends. And it's important not to annoy your single friends, because you never know when you're going to need them."

She laughed, and suddenly I realized that I'd forgotten to heed Kristina's suggestion to throw sex into the conversation. So out of nowhere I blurted, "Oh, and while we're on the topic of Facebook, I don't recommend being Facebook friends with anyone you've slept with either. That can get a little dicey."

The entire camera crew cracked up. I think Wendy may have gasped, but I couldn't be sure.

Oops. Had I just made myself sound like a slut?

I panicked and threw a Hail Mary. "Um, I got that last nugget of advice from my good friend Andie. She's says it's a lot harder to do than you might think." As soon as her name flew out of my mouth, I wished I could reel it back in. Why hadn't I stopped at *good friend*?

Crystal laughed again and faced the TV audience. "Well, there you have it, America, advice from the experts. From all of us at NBC, I'd like to wish our viewers a happy Valentine's Day, no matter how you spend it. Wendy Davenport of Love, Wendy, Waverly Bryson of Honey on Your Mind, thank you so much for joining us. It's been a pleasure. Matt, Ann, back to you."

The stage manager cut to a commercial break, and the bright lights finally dimmed.

Crystal stood up and removed her microphone. "Thanks, ladies. That was great, really great."

"Thanks, Crystal," I said. *Had* it gone well? I was in a daze.

"It was just wonderful," Wendy said, standing up and giving Crystal a hug.

Crystal hurried off and disappeared, and I stayed seated, relieved it was over.

"Good luck with that little column of yours," Wendy said, her Southern accent suddenly way less noticeable. "If you get your readership up *and* work on your stage presence, maybe I'll invite you to appear on my new show sometime. You might want to do something about that hair, though."

I looked up at her bleached blonde helmet. *What?*

But she was already gone.

Chapter Twelve

"How could you let that happen, Scotty? She totally ambushed me!"

He reached over and put his hand on my shoulder. "I'm so sorry, gorgeous. Believe me, I'm flabbergasted, and I feel awful. I can't believe what happened in there."

It was about an hour later. Scotty and I were seated at one of the approximately fifty thousand Starbucks in Manhattan, a block away from Rockefeller Plaza. I opened a pack of sugar and stirred it into my latte. "Wendy Davenport, *blech*. Why was she so horrible to me? Why does she hate me so much? And why didn't you warn me about her at dinner last night?"

His shoulders drooped. I'd never seen him look so rattled. "Scout's honor, I swear that I literally found out *while you were on camera* that the network is launching a new talk show about relationships, and apparently Wendy is auditioning to be the host. I guess she saw you as a threat, so she wanted to make it clear that she's more qualified than you for the position. At least that's my take on it. I'm so sorry, hon."

"I can't believe she brought up my engagement. What a *bitch*."

"You did great." He put his hand over mine. "You held your own, and I don't think it was that obvious that she was trying to undermine you. She clearly had done her homework on you, though."

"You don't think it was *obvious*? Are you on crack? I kept waiting for her to pull out a photo of me in my heinous prom dress or something, just to make me even *more* insecure."

He winked. "Hey now, no one looks good at the prom. It's part of the fabric of American culture."

I half laughed, shaking my head. "After the segment was over, she even made fun of my hair. *MY* hair. I bet that woman sprays her way through a can of Aqua Net a week."

"I wouldn't be surprised."

I took a sip of my latte and set it down on the table. "Okay, Scotty, tell me the truth. Did I recover okay?"

"You were splendid."

"Are you just saying that because I'm upset? It's all kind of a blur right now."

"Positive. You were very entertaining. Witty, too." He looked remorseful, but sincere.

I narrowed my eyes at him. "You owe me for not hating you right now."

He reached across the table and touched my cheek. "I truly am sorry, and I feel just terrible. I hope you believe me."

"Well at least you're human. It's nice to finally know I'm not the only screw-up in this friendship."

"Waverly, you're hardly a screw-up. And I promise I'm not just saying that."

I half smiled. "Thanks. I admit I'm feeling a little better now. How do you always know how to pick me up, even when I'm face down in the emotional gutter?"

"It's part of the job description, princess."

"You mean the job of Mr. Perfect?"

He laughed. "Only for you."

* * *

When I got back to San Francisco late that night, there was another envelope slipped under my door. It had my name and address in the same neat handwriting as before, again in red pen, again with no return address. How inept was my postman to keep delivering my mail to the wrong apartment? And what did it say about me that I was more concerned with the intelligence of my postman than the possibility that I had a stalker? Call it a sixth sense, but I had a feeling that it was innocuous. I just couldn't believe someone would bother to stalk *me*.

I rolled my carry-on into the living room and sat down on the couch. I opened the envelope. Just as before, the note inside had just one word on it.

lie

"Lie about what?"

Suddenly I remembered what I'd said on *The Today Show* about not being in a relationship—and the stories about my "recent" dates.

"Oh my God," I said to the letter. "How did you know?"

I put the paper back in the envelope and tossed it onto the coffee table, then leaned my head back on the couch and stared at the ceiling. After a moment I sat up again. "Technically, I wasn't really lying, you know. I just moved up the timeframe of a few dates."

I chuckled and pressed my palm against my forehead. *Why am I talking to a piece of paper?*

I thought about my experience on the *Today Show* set and suddenly wished I had someone to share it with other than Scotty. I'd left a message for Andie before getting on the flight home, but she hadn't called me back and was now probably on a date with Gaslamp Guy. McKenna and Hunter were at her parents' ranch in Oregon, where she never got reception.

I looked at the old-fashioned clock on the wall above my pine armoire. It was nearly nine o'clock. Exhausted, I stood up and stretched my arms over my head, then wheeled my carry-on bag toward my room.

"Happy Valentine's Day, Jake," I said softly. "Wherever you are." I'd checked my phone every few minutes all day in hopes of seeing a Valentine's message from him, to no avail.

Chapter Thirteen

The next morning I overslept. When I saw the clock on my night-stand, I freaked.

OH MY GOD.

I had less than thirty minutes to make it to the *Sun* for my meeting with Eloise Zimmerman, which I was already looking forward to about as much as my next appointment with my ob-gyn. I leaped out of bed and sprinted to the bathroom, then ran back to my bedroom and opened my closet door. I threw on a dark blue dress, grabbed a strand of pearls and matching earrings from my jewelry box, and rummaged around for a pair of black flats. *Why do I have so many pairs of shoes I never wear?* I thought.

I looked over at the clock on my nightstand. Twenty-two minutes to go.

I'm so dead.

I tossed my makeup bag in my purse and raced out the door. I was lucky to find a cab on the corner. As I held up my arms to hail it, my phone flew out of my purse. When I bent down to pick it up, I noticed the large black button on the top of my right shoe was missing. In its place was a big shiny nub that looked like a screw.

Lovely.

I jumped in the cab.

"I'm headed downtown, but I need to make a quick stop at Walgreens, please. And I'm in a huge hurry."

The driver hit the gas, then the brakes three blocks down Fillmore at Walgreens. I sprinted inside while he waited for me with the meter running. Ninety seconds later, I was back in the cab with a roll of electrical tape.

On our way downtown, I performed a bit of creative surgery on my shoe. When I was done, I held my foot away from me to evaluate my work. *Not bad.* I pulled out my makeup kit and applied some lipstick and blusher, a high-risk maneuver without a mirror. Just when I thought I was finally done, I noticed that my dress was covered in lint.

Oh no.

I'm screwed.

Then I had an idea.

I opened my purse and pulled out the electrical tape. I ripped off a few large pieces and made circles with the sticky side facing out. Then I set to work de-linting. My dad, the MacGyver of our family, would be so proud.

I arrived at the *Sun* office at 9:58. In the elevator, I inspected my dress and shoes. As long as no one looked *too* closely, I could pass for someone who had been awake for more than half an hour.

* * *

When the elevator doors opened, I noticed how much quieter the administrative floor was than the editorial one, with fewer people and a lot less paper.

And, I suspected, a lot more anxiety.

I walked on eggshells down the long hallway to the far corner office in the back. Many of the cubes in the center of the room were empty. When I got to the corner office with *Eloise Zimmerman* on the door, I stopped and poked my head in. She was sitting at her desk, her back to the door, the phone to one ear. Her hair was indeed high. And big. And stiff.

"I don't *care* what he told you, he's a liar, and he's overcharging us," she hissed into the phone loud enough for me to overhear. "So fire him today, or I will."

Yikes. Who is she firing?

I tried to look busy by checking my messages on my phone, then getting myself some water and touring the floor, stopping by every few minutes to see if she was done. At ten fifteen I finally got up the nerve to tap on the door. She was still on the phone, clearly unhappy.

"Ms. Zimmerman?" I whispered and pointed to the air behind me. "Just wanted to let you know I'm outside?" *Why did I pose that as a question?*

I expected her to wave me away like a mosquito, but she smiled and motioned for me to sit down in the chair across from her desk. I raised my eyebrows, then sat down and folded my hands in my lap. *This should be interesting.*

"Okay, I need to go now, I have a meeting," she said to whoever was on the other end of the phone.

I stared at my hands.

"Okay, okay, sounds good. I love you too. Bye."

I looked up. *I love you too?*

She hung up, then swiveled around in her chair to face me. "I'm sorry to keep you waiting."

"Oh, it's no problem."

"That was my husband. He hired a contractor to paint our house, and the man is *completely* incompetent. But Joe, my husband, is such a pushover that he just can't let him go, even though we're getting robbed blind."

I tried not to laugh. There I was, thinking she was bringing the house down, when all she was doing was painting it.

She leaned back in her chair and narrowed her eyes. "So... you're Waverly Bryson." She wore a dark blue pantsuit and a long, fat-linked gold necklace.

I nodded, trying not to look too nervous.

"And you were on *The Today Show* yesterday." She removed her glasses and let them dangle around her neck on a thin chain, also gold.

"Yes ma'am. I got back last night,"

"How did it go?"

I shifted in my seat. "I think it went pretty well. It was a little awkward in the beginning, but it ended up fine. The producers and correspondent seemed happy with it."

She slowly moved her fingers over the gold links. I wondered if that necklace cost more than my monthly rent.

"I missed it, but I heard it was quite good."

I smiled. "You did?"

She sifted through a stack of papers on her desk. "We got a few calls from advertisers who really liked that you speak to the single community. That's a coveted demographic for advertising because no kids means more disposable income."

I didn't say anything because I had absolutely no idea what to say.

She put her glasses back on. "I want to bump you up to two columns a week, starting immediately. Can you handle that?"

"Twice a week? Yes, I think I can do that."

"Good. This paper is a sinking ship, so getting our advertising dollars up is top priority right now. You'd be amazed at how much content we've been paying for that no one actually *reads*."

I was surprised at her candor. I still had no idea what to say.

"Okay then, keep up the good work. We need it right now." She swiveled her chair away from me to face her computer. I took that to mean the meeting was over.

I stood up and slowly backed my way toward the door. "Thank you, Mrs. Zimmerman."

She nodded, not looking up from her computer screen.

I smiled to myself as I reached the doorway and turned to face the ninth floor. I hadn't been expecting that at all. She actually liked my work! That could mean a bright future for Honey on Your Mind…and for me.

I was two steps out the door when she spoke again. "Oh, and Waverly, my dear."

I returned and poked my head back inside. "Yes, Mrs. Zimmerman?"

"I think you've got something hanging off the back of your dress. It looks like *electrical tape*?"

* * *

Mortified, I sprinted to the nearest restroom to fix my dress. *Ugh.* Just when I thought I'd had it all together for ONE shining moment, a Waverly one spoke up to remind me I still had a long way to go. I checked for additional unwanted accessories clinging to my body, then dropped by Ivy's desk to say hi.

"Waverly! How are you? It's been ages." She cleared off a pile of newspapers from a chair and motioned for me to sit down.

"I know, it's been forever. How was your trip?"

"Honestly, I don't even want to go there. Kansas is bonkers, and I'll leave it at that. You look super cute, by the way. Nice dress."

"Thanks." I smiled, deciding to keep my latest Waverly moment to myself. "That bad, eh? It's not every day you hear someone use the word *bonkers*, especially about a whole state."

"Let's just say that in small-town Kansas, or at least in my family, it is simply not acceptable for a woman in her late twenties to be unmarried."

"They're on your case to get married *already*?"

"You have no idea." She pushed a strand of curly red hair behind her ear. "Both my sisters are under twenty-five and already married, with *babies*, so because I'm twenty-eight and don't have a ring on my finger, they've all come to the conclusion that I must be a lesbian. Especially since I live in San Francisco."

I laughed. "No way."

"My sisters, not so much. But my parents? Totally. Plus my mom is convinced that even if I *am* straight, once I turn thirty, I'll be too old for any eligible man to ever want me. She's even talked to her pastor about it."

"Too old at *thirty*?"

She nodded. "According to unofficial Kansas state law, I have less than two years to get Casey to marry me, or I will officially become an old maid. So I guess the countdown is on."

"Wow, I can see why you left Kansas."

"I'm never moving back there. Add in my tattoos and belly ring to my advanced age, and I might as well be from Mars."

"Aren't women supposed to be from Venus?"

She waved a hand in front of her. "Mars, Venus, Jupiter, whatever. So hey, nice job on *The Today Show*."

"You saw it?"

"It was very entertaining. I thought you did great, but what was up with that bitch sitting next to you?"

I pointed at her. "Exactly! Thank you!"

"Total bitch."

"She was faking that Southern accent too,"

"Really?"

"Well, maybe not faking, but definitely embellishing. You know what it made me realize?"

Ivy raised her eyebrows.

"Have you seen my Honey Note that asks *Is it worse to be fake or bitchy*?"

She smiled. "Of course, that's one of my favorites."

"Well that woman made me realize that it's actually possible to be both fake *and* bitchy, because she was one fake bitch."

She laughed. "I thought your dating stories were really funny. The married twenty-two-year-olds in Kansas might not agree, but I loved them. I didn't know you were dating so much, though."

"What?"

"I didn't realize you went out on so many dates. But it was good. Gave you some street cred." She punched the air. "Plus it put that big-haired fake bitch in her place."

I was about to explain how the dating stories I'd told weren't exactly recent, when the sound of Nick's voice made us both turn our heads.

"Now come on, ladies, you shouldn't talk about Eloise Zimmerman like that."

"Sorry, wrong big-haired fake bitch," Ivy said as he approached her cube. He was wearing a light blue shirt that said, "BRING BACK THE THREE-MARTINI LUNCH."

I stood up and smoothed my hands over my dress. "Eloise wasn't nearly as bad as you two said she'd be. I just met her, and she was actually pretty nice."

They both narrowed their eyes.

"I'm serious. She even asked me to double the number of columns I write. She said I'm doing a great job."

"Really?" Ivy said. "I've never heard of her saying that to anyone before."

I smiled. "She said to keep up the good work."

Nick squinted at me. "I reserve the right to remain suspicious."

I crossed my arms and squinted back. "Is it really *that* hard to believe my column is good?"

"Hey now, don't put words in my mouth." He put his hands up. "You know I think your column is amazing. We're just saying that Eloise Zimmerman isn't known for being nice to anyone, that's all."

I dropped my arms to my sides. "I'm sorry, I guess I'm just a little rattled after what happened on the show yesterday."

"You mean when you threw your friend under the bus?"

I winced. "You saw that?"

"I saw. That was pretty brutal."

I put my face in my hands. "I know, I totally panicked. I suck."

"Ah, she'll get over it." He waved a hand dismissively.

"You think so?"

He nodded.

I looked at Ivy. "Do *you* think so?"

"I've never met her, so it's hard to tell. But if you and she are as close as you say, maybe it'll be fine. She'll understand."

I looked back at Nick. "I hope you're right."

"I'm always right. I've already told you that."

Chapter Fourteen

As soon as I was outside the *Sun* office on Market Street, I called Andie on her work line.

"Andrea Barnett."

"Hey, it's me."

"Hi." Her voice sounded dry.

"I'm back from New York. Want to meet for a drink tonight to catch up?"

"I can't tonight," she said, not elaborating.

"Got a date with Gaslamp Guy?"

"Yep."

"So how's that going?"

"Fine. Listen, I'm really busy right now. I'll talk to you later, okay?"

I closed my eyes.

"Andie, is everything all right?"

"It's fine."

"Are you sure? Because I'm really sorry about that comment yesterday. I don't know what I was thinking, using your name like that."

She didn't respond.

"Andie?"

"I watched it here at the office," she said. "With my boss and about ten of my coworkers."

I stopped walking.

"Oh my God."

"I need to go now." She spoke in a tone I'd never heard before.

"Okay," I said softly.

"Bye, Waverly."

She hung up, and I hung my head. I stood there on the sidewalk for a few moments, not knowing what to do. I wanted to call Jake but couldn't. I wanted to call McKenna, but I knew I'd only get her voicemail.

I suck.

The whole bus ride home, my mind was consumed with a single thought.

I really screwed up.

* * *

When I got back to my apartment, I noticed a sticky piece of paper on the floor near the mailboxes. I saw it was a "missed delivery" notice, addressed to me. The return address read *Soulflower Floral Design.*

Flowers?

I unlocked my front door and pulled out my phone, then sat on the couch as I dialed the number on the card. The cheerful woman on the other end of the line said she had a "lovely arrangement" for me and would send it over within the hour.

A lovely arrangement?

It had to be Scotty.

I stood up and looked at my phone for a moment, then set it alongside the missed delivery notice on the coffee table. I decided to change into jeans and have lunch before reading through the deluge of e-mails that had come through in the past twenty-four hours.

Eloise Zimmerman had been right. My *Today Show* appearance had struck a chord with a lot of frustrated single viewers, dozens and dozens of whom had e-mailed to tell me just how frustrated they were.

I scrolled through the messages as I munched on my sandwich.

Hi Waverly, great job yesterday. I'm thirty-three and single and SO glad to see I'm not alone out there. Men can be such tools. Thank God for wine and girlfriends.

Dear Waverly, I'm dying laughing over your Fresno Gramps story. Thanks for sharing, and I'll be checking out your column for sure. Keep it up.

Waverly, you give me hope that I'll find my Mr. Right AND that I won't end up like that plastic Barbie who was on the show next to you. You go, girl!

Dear Waverly, did you see any hot guys while you were in New York? All the babes in San Francisco are cocky players. Or married. Or gay. Some of them are all three.

The comments weren't *all* positive, though. Hardly.

Ah, Miss Picky who thinks she knows it all, you need to take a reality check, my dear. If you don't get married soon, all the good ones will be taken. Then where will you be? That's right, ALONE. Oh, that's right, you already ARE.

As a God-fearing Christian, I'm appalled that an unmarried woman would mention having multiple sexual partners on national television. Where are your morals? I hope the Lord has mercy on you.

That one was signed "Good luck in Hell."

Okay then.

I was debating whether to call Andie again when I noticed a message near the bottom of the inbox.
It was from Jake, and it had been sent the night before.
Oh my God, he wrote back.
I put my sandwich down and clicked to open the e-mail.

To: Waverly Bryson
From: Jake McIntyre
Subject: Message received

Hi Waverly, I saw you on TV today and was a bit thrown for a loop, as you can imagine. We're clearly not on the same page, so I think it's best if we nip this in the bud. I'm sorry for not calling, but I think you probably know how I'm feeling at the moment.
Take care of yourself. You deserve to be happy.

Jake

My jaw dropped. I picked up my phone to call him, but before I could dial, my doorbell rang. I stood up to answer it.
"Yes?"
"Delivery for Waverly Bryson."
"Come on in." I pressed the button and opened the front door. A few seconds later a man approached with a vase full of red roses.
"These are really for me?"
"Yes ma'am." He handed me a clipboard. "Can you sign here, please?"

I signed the receipt and traded him the clipboard for the vase, which I set on the coffee table after he left. I pulled the card out of the little envelope.

Hi Waberly, I miss you so muck too. I also want you to be my Valentine. Good luck in New York this week. I know you'll be great because you always are. I'll call you on the big day to say hi from my new phone, which I'm picking up today.

Love, Jake

I set the card on the coffee table and picked up the missed delivery notice from the florist.

It was dated February 12.

Oh my God.

Jake had sent the flowers before my trip to New York, but I'd left a day earlier than planned.

He sent me a dozen red roses, and I went on national television and announced that I didn't have a boyfriend.

I had to talk to him.

I ran into my office and picked up the phone.

Please answer, please answer, please answer. I paced around the room.

His voicemail picked up after one ring.

You've reached Jake McIntyre with the Atlanta Hawks. I'm currently on leave and without access to this phone. If you need to reach me, please contact the Hawks main office at 404/555-HAWK and ask for Melissa. Thanks.

The message ended with no beep.

I sat down in my chair and closed my eyes. I could feel tears welling up.

After a few moments I realized I still had the phone in my hand. I was desperate to talk to him but didn't have his new number yet, and he didn't have a land line at his house. I put the phone on the desk. How did everything get so screwed up? What had I done? How had I made such a colossal mess of, well, *everything*?

I looked over at all the e-mails on my computer screen. Dozens and dozens of e-mails sent to a relationship advice columnist who had just appeared on *The Today Show*.

I felt like a fraud.

For a few moments I just sat there, not sure what to do. Then I opened my desk drawer and unfolded the latest mystery letter.

lie

How fitting.

* * *

At six o'clock I walked over to Andie's place two blocks away at Fillmore and Washington. I sat on the front step of her building and waited.

At six fifteen, I was cursing myself for not having brought something to read and for forgetting my phone.

To distract myself, I watched a woman in a tiny car unsuccessfully trying to parallel park across the street. It reminded me of my college days in Berkeley, when I had to master the art of squeezing into the teeniest of places or I never would have made it to class.

Thinking of college made me remember how I'd met Andie. It was our junior year, and McKenna and I were at a semiformal date party thrown by the SAE fraternity house. SAE stands for *Sigma Alpha Epsilon*, though I knew many a scorned sorority girl who called it *Same Assholes Everywhere*. Mackie and I were proud, anchor-wearing members of DG (Delta Gamma), and our pledge sister Whitney was dating an SAE named Bryan. For the record, Bryan was, and still, is a non-asshole. Thank God, because Whitney ended up marrying him.

Bryan set us up with two of his buddies, Marc (with a C, he pointed out) and Tyler. We met them at a pre-party at the SAE house, and while McKenna and I sipped wine coolers, they downed cheap scotch in plastic cups. We all thought we were so classy and mature. Ha. Then we were bussed en masse (again, so classy) to the venue for the evening. I briefly cringed as a vision of the strapless turquoise dress I wore flashed before my eyes. In addition to math, English, science, and history, I think that every teenage girl should be required to learn the immutable fact that *no one looks good in strapless turquoise*. No one.

Marc with a C was quite charming, especially to Waverly with a Buzz. We had a lot of fun together, so when he accidentally put his hand on my boob on the dance floor, I laughed it off. Later, when he was telling me about all the top law schools he'd been accepted to, he accidentally put his hand on my butt. Looking back, he was clearly an arrogant jackass. But he was also very good-looking, and he was paying a lot of attention to me. My youthful naiveté, blanketed in a blissful fog of alcohol, kept me from heeding the red flags everywhere. When the DJ played "Truly Madly Deeply" by Savage Garden, we made out like no one's business. I felt so cool, because when you're in college, making out on the dance floor is even more cool than drinking wine coolers.

I "fell asleep" on the bus on the way home, as did Marc with a C. I'd long lost McKenna and Tyler, whom I'd last seen swapping spit in a dark corner. When we pulled up in front of the SAE house, it was nearly two in the morning.

Marc nudged me awake.

"Waverly, we're home," he whispered.

"Dad?" I mumbled.

"What?"

OH MY GOD.

I sat up straight, pretending to be sober. "Um, we're home?"

He put his arm around me and gently helped me from my seat, then led me out of the bus and toward the front door of the fraternity. The front lawn was filled with similar couples in a quiet, drunken stupor. It reminded me of the "Thriller" video.

"I should really go home," I whispered. "It's so late." Even in my impaired state, I knew I shouldn't go inside with him.

Suddenly Mr. Super Nice Guy was in the house. "Are you sure?" He smiled and put his hand on my cheek. "Your skin is so soft," he whispered.

"I really should go." Ms. Super Mature Girl *also* was in the house, and she was just saying no to, well, to going in the house.

He hugged me close, then leaned down and kissed my ear. "Just come with me and lie down for a while."

I shook my head. "I really should go. But thanks so much. I had a lot of fun."

"Are you sure?" He kept his arms around me.

I looked up at him.

He was so cute.

So, so cute.

I hesitated for just a moment.

And then Ms. Super Mature Girl threw in the towel.

"Okay."

I only planned to make out with him, of course.

"Great." He took my hand and led me inside. "My roommate's out of town," he whispered, squeezing my hand.

"Okay, cool." I whispered back, following him in the shadows.

He pulled out his keys when we reached the end of his hall. Then he noticed that his door was ajar, and a light was on inside.

"What the…?"

"I thought your roommate was out of town," I said.

"He is."

He pushed the door open, and there was Andie, fully dressed and sitting on his bed, casually reading an Econ 150B textbook.

"Hi, asshole," she said calmly. "Did you have fun tonight?"

I stood there with my mouth open. Marc with a C wore a similar expression.

"Andie, what are you doing here?"

"You're an asshole," she said again. She calmly closed her textbook, then stood up and stepped toward us, not looking at me.

Then she flat-out punched him in the face.

"Ow!" He put both hands on his cheek. I gasped and covered my mouth with my hands.

Andie looked at me and smiled. "You can have him." She left and shut the door behind her.

"What a bitch," Marc said, still holding his face.

"I'm guessing that was your girlfriend?"

He shrugged. "Not officially."

Not officially?

Suddenly I knew I had to get out of there. "I should go." I turned toward the door.

"Hey now, don't leave." He reached for my hand.

I caught my breath. His touch was so warm on my skin.

"Please stay," he whispered. "Don't leave."

I wanted to do the right thing, I really did. But I also wanted to make out with him.

He's bad news, I thought. *Nothing good can come out of this.*

I closed my eyes for a moment, then pulled my hand away and opened the door.

"Bye, Marc."

I shut the door behind me, navigated the dark hallway, and finally made it back outside.

When I reached the front lawn, Andie was almost to the sidewalk. I stopped in my tracks, mortified. The dim streetlights were all that illuminated the block. I hoped she hadn't heard me.

But she had.

And she turned around.

Frick.

I stood there in my ugly turquoise dress, holding my purse along with my breath, wondering what she would do.

She looked at me for a moment, saying nothing.

I bit my lip.

And then I learned all I needed to know about Andrea Barnett.

She smiled.

She waved me over and introduced herself, and from then on we were friends.

I admired her for calling Marc out for lying (he'd told her he was sick and wasn't going to the party), and she admired me for leaving his room after I found out he had a girlfriend, even though they hadn't been "official." We never talked to Marc with a C again, but I hear he's balding with a paunch now.

* * *

At 6:32, I saw Andie walking up Fillmore Street. She was hand in hand with a tall, lanky blond with curly hair that fell just below his ears. I assumed he was Gaslamp Guy.

I stood up and wiped the dust off my jeans as they approached. "Andie, hey."

"Oh, hi."

She turned to Gaslamp Guy. "This is Waverly."

I held my hand out. "It's nice to meet you, um…" I'd forgotten his name. Or had I ever learned it? Then I noticed how familiar he looked. "Have we met before?"

"I don't think so."

"We're sort of in a hurry," Andie said.

"Do you have a moment to talk?" I hoped she could see the pleading look in my eyes but also that Gaslamp Guy couldn't.

"I'm sorry, I can't tonight." The coldness in her reply was something I'd never heard from her before, and it scared me.

"What about tomorrow night? Pizza at Dino's? Beers at the Kilkenny? You pick. It's on me."

She turned to Gaslamp Guy. "Are we hanging out tomorrow?"

He put his hand on her shoulder. "I have to go visit my uncle, remember?"

She looked back at me and sighed. "Okay then, fine. Tomorrow."

"Kilkenny at seven?"

"Whatever." She opened the front door of her building and went inside without making eye contact.

"Okay, see you then. It was nice to meet you…I'm sorry, what was your name again?" I couldn't call him *Gaslamp Guy* to his face, at least not until I knew him better.

"CJ," he said as the door shut behind them.

"Bye, CJ."

I stared at a crack in the sidewalk. I had to get Andie to forgive me.

Then something hit me.

Suddenly I knew why Gaslamp Guy seemed so familiar.

He looked a LOT like the guy in the photo on Ivy's desk. The photo of her boyfriend, Casey.

Chapter Fifteen

The next morning I went straight to the *Sun* office. I had to see that picture on Ivy's desk. What I saw when I arrived, however, was not what I expected.

Her desk was bare. As was her cube, and three others around it.

I scanned the room, hoping to spot a familiar face to find out what was going on, but I didn't recognize anyone.

Nick will know.

Then it occurred to me that I had no idea where his cube was. Or did he have an office? Maybe he was gone too?

I stopped a random girl walking by.

"Excuse me. Do you know what happened to Ivy Grant?"

"Ivy? I think she got laid off."

"What? I thought that was over."

Random Girl shrugged. "They're calling it the same round, just additional notifications, whatever that means. The latest group found out yesterday afternoon."

"Oh my God." I stood there for a moment, and Random Girl disappeared down the hall before I could ask her about Nick.

I sat down at Ivy's empty desk and ran my hand over the spot where the framed picture of her and her boyfriend had been displayed. So proudly displayed. Could Casey and CJ really be the same guy? I hoped I was wrong.

After a few moments, I stood up and asked the next person I saw about Nick. She pointed to a cube at the far end of the hall. I made my way past a sea of empty cubes and spotted him sitting at his desk, focused on his computer screen.

"Hey, Nick."

"What's up, Brysonator?" He was wearing a tan shirt that said, "HELEN MIRREN IS HOT."

"Nice shirt. And did you just call me *Brysonator*?"

"Indeed I did. I watched a little Arnold on TV last night. To what do I owe the pleasure of this visit?"

"What happened to Ivy?"

He slid a finger across his throat.

"I can't believe she's gone. What happened?"

He shrugged. "They came through here yesterday afternoon and brought the axe down, and *bam* she was gone. I told you, this place is falling apart."

"That's so sad. Ivy was really cool."

His expression said, *Are you that stupid?*

"But you already knew that," I added.

"Thanks for keeping up."

"So where did she go?"

Again, he looked at me like I was an idiot. "Well, Sherlock, I'm thinking...*home*."

"Okay, you're right. I'm not thinking clearly right now. But I'll tell you why." I lowered my voice. "I think Ivy's boyfriend might be cheating on her...with a good friend of mine."

"Talk to me." He cupped both his ears.

I sat down at the chair next to his desk and leaned toward him. "My friend Andie, you know the one I, um, threw under the bus on *The Today Show*?"

He nodded.

"Well she met this guy a few weeks ago, and they've been hanging out a ton ever since."

"Continue."

"I finally met him briefly yesterday, and his face was super familiar. At first I couldn't place it, but then I realized that he looked a lot like the guy in the picture on Ivy's desk. Like *a lot*, a lot."

Nick's eyes lit up. "What's his name?"

"CJ, but that could be his initials. Ivy's boyfriend's name is Casey, right?"

He nodded. "You really think it's the same guy?"

"Maybe. Do you know Casey's last name?"

"No idea."

"Me neither."

"So Ivy's Mr. Perfect could be, in fact, a total douche bag," he said.

"Could be."

"Which would mean that Ivy *isn't* my parallel universe girl. She could be headed for this universe right here."

"Could be."

He smiled. "I like it."

"So what do I do?"

"You have to tell her."

"Tell who? Andie or Ivy?"

"Both. If it's the same guy, that is."

I sighed. "I can't believe this. Andie is really into him, and she's never really into anyone."

Nick didn't say anything, but I could see the hope in his eyes.

"So how do I find out if it's the same guy? Do you have Ivy's phone number?"

He turned to face his computer and started typing. "I can probably get it out of the archived employee directory." He pulled up her file, then wrote her name and number on a sticky note. "Here you go. But if anyone asks, you didn't get this from me."

I took the paper and put it in my pocket. "Thanks, Nick, I'll look into this. But first, I have some serious damage control to do with Andie." I stood up and started to leave.

"Bring hyacinths."

I turned around. "What?"

"Hyacinths. They mean *I'm sorry.*"

"They do?"

"They do."

"How do you know that?"

He leaned back in his chair and interlaced his hands behind his head. "I speak flower."

"You speak *flower*?"

"Indeed. It's just one of many things that make me an amazing boyfriend."

I leaned down to give him a kiss on the cheek. "Ivy would be lucky to have you."

"I know."

* * *

When I got home I called the Atlanta Hawks hoping to track down Jake, but I was forced to leave a message with some perky yet entirely unhelpful assistant who had obviously never heard my name before. It clearly wasn't my day for finding people I needed to speak with. I copied Eloise Zimmerman when I e-mailed my column to Ivy's *Sun* account, just to make sure the file wouldn't end up lost in cyberspace. I hadn't heard anything from anyone about the latest layoffs, which made me wonder just how safe my freelance position really was. Or maybe that's exactly what it meant? That my job *was* safe? No news is good news?

I had some time to kill before meeting Andie, so I decided to go for a run to clear my head. Once outside my apartment I turned left on Sacramento to run west through Pacific Heights, which led to Laurel Heights, then Presidio Heights as Sacramento turned into the quaint Lake Street, one of my favorite parts of the city. There was a little bit of an incline, and as my breath got deeper I began to think about what to say to Andie, and also what to say to Jake, if I could reach him. I'd never excelled in the conflict department, so to be faced with two problems at once was making my head spin. I wished I could talk to McKenna, but she was still out of town and out of cell phone range.

It was up to me to figure out what to do.

I kept my eyes glued to the sidewalk ahead of me and timed my steps to match the lines separating the cement squares. *Step on a crack, break your mother's back...step on a line, break your mother's spine.* Breathing heavily, I wondered how my life would have been different if I'd grown up with a mother. Would I be better at expressing my feelings? At dealing with conflict? My dad had done his best, but he was a quiet man. And as a result, sometimes I felt all alone in my head, trapped with my thoughts, not sure how to share them because I'd never really learned. I'd gotten much better over the years with the help of Andie and McKenna, who I *knew* loved me and would always be there for me, but once in a while, even with them, I still froze up, relying on them to see what I was thinking through my actions...or my eyes. Sometimes, I just couldn't put my thoughts into words. At least verbally. On paper I was much better because I had time to think about things, to edit and perfect my thoughts, but that approach doesn't work in real-time conversations.

I blinked away a few tears. McKenna and Andie knew me well enough to see through the jokes and strong-girl façade, and I'd grown to rely on their ability to know when I was really hurting inside. Jake didn't know me as well, and he clearly had no idea what I was thinking.

I'd pushed away the first guy I'd really cared about since Aaron, and I didn't even know why.

Neither did he.

I turned right at Park Presidio, then looped up and around back along the green trails that run parallel to Lake Street, beginning the long, steep incline back to Pacific Heights. I passed by a small playground on my left and watched a young mother pushing her baby in a tiny swing. Nearby, another mother watched proudly as her toddler son barreled down a low plastic slide, plopping gently into a soft pile of sand.

My thoughts turned to McKenna and the baby growing inside of her. Would she be showing the next time I saw her? Even though I was sad things were going to change between us, I was excited because *she* was so excited. McKenna had always known she wanted to have kids, unlike me, who still had no idea, or Andie, who was dead set against it.

I looked ahead and soon reached the beginning of the steepest part of the hill, breathing heavier than I could ever remember at this point in the jog. I stopped for a moment and put my hands on my hips, looking up to the top. I wondered about what I would say to Andie tonight, hoping she'd forgive me for my latest Waverly moment. Then my thoughts turned to Jake. It was killing me that I hadn't been able to explain myself to him.

"Waverly Bryson, it's time to whip yourself into shape," I said out loud. A postman standing on the corner turned his head and smiled. I wondered if he knew I was talking about more than my burning lungs and thighs.

I put my head down and started to climb.

* * *

A couple hours later I was sitting on a barstool at the Kilkenny Pub, a particular favorite of mine. It was a Friday evening and the place was getting more crowded by the minute, but longtime owner Jack O'Reilly, as always, took the time to say hello.

"Waverly, muh luv, it's luvely to see ya." He leaned across the bar and kissed me on the cheek. "Ware huv ya buhn?" I loved his accent.

"Hi, Jack, I'm trying to cut back on the beer." I patted my stomach. "I'm thirty now, so I've got to watch my figure."

He pretended to stab himself in the heart. "Oh my, yur killan' meh." Then he smiled widely. "Now whut ken I get ya?"

"How about a Blue Moon with an orange slice?"

He winked. "Excellent choice, muh luv."

"Can you make it two? Andie will be here in a minute."

He disappeared for about fifteen seconds. Then, like magic, two frosty Blue Moons were sitting on the bar in front of me.

"Thanks, Jack."

He winked and left to attend to another customer, and over his shoulder I saw Andie walking through the front door. I stood up and grabbed my coat from the adjacent stool as she approached. I couldn't believe how nervous I was.

"Hi. I saved you a seat. Got you a beer too."

"Thanks." She took off her coat and glanced around the room, then sat down and picked up the glass.

I leaned over and removed a small bouquet of hyacinths from a paper bag next to my stool. "These are for you." I handed them to her.

She set her beer down and took the flowers, but she didn't say anything.

"They mean *I'm sorry*," I said softly.

She kept her eyes on the flowers, still not speaking.

I swallowed. "I totally choked and blurted that out because I got nervous. I...I feel awful."

Suddenly she looked me right in the eye, and for a moment it was like I was back in college the night we met, standing on the steps of the SAE house, afraid of what she would say. I could feel my throat tightening up, and for a moment I thought I might start to cry.

Then history repeated itself.

She waved a hand in front of her and reached for her glass. "Ah, don't worry about it."

I smiled. "Really?"

She shrugged. "I was pissed for like a day, but then I got over it. It was sort of funny, actually."

"You think so?"

"*Now* I do. At first I was mortified because all my coworkers saw it, as did my *mom*."

"Your *mom*?"

She sipped her beer. "Yep. And my aunt and grandmother."

"Oh my God." I put my face in my hands.

"Apparently I was wrong about not knowing anyone who watches *The Today Show*."

"Andie, I'm so sorry."

She pushed her hair behind her ears. "It's okay. I *have* been with a lot of guys. But it's not like I'm the only one. After that aired my coworker Alyssa told me she's actually *introduced* herself to guys she's slept with."

"No way."

"Way. She's done it several times too. Totally forgot ever meeting them."

"That's hilarious. How could you forget someone you've been naked with?"

"Oh believe me, you can. It's really not that hard."

I laughed. "You have the best attitude."

She took a sip of her beer. "Who really cares, right? I figure I'm single, so what's the problem?"

"That's the way *I* look at you, I mean, at *it*."

"I said more or less that exact same thing to my mom when she called me in horror."

"Your mom called you in horror?"

"Yep. It was actually a pretty fun conversation. It had been a while since I'd told her to back off, and she needed to hear it."

I laughed. "How are you so amazing?"

"You get thick skin when you have a mother like I do."

"I really am sorry. I hope you know…how much I love you, Andie."

She set her beer down and smiled. "I do."

I leaned over to give her a hug, which she briefly returned before pushing me away and opening her eyes wide. "So oh my God, what was *up* with that skank on the show with you?"

I laughed. "Thank you!"

"She was tragic. And that hair? Yowsa."

"I hated her. Scotty said she was trying to upstage me so NBC would hire her to host some new show about relationships."

"I bet my mom adored her." She shifted on the barstool and gave a dirty look to a tipsy girl who had just bumped into her. "I loved your dating stories, by the way. I'd forgotten all about Fresno Gramps."

"Ugh, me too. I hadn't planned to talk about my own dates at all, but that Wendy witch screwed everything up, which is why I was so frazzled. Not that that's an excuse, but I was totally caught off guard and had to pull something out of nowhere."

"I was wondering about that. What did Jake think?"

I made a sad face.

"Andie, it's not good."

"Oh no."

"*SO* not good."

"What happened?"

I told her all about the roses and his e-mail, and about how I called but couldn't leave him a voicemail because his phone had been shut off.

"Ouch."

"I know. I totally blew it. I can't believe it."

"Did you e-mail him?"

I sighed. "I thought about it, but I didn't know what to say. And maybe I'm old fashioned, but I feel like it's wrong to use e-mail for important things like that."

She shook her head. "That's because you're thirty. People in their twenties propose over text message these days."

Despite my sad state, I smiled. "How do you manage to make me laugh no matter *how* bad I feel?"

"It's a gift. So what are you going to do?"

"I don't know."

"What would you tell one of your readers?"

I thought about the question for a moment before responding.

"I think I'd say…go find him."

She raised her eyebrows. "Like *get on an airplane* go find him?"

"Yeah, why not?"

"Maybe because it's crazy?"

I put my finger on my chin. "You have a point. But you know how I feel about e-mail and texting and Facebook and all that fake communication. So yes, I think that's what I would suggest. I'd say something like, *If you can't speak to him on the phone, then get on a plane and go find him.*"

She smiled. "Are you going to do it?"

I took a sip of my beer and set it on the bar. "Are you joking? Of course not."

"Why not?"

"Because it's crazy."

"But you just said you'd tell someone else to do it."

"Yes, but that was for someone *else*…"

"Well, why not do it yourself?"

"Because…because…"

"Well?"

I slouched on the barstool. "Because…he might shoot me down."

"So?"

"And that would be mortifying."

"So?"

"So?"

"Yes, *so*. Who cares if you end up mortified? How is that worse than how you're feeling right now?"

For a moment I saw myself at the bottom of that hill hours earlier, looking up, wanting to make things right.

I blinked and looked at her.

"You're right."

"I know."

"I need to see him. I need to tell him how I feel about him."

She smiled. "That's my girl."

"But what if…what if he doesn't want me back?" I put my hand on her arm and squeezed.

"Then we'll come back here and get really drunk. Okay?"

I laughed. "Okay, deal."

* * *

When I got home, I went straight to my office and checked out flights to Boston. I had no idea how to go about finding Jake's sister's house, but I knew someone who did. I pulled out my phone and called him.

He answered on the second ring.

"It's nearly ten on a Friday night. Is this a booty call?"

I laughed. "You wish it were."

"Perhaps."

"I need your techy brain. Are you free?"

"You mean right now?"

"Yes."

"If I answer in the affirmative, will it damage the image you have of me as a player?"

I laughed. "Of course not, Nick."

"Okay, then how can I help you?"

I told him I needed to go see Jake, and that he was at his sister's house in Boston helping out with her kids. All I knew was that her maiden name was Natalie McIntyre, her husband's name was Tim, and they had two daughters and lived in the suburbs.

"Is that enough information for you to find an address?" I twirled a pen between my fingers.

"Do you doubt my powers?"

"Have I ever?"

"Give me fifteen minutes. I'll call you back."

"Should I book a ticket? It's nonrefundable."

"Book it."

"You sure?"

"Again with the doubt. Do you even know who you're talking to right now?"

"Okay, okay, I'll book it."

"Cool, talk to you in fifteen. And hey, did you find out about Casey?"

I made a fist. "Ack. I totally forgot to ask. I was so focused on getting Andie to forgive me, and then on this thing with Jake, that I completely spaced. I'm sorry."

"No worries, you'll figure it out."

"Couldn't you just look it up? You're the master at using the Internet to find private information about people, right?"

"Yes, but I don't use my genius for my own romantic pursuits."

"Why not?"

"Because it's creepy. I don't want to be creepy Internet stalker guy."

"Creepy Internet stalker guy? I like that. Maybe I should get you a shirt with that on it."

"And maybe you shouldn't, unless you plan on getting a matching one for yourself."

I winced. "Touché. Call me as soon as you can."

"Will do."

I hung up the phone and studied the flight options on the screen in front of me. I couldn't believe what I was about to do.

Chapter Sixteen

"I leave town for a few days and everyone goes crazy." McKenna opened the door to Pea in a Pod, a maternity store on Sutter Street that sold super cute clothes I wouldn't mind wearing after huge meals. If I could afford them, that is. It's amazing how adding a little extra belly room to a pair of jeans can add two hundred dollars to the price tag.

I nodded and followed her into the store. "I hope you've learned a valuable lesson here."

She stopped walking and turned around. "You hope *I've* learned a valuable lesson?"

"Yes."

"And what would that be?"

"That you can't leave town anymore."

She rolled her eyes and began looking through a rack of suits. "Okay then, as I was saying, everyone went crazy when I was gone."

"Hey now, I'm not crazy. I'm just following the advice I'd give any of my readers." I put my hands over my heart, then flapped my arms like a bird. "I'm following my heart to Boston. Do you think I'm crazy for that?"

She paused.

"I think you're crazy for many things, but no, not for that. I'm proud of you, actually."

I smiled. "You are?"

She held up a black pantsuit in front of the mirror. "I know how afraid you are of getting hurt, Wave. And this is really putting yourself out there, so yes, I'm proud of you." She turned to face me. "What do you think of this suit?"

"I like it. Try it on."

"So when do you leave, exactly?"

"Tomorrow morning at eleven. It was the first flight I could get that wouldn't break the bank."

"And you're sure he's in Boston?"

I nodded. "I called the Hawks office yesterday just to check, and they said he's still on leave."

She pulled out a blue suit and held it up. "And you're just going to show up at his sister's house? What about this one?"

"Too grandma. And yes, that's my plan."

"You're not going to get a hotel room? Showing up with no place to stay could make you look a little psycho."

I put my hand over my mouth. "Oh my God, you're totally right. In the movies, when people jump on a plane and show up on someone's doorstep, they never seem to book a hotel first, much less a rental car. But then again, in the movies they don't wait a whole week for a cheaper flight."

She tapped her temple with her index finger. "See? It pays to think like a Boy Scout."

"Oh my God. You're already acting like a mother. You do realize that, don't you?"

Her eyes got big. "I know! Isn't it awful? I found myself cutting up Hunter's steak last night. You think he'd be capable of cutting up his own meat, given that he's a *surgeon*."

I laughed. "You would indeed. Okay, I'll get a hotel room and drop my stuff off first. Now that I think about it, this reminds me of a dating story my friend Nick told me about."

"What about this?" She held up a plain black dress. "Could I get away with this at work? And what story?"

"I like that one. And the story was that Nick had gone on like two dates with this girl, and their third date was supposed to be dinner at his place on a Friday night. So when Friday evening rolled around, she showed up at his apartment...with a small suitcase."

"She showed up with a suitcase? Why?"

"Because apparently she assumed she was going to spend the weekend with him."

"No way. Did she live far away or something?"

"He said she lived in the Marina."

"Where does Nick live?"

"Prodromou Gulch."

"Prodromou what?"

I tried not to laugh. "Prodromou Gulch. According to Nick, it's an up-and-coming neighborhood nestled between North Beach and Telegraph Hill."

"Never heard of it."

"Give it time, you will."

She shrugged and returned to the rack. "Anyhow, that girl was clearly a psycho, and you don't want to be *that girl*, right? Quirky's cute. Psycho, not so much."

I pointed at her. "You're totally right. See? You can never leave town again." I leaned down to whisper to her stomach. "Did you hear that, baby Kimball? Auntie Waverly says your mommy can't ever leave town again."

* * *

Monday morning I did leave town.

I got on a plane and flew 2,712 miles. As we crossed over the country, I tried to read a book, but inevitably my thoughts turned to what I would say to Jake and, of course, whether I was doing the right thing.

When we finally landed, I had to track down my rental car. Doubt enveloped me again.

Was this a mistake? Am I headed for an epic Waverly moment?

I closed my eyes and focused on the flowers Jake had sent me for Valentine's Day. I nodded and chanted to myself.

I'm doing the right thing. I'm doing the right thing.

In no time I had the keys to a purple PT Cruiser with wood paneling. *Sleek.* Directions in hand, I made my way to my hotel, a Hyatt smack in the middle of a sterile suburban corporate park in Waltham. I had to be the only person there who wasn't in town on business.

The man behind the counter smiled at me. "Welcome to the Hyatt Summerfield. Are you here for the insurance conference?"

I shook my head. "No, just a regular room. It should be under the name Waverly Bryson."

"Oh, well, okay then." The look on his face showed he clearly had no idea what to make of the likes of me, a young woman unaffiliated with any corporate entity. I highly doubted Waltham was a hot tourist destination for singles.

Key card in hand, I made my way to the third floor. I washed my face and changed my clothes, then stood in front of the full-length mirror to evaluate the severity of the situation. I had the inevitable flat airplane hair, but because of the long flight and three-hour time difference I didn't have time to wash and dry it. I was already risking being branded a stalker by showing up unannounced at Jake's sister's house. Doing it late at night would only make it worse. A black headband was my only hope.

On the way out to the car, I called Andie. She answered on the first ring.

"Talk to me."

"I just left the hotel. My heart's beating so fast, I think I might have a heart attack right here in the parking lot of the Hyatt Summerfield, which is in a corporate park in Waltham, in case you were wondering. Waltham is a suburb of Boston, in case you were wondering."

"Chill," she said. "Deep breaths, deep breaths."

I smoothed my hair with my hand. "I can't believe I flew all the way here. I don't know if I can do this."

"You're already doing it. Remember, you have nothing to lose, right?"

"Okay, okay. I keep telling myself to think about those roses he sent me. Those were good, right?"

"Exactly. He wanted you to be his Valentine. No matter what happens now, remember that, okay?"

"Okay, I will."

"Good girl."

I fished the car keys out of my purse. "Will you fill McKenna in? I think she's at her ob-gyn."

"Consider it done. Now get in that car and go."

I hopped into my so-not-hip PT Cruiser. "Okay, okay, I'm in the car. Wish me luck."

"No wishing for luck. You don't need luck."

"I hope you're right. Okay, I'll check in later."

"You'd better. Now *go*, before you change your mind."

"Okay, okay, I'm going. Bye."

Here we go.

* * *

Fifteen minutes later, I found myself driving through the streets of Waltham, approaching what I hoped was the correct house. I parked and tilted the rearview mirror to have a peek at my face. *Yikes.* I was as pale as a celebrity in a mug shot. I dug out a blusher and some sheer plum lipstick from my purse and applied just a touch of each. I removed my headband, ran a brush through my hair, then put the headband back on. I checked myself in the mirror again.

That's better.

I took a deep breath and got out of the car. My legs felt weak and wobbly. I willed them to start moving.

When I reached the front walkway, I paused to admire the house. It was quite pretty, very typical New England, with two stories, white wood and green trim, and a well-manicured front yard with wide steps leading up to the front door. There was a Radio Flyer wagon next to a swing on the porch. Several lights were on inside, but it was quiet.

I started toward the front door. When I realized I'd made it all the way across the yard and up the steps without tripping even once, I hoped that meant good things were on the horizon. I hesitated for a moment, then rang the bell.

I tried to remember to breathe.

After a few moments I heard footsteps. The door opened to reveal an attractive woman with shoulder-length brown hair. She was about five-six and had bright blue eyes like Jake's. I recognized her from the photos in his house.

"May I help you?"

I smiled. "Yes, hi, I'm looking for...Jake?" Again with the unnecessary question mark. *Ugh.*

"Jake?"

"Yes, I'm a friend of his. My name is Waverly Bryson."

Her face softened, and she opened the door wide. "Oh, of course, please come in. I'm Natalie, Jake's sister."

I took a step inside the foyer.

"We saw you on *The Today Show*."

I froze.

"You did?"

She smiled. "It was very entertaining. So what brings you to Waltham? Are you in town for work?"

Suddenly I wished I knew the name of that conference everyone at the Hyatt was attending. Throwing it out now seemed like a smart idea. Throwing out *any* reason for why I was standing there, other than the truth, seemed like a smart idea.

I bit my lip. "Not really. Is Jake here?"

She kept smiling, but her eyes showed pity. "Oh, Waverly, I'm so sorry, but no, he's not."

I hoped she meant he'd gone out for ice cream, but I doubted it.

"He went back to Atlanta last week."

What? I'd just called the Hawks office, and they'd said he was still on leave.

"Come in, please sit down." She gestured toward the living room. "Tim's upstairs putting the girls to bed. He'll be down soon though. Please, take off your coat. Can I get you something to drink?"

"Oh no, thanks, I'm fine." I carefully sat down on a pale green couch with thick white stripes, wishing I could disappear into its folds and reappear on my own couch in San Francisco. What had I done?

Natalie sat down on a love seat across from me. "How long have you lived in San Francisco?" The look on her face was kind, and I hoped she couldn't see how foolish I felt.

I forced a smile. "I grew up in Sacramento, then went to college at Berkeley. I've lived in the city since I graduated."

"I just love San Francisco. You went to visit Jake in Atlanta once, didn't you?"

I wondered how much she knew about that. "Yes, he's been a good…friend to me. I'm…I'm really sorry about your baby," I added softly.

"Thanks." For a brief moment her expression turned solemn, and I thought she might cry. Then she snapped out of it and smiled. I was impressed by her strength. "Are you sure I can't get you something to drink? Some water? Or maybe a glass of wine?"

Wine? Hmm...maybe you could insert an IV into my arm and drain the whole thing right here. That would certainly have eased my anxiety.

"Thanks, but I'm fine. I should probably get going anyway. My...my friends will be wondering where I am." I knew I was stretching the truth, but my friends *were* wondering where I was. She just didn't know the friends I was talking about were Andie and McKenna, 2,712 flight miles away.

Just then I heard someone coming down the stairs. Even though Natalie had already said Jake wasn't there, for a second I hoped to see his face. I turned to look, but the face that appeared was bearded, and its owner was probably wondering what a total stranger was doing on his couch at eight thirty on a Monday night. Bounding down the stairs with him was a huge golden retriever.

"Well, hello there." He held out his hand. "I'm Tim O'Connell."

I stood up to shake his hand, but before I could speak, the dog ran right at me. With its enormous snout leading the way, it beelined...for my crotch.

Nice.

I tried to push the dog away, but it wasn't having any of it. All I could do was laugh.

"Cooper!" Natalie jumped up to grab the dog, apparently a male, thus making our encounter even more awkward. She yanked him away by the collar and scolded him. "Cooper, that's terrible. Terrible!" She said *I'm so sorry* with her eyes as she led him into another room and shut the door.

Tim was clearly trying not to laugh. "Sorry about that. Cooper's quite a curious fellow." There was something in his demeanor that made me like him immediately. He didn't take things too seriously, so how could I?

I smiled and held out my hand. "I'm Waverly, a friend of Jake's. I like to make an entrance. How did I do?"

His handshake was firm. "Not bad, not bad at all."

Natalie rejoined us and put her hand on Tim's back for a moment, then gestured toward me. "Waverly was in town and thought she'd stop by to see Jake, but she didn't know he'd already gone back to Atlanta." I exhaled as I realized how plausible the story sounded as she told it. Apparently I was a better actor than I thought.

Tim motioned me back to the couch. "Please, sit back down. Let me get you a drink. How does a glass of wine sound? Maybe a scotch and soda to calm the nerves? You've just survived a vicious dog attack, after all."

I laughed. "You're so kind, but I should get going. I'm so sorry to just show up like this. I really…I really thought Jake would be here."

Natalie stood up and put her hand on my arm. "Don't worry about it for a minute. It was lovely to meet you, Waverly. Jake's spoken very highly of you."

"He has?"

She sensed the surprise in my voice. "I hope you realize it's nothing personal that he didn't tell you he was going back to Atlanta. That's his way sometimes."

"It is?"

"Definitely. You know how men can be when they're stressed. They clam up, and Jake is textbook like that. I'm sure he'll be sorry to hear he missed you."

I stiffened. "Please don't tell him I was here. He didn't know I was going to be in town, so I really would rather he didn't know."

"You don't want me to tell him?"

"If you don't mind. I…I don't want him to feel bad."

She smiled. "Okay then, we won't say a word."

"Scout's honor," Tim said.

I hoped they would keep their word, however odd the request.

I waved goodbye to Tim as Natalie showed me to the front door and handed me my coat. "Thanks for coming by, Waverly. I'm so sorry you missed him."

I smiled and put my coat on. "He *is* a popular guy."

"Always has been."

"It was so nice meeting you. Again, I apologize for stopping by unannounced. And I'm…I'm so sorry about the baby."

"Thank you." She took my hand and squeezed it gently. "Maybe we'll see you again sometime."

I hope so, I thought.

* * *

The second I sat down in the PT Cruiser, I pulled out my phone and called Andie. She answered immediately.

"You're calling me already? What happened?"

"You're not going to believe it."

"I don't think I want to know. Was he there with another girl? Did he make you cry? Did he kick you to the curb? Do I need to fly out there and kick his ass?"

"He didn't do anything."

"What?"

"He wasn't there."

"Where was he?"

I sighed. "In Atlanta."

"What? I thought you were sure he was in Boston."

"I really thought he was, but his sister said he went back to Atlanta last week."

"Oh lordy. So where are you now?"

"Sitting in the rental car, half a block down from her house."

"So you spoke to her?"

"Yes."

"What did she say?"

"She was nice. Really nice, actually. So was her husband. They said he went home last week, and that was about it."

"Did they know who you are?"

"Yes. They saw me on *The Today Show.*"

She laughed. "As did the whole world, apparently. So what are you going to do now?"

"I don't know. What do you think I should do?"

"You tell me. You're the famous advice columnist."

"Not helpful, Andie."

"Hey now, I'm just speaking the truth. What would you tell your readers?"

I sighed. "I think...I think..."

"Well?"

I waited a moment before finishing the thought.

"I think...I think I need to go to Atlanta," I finally said.

"That's my girl."

"Am I crazy?"

"Yes," she said immediately.

"Thanks for that. It's just what I needed to hear right now."

She laughed again. "You're welcome. Now get yourself on a midnight plane to Georgia."

Now I was laughing too. "*A midnight plane to Georgia*? How long have you been waiting to use that?"

"A while. I wasn't sure when I'd get a chance, but that was pretty sweet, wasn't it?"

"Definitely good timing, I'll give you that. Although I doubt I could actually *get* on a midnight plane to Georgia at this point."

"I imagine you can take a morning plane to Georgia too."

"Ha. Okay then, I guess I'm headed south. I'll keep you posted."

"Good luck."

"I thought you said I didn't need luck?"

"Oops, you're right. Then go get 'em, cowgirl!"

"*Go get 'em, cowgirl?* Have you been drinking?"

"Just a glass of wine. Okay, maybe three. I'm hanging out at my place with CJ."

"I could use a glass of wine myself right now. Hey, Andie, why do you call him CJ?"

"Everyone does. It's his initials."

I was about to ask what his initials stood for, but I didn't get a chance. "Listen, speaking of CJ, I'm being rude to him by yapping on the phone, so I'm gonna hang up, okay? Call me from Atlanta?" she said.

"Will do. Bye."

I called McKenna but got her voicemail. I left a long, rambling message that included all the relevant details, plus the unfortunate snout-to-the-crotch incident. I sighed and leaned my forehead against the steering wheel for a long moment, then fired up the PT Cruiser and drove back to the corporate park.

* * *

Back in the hotel, I changed into my pajamas and sat cross-legged on the bed. I booted up my laptop, planning to work on the first of my two columns for the week. As I read through e-mail after e-mail from readers wondering why it's so hard to find love, one in particular caught my eye. It was from a woman named Tamara, whose latest crush had just *texted* her to cancel their first date. Her note said that was the last straw, she'd been hurt so many times she was ready to cash in her chips and walk away from the table. I closed my eyes and leaned back against the headboard, thinking about Tamara and her chips. Gambling was the perfect analogy for what *I* was doing at the moment.

After I finished the column, I called United Airlines. The customer service representative said there'd be no fee to move the date up for my direct flight back to San Francisco if I was willing to fly standby, but she put me on hold to check on how much it would cost to reroute me through Atlanta. As I waited for her to throw out a number, I wondered if I'd have to sell my car to pay for the ticket.

"Ms. Bryson? Are you still there?"

I held my breath.

"Still here."

"We can get you on a flight leaving Boston at two forty-five tomorrow afternoon, arriving in Atlanta at five thirty-three."

Then she told me the change fee, and I flinched.

"Do you want me to make the change, Ms. Bryson?"

I studied my reflection in the mirror, thinking about what Andie had said.

You can do this. You're already doing it.

Then I thought about the roses Jake had sent me.

He wanted to be your Valentine. Remember that.

Suddenly I heard my voice saying the opposite of what I was thinking.

"I think I'll just fly directly to San Francisco," the voice said. "You think I can get on that flight tomorrow?"

"It shouldn't be a problem, Ms. Bryson."

I shut my phone and looked at my reflection again.

"I'm sorry," I said to the mirror.

Chapter Seventeen

I still had loads of time after I checked in the next morning, so I decided to do something I'd never done at an airport: have a real sit-down meal. Usually I raced my way through airports, always on the verge of missing my flight, but today I wasn't in the mood to spend any more time in the greater Boston Area than absolutely necessary.

I sat down at a table in Legal Seafoods. While I was scanning the menu, I heard a familiar voice behind me.

"Waverly?"

I turned around.

No way.

"Scotty? What are you doing here?"

He kissed me on the cheek. "I should be the one asking, my love. *I'm* the one who lives on the East Coast and travels all the time for work."

I laughed. "This is true."

He picked up his coffee mug. "Shall I join you? Or are you still mad at me?"

"Of course you should join me. And no, I'm not still mad at you. I could never stay mad at you. You're too pretty."

He moved his bag to my table and sat down. "So talk to me, princess. Why on earth are you in Boston?"

"You don't want to know."

He raised his eyebrows. "I don't want to know?"

"It's a little embarrassing."

"Oh now you *have* to tell me. Come on, sweetheart, talk to me."

I grimaced.

"Waverly…"

"Okay, fine, I'll tell you."

And I did.

As I finished the story, Scotty finished his lobster omelet.

"So that's it." I shrugged and dug into my French toast. "You may proceed to heckle."

"Oh kitten, I'm not going to heckle you."

I pointed my fork at him. "I already told you I'm not mad at you anymore, so you don't have to suck up. It's okay, really, heckle away. I deserve it."

"I can't believe you came all the way to Boston and he wasn't even here."

I sighed. "I really thought he would be. I called the Hawks the day before I left, and they said he was still on leave."

"Did you think about flying down to Atlanta?"

I poured more syrup on my plate. "I did, briefly, but I just couldn't pull the trigger. Plus it was crazy expensive to change my flight, so that made my decision a lot easier."

"So that's it? You flew all the way across the country, and now you're just turning around and going back to San Francisco?"

"So it seems."

"You sure you want to do that?"

"What *can* I do, Scotty? I mean, am I supposed to just go show up at Jake's house in Atlanta? Who *does* that?"

"Maybe *you* do."

"But isn't that, like, insane?"

"Maybe, maybe not."

"But won't it just scare him away?"

"Maybe, maybe not."

"You're not being very helpful." I took a sip of my coffee. "Besides, I already showed up at his sister's house, remember? Even though I'm pretty sure she thought I was in town visiting friends, I already feel enough like a stalker."

"What would you tell a reader who was in the same situation?"

I put my coffee mug down. "Again with the *What would you tell your readers?* question. Like my readers actually care what I have to say."

"Hey now, don't sell yourself short. You're really good at what you do. Everyone thought you did a great job on the show."

"They told you that?"

He nodded. "You were refreshing and honest and *different*, Waverly. People like different."

Ha. Different was *one* way to put it. A polite way.

"So what happened with that horrible Wendy Davenport anyway? Did she get her own show?"

He nodded. "Sad to say, but she did. It's starting pretty soon, actually."

I stuck my tongue out. "Blech. She's gross."

"My dear, there's no accounting for taste where big advertising dollars are concerned."

"I know, I know. I just hate to see her rewarded for being such a...*bitch*. It doesn't seem fair."

He opened his mouth to say something, but I interrupted him. "And please don't say life isn't fair. I don't feel like hearing that right now, okay?"

He smiled. "That's not what I was going to say."

"I don't believe you."

"Fine, don't believe me. All you need to do is listen to me."

"Listen to you?"

"Yes, listen to me."

I narrowed my eyes as he pulled out his phone.

"You, my dear, are going to Atlanta. *Today.*"

"I am?"

"You are. You need to go see Jake. Tell him how you feel."

"I do?"

"You do. And I'm paying for the flight change *and* upgrading you."

"You are?"

"I am. And I won't take no for answer. Think of it as my way of paying you back for the *Today Show* incident, okay? Now hang on a minute."

He dialed the in-house travel agent for NBC, and before I knew it, I was on the two forty-five flight to Atlanta.

In first class.

* * *

Several hours later I found myself in another rental car, this one a scary teal Pontiac. I had Jake's address displayed on my phone, as well as directions to his house. I drove by all the T.G.I. Friday's again, this time with even more butterflies fluttering around in my stomach. As I headed toward the burbs, I adjusted the radio and listened to the latest Kelly Clarkson song, which was followed by a Scotty McCreery song, then a Carrie Underwood song. I put my hand on my heart and gave a mental shout-out to some of my favorite *American Idol* alums, out there tearing up radioland and making one of their biggest fans proud.

It wasn't that late, but it was long past dark when I finally made it to Virginia Highlands. I turned left on Jake's street and caught my breath when I saw his house up the road, the memories of our weekend together flooding my brain—and heart. As I approached his place, everything about it was exactly the same as I remembered.

There was just one little glitch.

A car was parked on the street in front of his house, but his dark green Tahoe wasn't in the driveway.

It was nearly seven.

Maybe the Tahoe was in the garage? Did he have two cars? *Please don't let him be out of town.*

Just as I'd done at his sister's, I drove past the house and parked down the street, trying to ignore the fact that this was the *second* time in less than twenty-four hours I'd engaged in semi-stalker behavior. (Or full-blown stalker behavior, depending on whom you asked.) I checked my face in the rearview mirror, then retrieved the small bouquet of hyacinths I'd bought on the way. Given how hard I found it to speak English when I was nervous, I thought I might as well try speaking in flower.

I got out of the car and walked toward his house, part of me hoping he was home, part of me hoping he wasn't, and part of me wondering if the crazy police were going to show up and haul me away. As I neared the front door, I practiced the beginning of my little speech in my head. As long as I could remember the beginning, I knew I could get through the rest. *Hi, Jake, before you say anything, I have something to tell you...*

I reached for the doorbell but stopped just short.

I squeezed the bouquet, took a deep breath, and pressed the button.

Then I waited.

And waited.

And waited.

Is the doorbell broken?

I knocked on the door, but still he didn't answer. Hoping maybe he was in the shower, I gave it five minutes and knocked again, but still no answer.

Crap.

I exhaled and sat down on the front step, wrapping my coat around me. I'd always had a secret fantasy of coming home from a long day at work to find a guy I liked sitting on the steps to my building, holding a flower, or maybe even a whole bouquet. I'd walk up and smile, and before I could speak he would stand up and smile back at me, then apologize, or say he missed me, or maybe even that he loved me. I'd never thought too much about the details because the fantasy never really got past the part where I saw him sitting there. (It also had never happened. But hope springs eternal.)

It was now seven thirty.

I decided to call McKenna. I was doubtful that I'd actually reach her, but if anyone could calm me down, she could. Lucky for me, she answered.

"Hey, Wave, where are you?"

"Atlanta. I'm sitting in the dark on the front step of Jake's house, waiting for him to come home. Oh my God, that sounds *SO* stalkerish when I say it out loud."

"You're really sitting on his doorstep?"

"I kid you not, I'm literally sitting on his doorstep, in the dark, holding a bouquet of flowers."

"That's sweet."

"I feel ridiculous, Mackie."

"It's sweet. Do *not* feel ridiculous."

"I love you for saying that. Can I just tell you that?"

"I love you too. So when is he getting home?"

"No idea." I set the flowers down and wrapped my arms around myself. "I just hope it's soon. It's getting really cold out here."

"He'll be so happy that you're there."

"You think?"

"How could he not? It's so romantic."

"I like to *think* it's romantic. That keeps me from thinking it's ridiculous."

"I promise, he'll love it."

"So what's up with you? All good on the baby front?"

"Actually, I have a little news."

"News? Good news, I hope?"

"Definitely good news. We're having a girl!"

"Oh my gosh, a baby girl?"

"Yep, can you believe it?"

"Wow, that's so exciting. Congratulations."

"Thanks. We're so happy. And there's one other thing..."

"One other thing?"

Silence.

"You sure nothing's wrong?" I asked.

"Nothing's wrong."

"Then what?"

"It's just that...I think we're going to move to Mill Valley."

"NO!" I covered my mouth and hoped I hadn't disturbed the neighbors. "You said you'd never leave the city."

"I know, I know, but Hunter and I have been talking about it a lot lately, and it will make things so much easier. I mean, a baby in the city would be really hard. I love our apartment, but I just can't imagine raising a child three floors up with no elevator. Plus I feel like she deserves to have a real yard, to run around and feel the grass under her feet, you know? I think it would be selfish for us to stay in the city."

"You could make it work."

She laughed. "Mill Valley is ten minutes over the Golden Gate Bridge, Waverly."

"I know. But what about Dino's? What about the Kilkenny?"

"We will *always* go to Dino's for pizza and frosted mugs of Bud Light, no matter what. Just maybe not every week, okay?"

I sighed. "I just wish things could stay the same, Mackie. You know I don't handle change very well. If it were up to me, we'd all still be living within a block of each other when we're old and gray."

"Nothing can stay the same forever, you know that. But don't worry. I'll make sure we have an extra bedroom so you can come have a slumber party anytime you like. You know you're family to us."

"I know, but I'm just really going to miss seeing you all the time."

She sighed. "Can we please put the dramatics to bed? It's not like I'm moving across the country. I'm not dropping off the face of the earth. I'm having a baby. I'll be ten minutes away. We'll just be shopping for baby clothes instead of getting mani-pedis. Deal with it."

I laughed. "Okay, okay, I get it. I will learn to embrace life change."

"There you go. There's the Waverly Bryson I love."

"Actually, that reminds me. I've been thinking about a new—"

Just then I saw the lights of a car pulling up to the house. "Oh Jesus, he's here, Mackie. I gotta go."

"Okay, good luck! I love you!"

"Love you too. Bye." I hung up and threw my phone into my purse. Then I scrambled to stand up and collect myself. As Jake's car pulled into the driveway and out of my line of sight, I smoothed my hand over my hair and reached down to pick up the flowers.

I heard the sound of a car door opening and shutting.

Then I heard the sound of another car door opening and shutting.

I heard the sound of Jake's voice.

Then I heard the sound of a woman's voice.

OH MY GOD.

I had to get out of there. The only route away from them was to the side of the house, so I sprinted toward the side yard. When I got to the end of the house, I turned left out of their view.

Or so I hoped.

As I rounded the corner, I bit my lip.

Then I bit *it*.

I slammed right into a trash can and sent it flying, me along with it. I banged my knees against the cement and landed on my chest with a painful thud. The trash can was empty, but it was very *loud*, and it clanked and clattered as it rolled along the cement walkway. I managed to get myself up quickly and ran to the can to right it—and shut it up. But it was too late. Jake had heard the commotion, and I could already hear him headed toward me.

Sweet holy mother of Jesus.

I had to hide.

In the darkness all I could see was an enormous tree in his neighbor's yard, about ten feet away. I made a run for it and flattened myself against its back side. The trunk was big enough to shield my entire body.

Breathing deeply, I held my arms tightly against my chest and prayed Jake wouldn't see me. Or hear me.

A moment later I heard footsteps. Jake was walking along the side of the house to check out the scene. Then I heard the click of high heels on the cement.

"What was it?" a female voice asked. She sounded a bit scared.

"I'm not sure. I think maybe a raccoon."

A raccoon! I thought. *Yes! Please think it was a raccoon!*

"What are those?" the female voice asked.

"What are what?"

"Right there, on the ground. Are those flowers?"

I looked down at my hands, one of which was holding my purse. The other was holding half of a tattered bouquet of hyacinths.

Oh no.

"Stay here," I heard Jake say.

Then I heard footsteps on the grass.

They grew louder as he approached the tree.

"Is someone there?" he said tentatively. His voice sounded so close.

I didn't speak and didn't breathe. All I could bring myself to do was close my eyes.

Then I heard footsteps again, walking around the huge tree.

"Waverly?"

I opened my eyes, and there he was, standing right in front of me. The look on his face was a combination of confusion and surprise.

I tried to smile. "Surprise?" I whispered.

"What are you doing here?"

"Now *that* is a great question."

He opened his mouth to speak, but before he could say anything, the woman's voice called out from the side of the house. "Jake? Are you okay?"

He held a finger to his lips. "Don't move," he said softly.

The sound of his voice faded as he approached the side of the house, so I couldn't tell what he was saying. A few moments later, I heard two sets of footsteps heading toward the front yard.

I didn't know what to do, so I just stood there and waited. Was he coming back? Was he mad at me? What was going on? I was tempted to pull out my phone and call McKenna, but I knew that would only make the situation worse. I slid down the side of the tree and sat down on the ground. The grass was damp, but I didn't care. My coat was probably ruined from my fall anyway. My knees hurt, and I wondered how badly I'd scraped them underneath my jeans.

After what seemed like a long time, I heard the sound of a car door opening and shutting, then a car driving away. A single pair of footsteps came back around the side of the house.

"Okay, Marco Polo, you can come out now," Jake said.

I stood up and wiped the grass off my backside as I emerged from behind the tree.

"Hi there." I waved nervously at him. "Fancy running into you here."

"What are you doing here?" I could tell he wasn't angry, just curious.

I looked at the remnants of my broken bouquet, the memory of my carefully prepared speech also shattered. "I came to say I'm sorry." I held the flowers up. "Hyacinths mean I'm sorry."

"Sorry for what?"

"For everything, I guess." I smiled, but I could feel tears slowly forming in the corner of my eyes.

"Let's go talk inside." He gestured toward the house. "It's cold out here."

I followed him to the front door, but I couldn't bring myself to keep quiet for long. "I got your roses, but not until the day after I was on *The Today Show*."

He didn't say a word. He pulled out his keys to unlock the door, then held it open for me. I took a step inside and spoke again.

"I'm so sorry for the mix-up. And I'm so sorry for your sister. I'm so sorry for…everything."

He passed through the foyer and turned on a floor lamp, still not saying anything.

The silence was killing me. I felt a few tears trickling down my cheeks.

He turned to face me, and behind him I noticed a big suitcase in the hallway. I wondered exactly how long he'd been back in town.

"Jake? Will you please say something?"

For a moment he stood still.

And then my dreams were answered.

He hugged me.

"You came all the way to Atlanta to tell me you're sorry?" he said softly.

I nodded through my tears. "I'm so sorry."

He smoothed my hair and held me close. "It's okay," he whispered. "It's okay."

I closed my eyes and leaned against him, so relieved to be in his arms again. I inhaled deeply to take in the scent of his skin, but quickly stopped at the unfamiliarity of it.

He smelled like...perfume.

I stiffened.

"Jake?"

"Yes?"

"Tonight, were you...on a date?" I kept my eyes closed tight, not really wanting to know the answer.

He smoothed my hair again but didn't say anything.

"Jake?"

"It's complicated."

My heart sank.

"Is she...is she the girl in the picture?"

"What picture?"

"The picture on your mantel. The one with...your whole family?"

He broke our embrace and walked toward the living room. He took off his coat, then sat on the couch and leaned forward, putting his elbows on his knees. I followed him and took a seat, next to him but not touching him.

He looked at the mantel, then at me.

"Yes," he finally said.

"Oh." I hoped he couldn't see the strain in my face. "Is she... is she the girl you took to Cynthia and Dale's wedding last year?"

"Yes."

I swallowed.

"Her name is Holly. Our families were friends growing up."

"But you dated her?"

"On and off."

"And…now?"

He sighed. "She's been a good friend to me, especially lately, with everything that's been going on with my sister, because she knows my family so well. So we've been…talking."

I could feel a lump forming in my throat.

"She lives in Atlanta?"

"She does now."

"Oh."

I probably didn't have the right to ask the next question, but I did anyway.

"Are you…getting back together?"

He looked at the ceiling.

"That isn't something we've talked about."

"Do you think she wants to?"

He hesitated a moment before answering.

"Yes."

"Do…you want to?" I whispered.

"I don't want to have this conversation right now. It's late, and I have a lot to do tonight."

I tried to smile. "I guess I don't have very good timing."

"I'll give you that," he said, sort of laughing.

I reached over and put my hand on his arm. "What I said on *The Today Show* wasn't true."

He didn't respond.

"About those dates I'd been on? It wasn't true."

He still didn't respond, so I removed my hand and looked away.

My voice began to crack. "I mean...I went on the dates, but a long time ago. I don't know why I blurted them out like that, or didn't explain it better. I...I guess I sort of choked."

"It's okay, you don't owe me anything."

"But I...I *want* to owe you something. I *do* want to be your Valentine, Jake. I hope it's not too late for that." I searched his eyes, hoping they would tell me I hadn't ruined everything. I wanted to throw my arms around him, but I couldn't bring myself to do it. Regardless of what my heart was feeling, my body was literally frozen by fear.

He sighed, then stood up and went into the kitchen, returning a few moments later with two glasses of water. He handed me one, then took a sip of his and put it on the coffee table. "I need to ask you something," he said.

"Sure, Jake, anything."

He paused for a moment, then looked at me.

"Did you take a pregnancy test?"

I felt like the wind had been knocked out of me.

"What?"

"Did you take a pregnancy test?"

"How did you know that?"

He didn't respond.

"How did you know that?" I said again.

"Shane said you told Kristina about it when you were in New York."

I looked at the glass in my hands.

He scratched his eyebrow and sighed. "Were you planning to tell me?"

I opened my mouth to speak, but I couldn't think of the right words. He stood up and smoothed his hands down the front of his jeans, then picked up his glass and returned to the kitchen.

I put my water down and followed him. "I was going to tell you. But then your sister lost her baby, and I...I couldn't do it. I didn't want to upset you more."

He emptied his glass into the sink and leaned again the counter. "Kristina said you were really scared. Is that true?"

A few tears trickled down my cheeks, and I used both hands to wipe them away. "Yes."

He put his hands on my shoulders. "You were scared and didn't feel you could tell me?"

"I just...didn't want to burden you, that's all."

He removed his hands and put them on his head. For a second I thought he might pull his hair out. Then he walked back into the living room.

I followed him again, determined to make things right. He picked up the big suitcase in the hall and went into his room.

"What are you doing?"

He put the suitcase on the floor by his bed and opened it. It was empty. "I'm packing."

"Packing? Are you leaving with the team again?"

He stood up and looked at me.

"I took the job."

"What job?"

"The one in Argentina, in Buenos Aires."

"What? When are you leaving?"

"The day after tomorrow."

"For how long?"

"Three or four months, maybe more."

"You're just going to leave?"

He nodded.

"Just like that?"

"I need to go, Waverly."

"But why?"

He didn't respond.

"Can you at least tell me what you're thinking?"

More silence.

"I...I know I don't have the right to expect anything, but I've come all this way. Will you please...talk to me?" The words came out as a whisper.

He gestured to himself and then to me. "This *thing* we have, whatever you want to call it, it isn't working."

"But I explained why I didn't tell you about the test. I said I was sorry."

He sighed. "It's not that you didn't *tell* me, Waverly. It's that you were *scared* but didn't tell me. Don't you see the difference?"

I didn't say anything.

"Besides, it's not just the pregnancy thing. And it's not just the *Today Show* thing. It's *everything*. You've been resisting *everything* from the beginning."

I still didn't say anything.

"I want someone who needs me, Waverly, not someone who's afraid of me. You're not ready to need anyone other than your girlfriends."

I looked at the floor and thought about the times I'd leaned on Mackie or Andie instead of him, how I was afraid to trust him... even though I adored everything about him.

He was right.

"But...I don't want to be afraid anymore. I want it to work."

"I did too. I really did."

I looked up at him. "You *did*? Not you *do*?"

"You're not ready, Waverly."

"But I want to be ready," I whispered. I felt a lump in my throat again.

"I wish I could believe you."

"Then believe me, Jake. Please believe me."

He put his arms around me and held me tight, but only for a moment. Then he backed away and put his hands on my shoulders.

"You need to believe it before I can." He wiped a tear from my cheek and slowly shook his head. "I'm sorry."

Chapter Eighteen

I picked at the paint on my pint glass. "I can't believe I made such a fool of myself." I was sitting on a stool next to Andie at the Kilkenny the following evening.

"Hey now, you did *not* make a fool of yourself. Far from it."

"You are a total liar, but thanks."

"Waverly, that was a big step for you, going all the way to Atlanta to tell Jake how you feel. You wouldn't have been able to even *think* about doing something like that a couple years ago."

I took a sip of my beer and remembered how crushed I'd been after Aaron had broken off our engagement. At the time I thought I'd never leave my *apartment* for a guy again, much less California. "This is true."

"Maybe it's just not the right time for you two."

"Bad timing is right. My timing couldn't have been worse. From day one, I've messed it up."

"Come on, you're being way too hard on yourself."

"No, I'm not. This one's all on me. He's amazing, and I blew it."

She shrugged. "Okay, maybe you're right. What are you going to do about it?"

"I don't know."

"What would you tell your readers to do?"

I looked at her. "Are we really going there again?"

"I guess we are. What would you tell them?"

"I think I'd tell them to stop asking me for advice, because clearly I don't know anything."

"Please. Know what *I* think you'd say?"

"I have a feeling I will soon."

"I think you'd say to get on with your life, maybe throw yourself into your work, try to figure out if you even *want* to be in a relationship right now. I mean, do you?"

"You sound like Jake."

"Well, do you?" She raised her eyebrows.

I drooped my shoulders. "I thought I did, but now I honestly don't know. I mean, just look at how I acted. First, I didn't sleep with him. Then, I did sleep with him. Then, I basically ignored him. Then, when he decided to break things off, I flew to Atlanta and showed up uninvited at his house. What is wrong with me? Who does that?"

"A lot of people. They call it playing games."

"But I don't want to be one of those people. I don't like those people."

"Hey now, I'm one of those people."

"Except you, of course. You know I love *you*."

"So he's really gone off to Buenos Aires?"

"Yep."

"For how long?"

"Three or four months, but maybe longer."

"Ouch. Talk about crying for me, Argentina."

I lightly pushed her shoulder. "Thanks."

She laughed. "I'm sorry. I couldn't resist."

"The midnight plane to Georgia one was much better."

"Agreed. So do you think you'll hear from him ever again?"

I pointed at her. "Now *that* is a good question. Now if you'll excuse me, I need to use the restroom." I stood up and weaved through the crowd to the back of the bar, then pushed open the ladies' room door. The two stalls were full, so I waited against the wall. Two pretty blondes in their early twenties were washing their hands.

"No way," the first one said. "He showed up for the date in a black turtleneck sweater?"

The second one nodded. "With a gold chain on the outside."

"Ugh, *gross*," the first one said.

"*So* gross," the second one said. "I wanted to ninja out of there right then, but I just couldn't be that mean."

I half chuckled, even though the other half of me felt like crying. *I've been there*, I wanted to say. *And I'll probably be there again soon*, I thought as I looked at the floor.

"You should totally e-mail that story to Honey on Your Mind," the first girl said. "Maybe they'd print it."

I looked up. *What? What?*

The second girl laughed. "Maybe I will."

"You guys read Honey on Your Mind?" I said.

They both turned around.

"Always," the first one said.

I smiled. "I write it."

Their eyes got big. "No way, really?" the second one said. "You're Waverly?"

I nodded.

"That's awesome," the first girl said. "I love that column."

"Me too," the second girl said. "It makes me feel like no matter how much my life might suck, I'm not alone."

I smiled but hoped they couldn't see how sad I really was. That would be so, well, *sad*.

They opened the door to leave. "Keep up the good work, *honey*," the first girl said, laughing.

As the door shut behind them, I didn't feel quite so alone either.

And then it hit me.

That's exactly it.

I hurried back to the bar. "I know what I'm doing next," I said to Andie as I sat down.

She narrowed her eyes. "What happened in the restroom?"

I smiled. "I'm serious. I think I just figured it out. I'm ready to move forward with my career, with my life, with everything."

"Care to share?"

"I will soon."

"Does this next step involve Jake?"

"We'll see. If it doesn't, it doesn't, no matter how much it hurts."

She looked at me sideways.

"For now, I'm going to stop talking about him all the time, or at least I'm going to try," I said.

"Seriously, Waverly, what happened in there?"

"I guess you could call it a new kind of Waverly moment."

"I'll drink to that." She stood up and raised her hand toward Jack to order more beers, then dashed off to the restroom herself.

Chapter Nineteen

That Saturday morning I walked to Noah's Bagels for a bagel and a coffee, then hopped in my car to drive to Sacramento. My dad wanted to take me to lunch at Applebee's.

I pulled into the parking lot a few minutes before twelve thirty. His truck was already there. When I opened the front door to the restaurant, I saw him sitting on a bench in the waiting area, working on the crossword puzzle in the *Sacramento Bee*.

"I hear the one in the *San Francisco Sun* is trickier," I said.

He looked up and smiled.

"Well hello there," he said.

He stood up, and for a moment we faced each other in silence, as awkwardly as always. Finally I leaned into him to give him a hug, which clearly surprised him. He sort of returned the gesture by stiffly putting one hand on my back and patting me a few times. It must have been painful to watch, but it was a big step for us both.

"It's good to see you, Dad."

He cleared his throat. "I'd like you to meet someone." He turned to a pretty blonde woman on his left. She had short yet poofy hair and bright green eyes. She seemed about his age. "Waverly, this is Betty."

Betty smiled warmly and held her hand out. "It's lovely to meet you, Waverly. I've heard so much about you."

I was totally thrown off guard. My dad was introducing me to a woman? He'd never done that before. As far as I knew, he hadn't been on a date since my mom died.

"Hi." I reached out my hand, which Betty covered with both of hers and squeezed.

"Betty works at the restaurant. She's our top waitress," my dad said.

I was in uncharted territory and had no idea how to respond.

"Sir, we can seat you now." The perky voice of the hostess temporarily saved me. We followed her to the back of the restaurant, which smelled like maple syrup and was filled with families. I also spotted several college students, who, I couldn't help but notice, were looking more like children to me every day.

The three of us settled into a booth, me on one side, my dad and Betty on the other. The waitress handed us menus and promised to return with water in a minute.

I unfolded my napkin across my lap. "How long have you two been, um, seeing each other?" Talk about an awkward question to ask your own father. But I was dying of curiosity.

Dad grinned, something I hadn't seen him do in a long time. He put his arm around Betty. "How long has it been, sweetie? Two months?"

Sweetie?

She smiled up at him, then looked across the booth at me. "Nine weeks."

"We met back when I started at the restaurant, but I didn't have the nerve to make a move until right after New Year's," my dad said.

I flinched. Who wants to hear about your dad making a move? I hoped they couldn't see how uncomfortable I was.

The waitress returned with a tray of waters, and as soon as she left Betty put her hand over her heart. "Waverly, I'm just so thrilled to meet you. Your father talks about you all the time."

I smiled at her, feeling guilty for not having called my dad for so long, for not having visited since Christmas. Nine weeks they'd been dating, and I didn't even know? Then again, I hadn't told my dad a word about Jake. I made my hands into fists under the table. *Stop thinking about him,* I told myself.

"You write an advice column for the *San Francisco Sun*?" Betty said.

I blinked, snapping myself out of my thoughts. "Yes ma'am. Print and online. It's called Honey on Your Mind. It's mostly about dating, but a lot of people write in about other things too."

"We don't get the Internet, dear." She turned to my dad. "Darling, we should have asked Waverly to bring us a copy to read."

I took a sip of my water and wondered how people survived without the Internet.

The waitress reappeared, and after she took our orders, Betty interlaced her hands on the table. "How's *your* dating life, Waverly? Your dad says you two don't chat much about that."

I looked at her.

Did she just ask me about my dating life?

In my thirty years on earth, my dad had asked me about my love life exactly twice, once after I told him I was getting married, and once after I told him I wasn't getting married. Otherwise, our conversations were superficial, innocuous, light. We played Scrabble and talked about movies, weather, occasionally his latest get-rich-quick scheme, an interest that, thank God, had waned now that he was working steadily. The closest we ever got to a serious topic was around the presidential election every four years. And now, after ten minutes, *Betty* was asking me about my love life?

I took a huge drink of water. "It's okay." *If you only knew.*

"Just okay?" She clearly had no idea how much she had freaked me out simply by asking a question that I imagine is totally normal in most American families.

"I told you," my dad said to her.

I shot him a look to say, *What are you doing?*

Betty put her hand on his shoulder. "Isn't that just a shame, Paul? Such a beautiful girl should have men knocking down her door to get a date."

He stared at his napkin, suddenly looking like he wanted to crawl under the table.

"Well, I think it's just terrible," Betty said. "Don't you worry, Waverly, you'll find him when it's right."

"Thanks." I wished our food would arrive to put an end to this excruciating topic. I turned my head toward the kitchen, willing our waitress to emerge with a tray.

"So, tell me about this column of yours. Your father says you haven't told him much about that either."

My dad, who was now studying his fork, slowly looked up at me.

He didn't speak, but I noticed something unfamiliar in his face.

It was...*interest.*

I turned from him to Betty, who had the same curious expression on her face.

Then I realized something.

He does want to know about me.

I was grown and long out of the house, but apparently my dad wanted to get to know his daughter better. And Betty was trying to help him do it.

* * *

Once we got off the topic of my love life, I was surprised at how much I enjoyed chatting with Betty. She was quite funny, and she clearly cared a lot about my dad, who sat next to her the entire meal in near total silence. But I could tell he was listening.

Only when we ordered dessert did my dad, who loves sweets even more than I do, finally speak up to vote for apple pie à la mode. A few minutes later, the waitress set a huge, steaming slice topped with an enormous scoop of vanilla ice cream before us, along with three spoons and three cups of coffee. We all dug in.

"So the new editor doubled your workload?" Betty said.

I stirred sugar into my cup. "She did. Everyone told me to be afraid of her, but she's actually pretty nice. And she really seems to like my work."

"That's just wonderful. Paul, isn't that wonderful?" She nudged my dad with her elbow, and he coughed into his pie. I tried not to laugh. Now that I'd gotten to know Betty a bit, I found their interaction endearing.

"Thanks. I've been having fun with it. And it's given me an idea for something else I could do as well," I said.

"More writing?"

I took a sip of coffee. "Sort of. It's in the beginning stages, but I'm excited about it."

"We think it's great to stretch yourself like that. Don't we, Paul?" She put both her hands around my dad's arm.

"Yes." I think it was his first non-food-related word of the entire meal. "Waverly's always been the creative one in our family, the smart one too."

I looked up from my coffee.

He cleared his throat. "She just needs to believe in herself a little more, not worry so much about how things will turn out."

This was coming from...my dad? Was that really how he saw me? I thought I'd kept that side of myself hidden from him.

Betty smiled into his eyes. "I can tell she's just wonderful, Paul."

When we left Applebee's, Betty hugged me like she'd known me forever. I hugged her back, truly glad to have met her. Then I looked at my dad, and we repeated our awkward half embrace, which was progress for us. I said goodbye and walked to my car. As I was about to unlock it, I looked back across the parking lot. My dad had opened the passenger door of his truck for Betty and was leaning in to give her a quick kiss as she buckled her seatbelt. He shut the door, tapped his hand on the top of the truck, and trotted around to the other side.

He was smiling.

I found myself smiling too as I got my in my car.

I hoped Betty would stick around.

* * *

Later that afternoon I met up with Andie at Royal Ground Coffee on the corner of Fillmore and California. We grabbed a table near the front door and sat down.

"So what's going on with CJ?"

She picked up her latte and smiled. "He's still great. We're going out to dinner later."

I hesitated. I didn't want to cause trouble until I'd spoken to Ivy, so I wasn't sure how exactly to proceed. "How often are you seeing him?"

"It's been about three nights a week. Unless he's traveling for work, which unfortunately is a lot."

"He's out of town a lot?" I raised my eyebrows.

"He takes a lot of overnight trips, for sales calls mostly. Like next weekend, for example, he'll be gone from Friday morning until Monday evening."

Hmm. It sounded so innocent and yet so suspicious, depending on your perspective.

She took another sip of her latte. "Maybe one of these days you can finally meet him for real. I know you'll like him."

"I'm sure I will. I'm glad to hear it's going so well."

"I know, can you believe it? I don't even have another guy on deck. *Me.* It's been a long time since I liked a guy this much, Waverly. Maybe even since college."

I sighed. "Ah, the good ol' days. Remember Marc with a C?"

She laughed. "Oh God, how could I forget? Although that guy's hardly worth remembering. What an ass."

"Would you still do that now?"

"Do what?"

"Break up with a guy if you found out he was seeing someone else?"

She paused to think, then nodded slowly. "If we were exclusive, then yes, I'd have to. Why do you ask? Are you thinking about Jake and that girl?"

I wasn't before that moment.

"Yes," I said, looking at the floor.

Chapter Twenty

Monday I took the bus to the *Sun* office to work on my column in an empty cube. I was feeling restless at home, so I thought a change of scenery would help me focus. I plugged in my laptop, then went to grab a cup of coffee in the kitchen. On the way I pulled the crumpled yellow Post-It that said HONEY BRAINSTORM from my pocket. For nearly two weeks I'd been doing my best to concentrate on that piece of paper and not on Jake. I hadn't been entirely successful, but I'd made a ton of progress on the project. At least I was moving forward with my career, if not my heart.

On my way back from the kitchen, I ran into Nick. He was wearing a plain white button-down shirt.

"What's wrong?" I pointed to his chest.

He shrugged. "Even the president needs a day off now and then. So what happened on your trip? You can't leave your fans hanging."

I made a sad face.

"Not good?"

"Not good. Want the executive summary?"

"Lay it on me."

I gave him the highlights. Or rather, the lowlights. When I was done, I crossed my arms in front of me. "So what do you think?"

"You really hid behind a tree?"

"Oh yes. And did I mention I ripped my jeans when I fell on my face?"

"Impressive."

I laughed. "That's hardly the adjective I'd choose to describe it, but thanks. So what's going on with you? Have you heard from Ivy?"

"Wasn't that *your* move?"

"Oops, you're right. I'm sorry, I've been a little distracted lately."

"So I've heard. Just don't forget. You *owe* me."

"I know I do, and I won't forget. I promise. I'm going to owe you even more soon."

"For what?"

"You'll find out soon enough."

"Okay then, hang in there." He blew me a kiss and started walking backward down the hall.

I sat down at my computer and scrolled through my e-mails. One was from a woman who went on a first date with a man who casually pointed across the bar and said, "That's my probation officer." Another woman wrote that she'd briefly dated a policeman, who apparently used his access to classified information to mysteriously show up everywhere she went, even after she'd stopped returning his calls. A third e-mail was from a male attorney who signed up for an online dating service and was unexpectedly matched up with a senior female partner in his firm—who, as far as he knew, was married with three kids.

Nothing to brighten your day like a reminder that we have kinks in all three sides of the legal triangle. No wonder *Law and Order* has been around for like fifty years.

* * *

I called Ivy later that afternoon, after I'd returned to my apartment. We'd never chatted outside the office, so I wasn't sure exactly how to approach the call.

"Ivy, hey, it's Waverly."

"Waverly! How nice to hear from you. How are you?"

"I should be asking you that. I can't believe the layoffs. I was so sad when I heard what happened."

"I'm doing fine. Great, actually. I hated it there anyway, so this is forcing me to really give the photography thing a try."

"Did they at least give you a severance?"

She laughed. "If you can call it a severance. I think I already spent it at Starbucks. But it's all good. I'll be fine."

I swallowed. "So how are things going with Casey?"

"The same. I was hoping we'd be living together by now, but he's been so focused on work lately I hardly ever see him."

"Work?"

"Yeah, he's been traveling a lot."

"What does he do again?"

"He's in pharmaceutical sales. He loves it though."

I scratched my cheek, trying to figure out how to ask his last name without blowing it. I would have been a horrible trial lawyer. "So what's going on with the photography thing?"

"I'm going to try weddings. I *was* thinking children, but then I realized that I don't really know any kids out here, and I didn't think putting an ad on Craigslist looking for *children to photograph* would be a good idea."

I laughed. "You're probably right. I'd hate to see you end up in jail."

"So I thought maybe I should go the wedding route. You know how much I love weddings."

I bit my lip. If Casey *was* cheating, I felt horrible for her.

"Good for you. I'd plug you in my column, but something tells me that most people who read it aren't in the market for a wedding photographer."

She laughed. "Actually, I already have a gig lined up. Well, sort of. They're friends of friends. I'm taking their engagement photos on Saturday, and if that goes well, they'll let me do their wedding."

"Really? That's great."

"Thanks. It's near your hood, so you should stop by to say hi if you're out and about. Casey and I are meeting them at two o'clock at Crissy Field."

"Casey?" Andie's CJ was supposed to be out of town for the weekend.

"He's my staff until I actually make some money. He's going to help with the lighting and stuff."

"At two o'clock on Saturday?"

"Yes."

"Okay, I'll try to stop by," I said casually, trying to sound, well, *casual*.

"Cool. I've got to run now. Casey's on his way over. I'll see you Saturday, I hope?"

"I'll do my best."

"Okay, cool. Bye."

"Bye."

I hung up the phone, then called Andie at work.

"Andrea Barnett," she said in her work voice. I loved Andie's work voice.

"Hey, it's Waverly."

"What's up?" Her work voice disappeared.

"Just checking in. Want to have brunch at the Grove on Saturday, then maybe take a walk on the beach?"

"A walk? As in exercise?"

"Okay, let me rephrase. How about we take a stroll along the beach, drinking coffee and making fun of the windsurfers when they bite it?"

"Much better."

"Okay cool, I'm going to see if Mackie can join us."

I hung up and called McKenna but got her voicemail. I left a message, then pulled out the HONEY BRAINSTORM Post-It again and stared at it.

I took a deep breath and dialed Smithers Publishing. I made an appointment to go see them in three weeks' time, then hung up the phone and made fists with my hands.

Crunch time.

Chapter Twenty-One

That Saturday was bright and clear and crisp, and as I began to descend the Fillmore Street steps toward the Marina to meet Andie, I stopped for a moment and gazed out at the sailboats moving gently across the San Francisco Bay. After nearly ten years, I still found it breathtaking. A jogger slowly trekked up the hill toward me, and I smiled at him as he passed by. *Just try to find a better place to live than this,* I thought. It was March and at least sixty degrees. Behind me I heard a noise. I turned around to see a couple cruising down Broadway on a Vespa, and I smiled again. *I bet it's snowing in New York right now.*

Ten minutes later, I entered the Grove on the corner of Chestnut and Avila. I scanned the room for Andie but didn't see her. As usual the place was packed, so I went outside to check the benches on either side of the entrance. I saw about a dozen dogs and nearly as many owners, plus at least twenty dog lovers petting the dogs. I knew at least half of them were complaining that they wanted to get a dog but couldn't because their building didn't allow it. It's amazing what people will put up with to live in San Francisco: no parking, no pets, high rent, awful public transportation, freezing summers, lame cell phone reception, and a terrible football team that makes the whole city long for the glory days of Joe Montana. You name it, we deal with it. And we love doing so.

No sign of Andie.

"Hey, Waverly."

I turned around to find a face I hadn't seen in months.

"Brad?" It was the ubiquitous Brad Cantor, or should I say, the formerly ubiquitous Brad Cantor. He had moved to Los Angeles several months earlier for his job, and when he left, a little piece of small-town San Francisco went with him. Running into congenial yet dorky Brad Cantor everywhere I went used to drive me nuts, but now that it didn't happen anymore, I had to admit that I missed it. I even missed *him* a little bit.

I gave him a hug. "How are you? How is LA?"

He shrugged. "It's okay."

"Not your scene?"

"Not really. It's just so big and spread out. I can go weeks without running into anyone I know. Not that I know that many people yet."

I patted him on the arm and smiled. "It's only a matter of time. So what are you doing back in town? Are you still seeing Mandy?"

His face lit up. "Yes."

"How's it going with the distance?"

"It's not ideal, but we make it work." The way he said it made it sound so...*easy*.

"That's...great." I hoped he couldn't see what I was really feeling behind my smile. "So you're in town to visit her?"

"Yes and no. The real reason is for a buddy's wedding. Seems like everyone I know is getting married these days, or having kids."

"I'm not!" I blurted, then covered my mouth when I realized I'd practically shouted. "Oops, sorry. How long are you in town?"

"Just for the weekend. And hey, I'm glad I ran into you. I wanted to tell you that I've been reading your column online. It's funny."

"You think so?" I was intrigued. Brad was as kind as they come, but he was completely lacking in the humor department.

He nodded. "I'm impressed. I never thought of you as being funny."

I nearly laughed out loud. Given how many times I'd made fun of him behind his back, I totally deserved that. I smiled. "Thanks, Brad. I appreciate that."

"Well hey, I've got to head back to Mandy's place before these get cold." He held up his Noah's Bagels bag. "It was nice running into you."

"It was nice running into you, too." For the first time maybe ever, I meant it.

I watched him disappear down Chestnut Street, thinking about what he'd said. Then I heard Andie's voice behind me. "Hey, woman."

I turned around and saw that McKenna was with her. I hugged them both before stepping back to admire McKenna's growing belly.

"Wow, baby Kimball's getting big."

"Tell me about it," McKenna said. "I've think I've got a sumo wrestler growing in here."

"You've *got* to see her butt when she sits down," Andie said. "It spreads out behind her like a fan. It's fantastic."

"Thank you for pointing that out," McKenna said.

Andie put her hands up in front of her. "Hey now, don't shoot the messenger. Was that Brad Cantor?"

I nodded. "Can you believe it? The first sighting in months."

"Doesn't he live in LA now?" McKenna said.

"Yep. He's just in town for the weekend. And now that I've run into him, I feel like order has been restored to the universe. I'm so glad you're here, by the way. I didn't know you were going to make it."

"Yeah, I'm sorry I didn't call you back. Just swamped."

"We're going to have to start calling you *McKenna MIA*," Andie said.

"I know, I know. Especially since after brunch I need to take off to meet Hunter."

"More house hunting?" I said.

She nodded. "It never ends. Every weekend is like *Groundhog Day*."

We walked into the Grove, and Andie pushed her sunglasses up to rest on her head. "So how's it been going?"

McKenna sighed. "They say real estate is all about location, location, location, but it seems like no matter *what* the location in Mill Valley, the operative word is expensive, expensive, expensive."

"That's why I go with rent control, rent control, and more rent control," I said.

We got in line and ordered three coffees (decaf for Mackie) and three veggie scrambles, then took our numbered flag stands and sat down at a table. When we finally had our meals, McKenna put her hand on my arm.

"How are you holding up?"

I smiled weakly. "I'm trying, but I wouldn't say I'm succeeding."

"Have you heard from him?"

I shook my head.

"Have you e-mailed him?"

"I wouldn't know what to say."

"I'm sorry, Wave."

"Thanks, Mackie. I'm doing anything and everything I can not to think about him for now and accept whatever the world is trying to tell me, although I fear it's telling me I suck and will be alone forever."

She laughed. "Please. You're way too loveable to be alone forever." Then she looked at Andie. "Am I right?"

Andie nodded and looked at me. "You rock."

I forced another smile. "Thanks. Actually, I'm making a big effort to focus on important things in my life other than romance. Like my *friends*, for example." I pointed to both of them with my fork.

"I like it," Andie said. "Anything that focuses on me, I like."

"Also, I went to see my dad last weekend." I was glad to change the subject.

McKenna reached for a napkin. "Your dad? Really?"

"Yep. He has a girlfriend. I met her. Can you believe it?"

"Your dad has a girlfriend? How did that go?" I could see the surprise in her face.

"It was weird at first. But it ended up going really well because she helped keep the conversation going. I mean, I love my dad, but we never seem to have that much to say to each other, you know?"

They'd met my dad. They knew.

"It was nice to have someone else there, to help us, well, *talk*. Plus, he seems really happy. He's like a different person."

"I have something I need to talk about," Andie suddenly said.

McKenna and I both looked at her.

"What's up?" I asked.

She lowered her voice. "Actually, the problem is what's *not* up."

We both raised our eyebrows.

"You know, *down there.*"

Neither of us spoke.

She sighed. "Come on, people, work with me here."

McKenna sat up straight. "Oh, you mean…"

"I *mean* I'm not getting it," Andie said.

"Sex?" I said.

She nodded.

"You aren't getting enough?"

"I'm not getting *any*."

"Any?" McKenna said.

"None."

"Like, *ever*?" McKenna said.

"Like, *never*."

I narrowed my eyes. "Wait a minute. Are you saying that you haven't slept with him even once?"

She picked up a piece of toast. "I prefer to think of it as *he* hasn't slept with *me*. God knows *I'm* able and willing."

"I don't get it," McKenna said.

She sighed. "Welcome to the club. At first I thought it was cool, because it was nice, for once, to be with a guy who doesn't take sex so lightly. For a while it made me feel respected, but now it's just driving me crazy."

"Has he said why? Or I mean, why not?" I asked.

She waved the toast in the air. "It's always some excuse, like he has to get up early, or he's not feeling well, and lately it's been that he wants to wait until it feels right."

I coughed. "He said he wants to wait until it *feels right*? In the history of time, I don't think any man has ever uttered those words."

"Tell me about it. It's so weird. I mean, he kisses me, and we cuddle, and he says the sweetest things, but that's where it always ends. I'm beginning to think that...maybe...he's not into me. Either that, or he's seeing someone else and doesn't want to sleep with more than one person at the same time."

My ears perked up.

"You think so?" McKenna said.

"I don't know. But what else could it be? I mean, what's the problem? I'm attractive, right?"

McKenna put her hand on Andie's shoulder. "Of course. Don't think for a second you're not."

"You're hot," I said, nodding.

Andie smiled. "Thanks. Good lord, ladies, what has it come to that *I'm* questioning how attractive I am to men? *Me?*"

"Talk about a disturbance in the Force," I said, pretending to wave a lightsaber.

"Maybe he really *is* just waiting for the right moment," McKenna said. "Maybe he's really that into you."

I hoped Andie didn't see the look of concern in my face. "Yeah, maybe that's it."

She tossed the toast on her plate. "This is brand new for me. I've never been turned down by a guy in the bedroom, so I've got to admit that I'm a little freaked out."

"Wow, you're never freaked out about *anything*," I said.

"I know. So the fact that I'm freaked out has me even more freaked out."

"What are you going to do?" McKenna said.

Andie shrugged. "I guess I'll just wait and see what happens. Although knowing me, what will happen is that I'll crack after a couple glasses of wine and ask him why the hell he doesn't want to sleep with me."

I laughed. "What does *CJ* stand for anyway?"

"Casey James."

I sucked in my breath.

This is unfortunate information.

Then something else occurred to me. "You mean Casey James, like that hot guy who was on *American Idol* a few seasons ago?"

She looked at me. "Are you really bringing up *American Idol* right now?"

"You're right, not good timing, sorry. Do you think...maybe he's acting weird because of that comment I made on *The Today Show*?" I was afraid to hear her answer. Which was worse? For CJ to be cheating on her? Or for him to be thinking she was kind of a slut because of what I'd said? Maybe the unfortunate truth was... both? However you sliced the problem, the answer was not pretty.

"It's definitely not that," she said quickly. "He didn't even see it."

"Are you sure?"

"Totally sure."

McKenna checked her phone. "Damn it, I've really got to go. I'm so sorry to eat and run yet again, ladies. I hate leaving in the middle of this."

Andie finally took a bite of her toast. "It's okay, you've got a lot on your plate right now besides food."

I nodded. "Totally okay, we still love you." I pointed to her stomach. "And we love her too."

"Thanks for understanding. I really wish I could stick around and hash this one out." She stood up and unhooked her purse from the back of her chair, then leaned down to give us each a quick hug. "Love you both. Good luck with CJ, Andie."

A few minutes after McKenna left, a woman wearing a skintight white unitard walked in. I mean *skintight*. She was carrying a yoga mat, a purse, and nothing else. As she walked toward the counter to order, Andie and I turned our heads in disbelief. So did everyone else in her path.

"I just saw the full outline of her vagina," Andie said, not in a quiet voice.

I laughed out loud. "Andie!"

"I saw it too," said the guy sitting at the table next to us.

Andie looked at me. "See?"

I kept laughing. "No thanks, I don't need to."

* * *

Ten minutes later Andie and I gathered our things and headed west on Chestnut toward Crissy Field. I felt uneasy about my stealth approach to the situation, but I didn't want to rock the boat unless I was certain that her Casey and Ivy's Casey were one and the same.

We soon passed the Palace of Fine Arts, where we navigated our way through a throng of families on their way to the Exploratorium. Finally we reached the entrance to Crissy Field. It looked like the entire city was out and about, walking, jogging, picnicking, frolicking. Kids were catching baseballs, windsurfers were catching waves, and even a few brave sunbathers were catching rays. Or trying to. It's not easy to get a tan in San Francisco.

"Where did your friend say she'd be?"

I pointed toward the Golden Gate Bridge. "That way."

We walked along the beach, and as we got closer to where Ivy was supposed to be, I started getting nervous. Was this the right call? I really didn't know. Andie was busy watching the windsurfers and didn't seem to notice my anxiety. I kept my eyes peeled for Ivy. Finally I spotted her along the shore about fifty feet ahead of us, a huge camera hanging around her neck. She was talking to two people whom I assumed to be the betrothed couple. A few feet away I saw a tall guy with blond hair adjusting some lighting umbrellas in the sand, his back to us.

"There they are." I tried to contain the stress in my voice.

Andie turned her head to follow my gaze. "Cool, let's check it out."

We approached them, and as we got closer I noticed that my shoelace was untied. Just as I kneeled down, Andie gasped and grabbed my shoulder.

"Oh my God."

"What?"

"Oh my God, he's a liar." She squeezed my shoulder. Hard.

I finished tying my shoe and started to stand up, but she pulled me in the other direction before I could see anything.

"We're getting out of here."

"What?"

"I can't believe this. He said he was going out of town." She kept pulling me, walking faster than I think I'd ever seen her move.

"Andie, what's going on?"

"He's cheating, that's what's going on. I can't let him see me." She kept one hand on my arm as we hurried back along the beach. She didn't stop until we reached the sidewalk that led to the entrance.

"What did you see?" I said, out of breath.

"He's cheating. I just saw him kiss her."

"Who?" At this point I figured my best bet was to just go with it.

She put her hands on her hips.

"Josh."

Josh?

"Who's Josh?"

She pushed her hair behind her ears. "He's this guy who's been sleeping with my friend Alyssa from work. I've met him like five times, Waverly. And he's out there getting his *engagement* photos taken?"

I was speechless. I opened my mouth, but nothing came out.

"What a jackass. I had drinks with Alyssa last night, and she said Josh was visiting his grandparents in Arizona this weekend."

I tried to speak again, but all that came out was, "Oh."

"They've been dating for like two months," she said, shaking her head. "Alyssa *really* likes him. She lives over in Alameda, so I guess he figured he wouldn't run into her in the city. What a tool."

"Are you going to tell her?"

"Hell YES. Wouldn't *you* want me to tell you something like that?"

I swallowed. "I guess so. I mean, if you were sure about it."

"Well I'm one hundred percent sure about this. What a dick."

I bit my lip. Because she'd yanked me out of there so quickly, I wasn't *one hundred percent* sure that Andie had even seen Casey. I was trying to decide what to do when she put her hand on my arm.

"Listen, I'm going to go call Alyssa, okay?"

"Sure."

"Why don't you go back and say hi to your friend? I'm sure she'd like to see you. Just don't say anything about this, okay?"

"Of course."

"Cool. I'll talk to you later?"

"Okay, bye."

She started to walk away, then stopped and turned around. "And by the way, I'm proud of you for going to see your dad. I know how much that stresses you out."

"Thanks, Andie. I'm glad…I'm glad he has a girlfriend."

"Remember, Waverly, no matter what happens with that, we're your family too, okay?"

I smiled. "I know."

She left, and I stood there, not sure what to do next.

I watched her walk away until she rounded a corner and disappeared. I sighed and turned back to face the beach, thinking I would go say hi to Ivy, but my feet didn't move.

Do I want to go back?

After a few moments, I decided to climb the hill back to my apartment. I'd had enough Nancy Drew for one day.

* * *

Early the next evening, I changed into my pajamas and slippers, poured myself a big glass of merlot, and called Ivy.

"Hey, it's Waverly." I carried the glass to the couch and sat down, tucking my legs underneath me.

"Hi, Waverly. How are you?"

"I'm good." I took a sip of wine. "I just wanted to apologize for not making it to your photo shoot yesterday. I wanted to stop by, but…I wasn't feeling all that well." I figured that was true, given how sick I'd felt about the whole situation. I was beginning to feel like Bill Clinton with my liberal employment of semantics. For just a moment I thought about how Jake would call me out on that, but then I called myself out for thinking about Jake. *Be strong,* I thought.

"Oh, don't worry about it. There must be something going around. Casey was knocked out too."

"He was?"

"Yeah, he came down with a terrible bug Friday afternoon. I had to rally my neighbor to help me with the lighting by promising to make him dinner."

"So Casey didn't go either?"

"Nope. It went great though. Josh and Jill, the engaged couple, were really happy with the results. They want me to shoot their wedding."

So Casey *hadn't* been there? *Ugh.* Enough of the mystery. I had to cut to the chase and figure it out. I decided to be as direct as I could without seeming too suspicious.

"Glad to hear that." I paused, then took another sip of wine. "So, hey, what's Casey's last name? I…I met a blond guy named Casey the other day and am wondering if it's the same person."

"Casey? His last name is Thompson."

"Thompson?" *As in NOT JAMES?* I hoped she couldn't hear my loud exhale of relief, which nearly blew ripples in my wine.

"Did you meet him? Isn't he great?"

"Nope, guess it was a different guy. But I'm sure your Casey is great."

"He is. He's the best."

"I'm sure he is." I hoped the other Casey was too. "So listen, I wanted to ask you something. Do you think you could maybe do a short photo shoot for me?"

"Did I miss something? Are you getting married too?"

I laughed. "Hardly. But I *do* need to document a labor of love with some photos, nothing fancy. It's just something I've been working on, and if things work out, I think I could use your help even more. You think maybe we could get together soon? I'll explain more later."

"Sure, just let me know where and when, and we'll make it work."

"Cool, thanks Ivy."

"No problem."

I hung up and leaned back into the couch, wondering if any good reader e-mails had come in over the weekend. I could use a laugh, not to mention some additional material for my new idea. I picked up my wineglass and walked into my office.

Dear Waverly: I recently started dating a woman who has a little dog that she dresses up and carries around in her purse. She takes the dog absolutely everywhere, even to the movies. I keep telling her how inappropriate it is, but she doesn't listen to me. What should I do to get through to her?

My reply: I'm sorry, honey, but did you just say you CHOSE to start dating, i.e., the opposite of CHOSE NOT to start dating, a grown woman who carries a dressed-up dog around? And if she takes the pooch, as you say, "absolutely everywhere," I assume it was present when you first met this woman, yet you still decided to ask her out. Hmm...methinks that makes you...a moron.

Dear Waverly: Why do women wear a face full of makeup to the gym? I can understand if they're coming from work, but I'm talking about a Saturday morning spin class here. I know it shouldn't bother me, but I think I hate them. Am I evil?

My reply: *Honey, I lump women who wear makeup to the gym into the same category as those who yap on their cell phones in restaurants or wear ski jackets when they're not skiing. As my yoga teacher says, you just can't argue with crazy. Namaste.*

Dear Waverly: My boyfriend just gave me a bouquet of yellow roses. Thoughts?

My reply: I hate to say it, honey, but you're gonna get dumped. For those of you out there who don't speak flower, yellow roses = not smitten. Now if you come home to find him waiting on your door-step with RED roses...that's another story. Note to guys out there: non-yellow flowers + waiting on doorstep = FANTASY COME TRUE. (Huge bonus points for red roses.)

Dear Waverly: I got my teeth cleaned yesterday, and my dentist told me I have stains from drinking too much red wine. Just wanted to share.

My reply: *OMG, honey, will you be my BFF? Oops, I just got so emotional that I spilled some on my keyboard. P.S. I heart you.*

I chuckled at the computer screen, then noticed that my wineglass was nearly empty. *Perfect timing.* I scribbled a few ideas in my Honey notebook before returning to the kitchen for a refill.

Chapter Twenty-Two

About a week before my meeting at Smithers Publishing, I was at my desk, looking through my Honey notebook, when I heard my doorbell ring. I put my pen down, closed the notebook, and put it in a drawer.

"Yes?"

"It's me. Will you buzz me in?"

"Andie?"

"Yes, will you please buzz me in?"

Why didn't she call first? I opened the door, and a few seconds later I saw her walking toward me.

She was crying.

"Andie, what's wrong?"

She passed me and went straight to my couch. "Do you have anything to drink?"

I followed her. "You mean something alcoholic?"

She gave me a look that said, *Are you really that stupid?*

"Red wine okay?" I said quickly.

"Bring the bottle."

I opened a bottle of pinot noir and poured two glasses, then went into the living room and sat down next to her.

"What's going on?" I handed her a glass.

She took a huge gulp, then wiped a tear from her cheek and looked at me.

"I was right."

"Right about what?"

"About CJ. He's seeing someone else."

"What? Are you sure?"

She nodded slowly and took another gulp of wine. Her eyes were watery and blank. I realized I'd never seen her cry before.

"What happened?"

She closed her eyes. "I can't believe this, Waverly. I feel so... sick."

I reached over and squeezed her knee. Andie was the strongest person I'd ever met. It was breaking my heart to see her so upset.

"My mom is going to go nuts over this if she ever finds out. Yet another reason to badger me about being single."

"Andie, what happened?"

She took another drink. "I...I saw him."

"You *saw* him?"

"I...I stopped by his apartment...to say hi...and I saw him through the window...with someone else...he was kissing someone else."

"No way."

"Way."

I put my hand over my mouth. I couldn't imagine what that must feel like. At least with Aaron, and then with Jake, I'd been spared *that*.

"I can't believe I didn't put the pieces together. From day one, it was right there, right in my face, but I didn't want to see it."

"Don't blame yourself. You couldn't have known."

"I should have known. All those times...in the bedroom...I should have known. I'm so stupid."

"You're *not* stupid."

"I certainly feel stupid."

"Well believe me, you're not. What *is* unbelievable is that you saw Mr. James with someone else."

"Mr. James?"

"Isn't James his last name?"

"That's his middle name."

Oh.

This was unexpected. I hadn't thought about middle names. So maybe CJ *had* been kissing Ivy? Was it really the same guy? I was totally confused.

"What's his last name?" *Please please don't let it be Thompson.*

"Myers."

Not Thompson!

I was so relieved, not for Andie, but for Ivy. *One out of two is better than nothing,* I thought.

For a long while Andie stared at her wineglass without speaking. Finally she turned to face me.

"Waverly."

"Yes?"

"That's not all."

There's more?

"He was…he was…"

"He was what?"

"He was…he was kissing a *guy.*"

"WHAT?"

She nodded slowly, a pained look in her eyes.

"A guy? As in he's gay?"

She nodded again.

I wanted to say something more, but nothing came out.

"It all makes sense now," she said. "Everything makes sense."

"But why didn't he tell you? I mean, this is *San Francisco.*"

"I know, I know. Leave it to me to fall for the one gay guy here who's still in the closet."

"I didn't think *any* gay people here were still in the closet. That's so, so *old school*."

She took a drink of wine and tried to laugh. "He's from Nebraska, remember?"

"Oh, Andie, I'm so sorry."

"Me too. I really liked him, Waverly. I *still* like him. How messed up is that?"

"It's not messed up. It's unfortunate, but it's not messed up. I mean, at least you found someone to care about, right?"

She looked at me. "Are you seriously trying to look on the bright side here?"

"Yes?"

"There's no bright side here."

"Hey now, that's not true. Remember what you told me when I got back from Atlanta?"

"Not really." She finished off her wine and looked over my shoulder. "Do you have any donuts?"

"Well, let me remind you." I stood up and backed into the kitchen. "You told me what a big step it was to put myself out there like that, how I wouldn't have even considered doing something like that a couple years ago. That I wasn't a fool for trying." I pulled a bag of Chips Ahoy! cookies down from the cupboard and held them up. "Will these do?"

She gestured for me to bring her the bag. "That's true, I did say that. And a couple years ago you *wouldn't* have done that."

"So look at *yourself*, Andie." I handed her the cookies. "You just had a relationship with a guy that wasn't purely physical, and yet you really cared about him. You just said yourself that you *still* care about him. Caring for someone hardly makes you a fool, right? Isn't that what you and McKenna have been telling me?"

She opened the bag and shrugged.

"Maybe it's even a step forward for you? For me? For both of us?"

She put an entire cookie in her mouth and shrugged again.

I pointed at her. "Come on, Barnett, you know I'm right."

She laughed just a little bit and choked down the cookie. "Maybe I should write to your column, see what your alter ego has to say about it."

I refilled both our wineglasses and took a sip of mine. "I'm guessing my alter ego would say that you can't stop believing in love, no matter how hard that may be. We all have to believe in love."

She pulled another cookie out of the bag. "That's *definitely* your alter ego talking."

"Why do you say that?"

"Because I get the feeling that *you* stopped believing in love the day Jake McIntyre got on a plane to Argentina."

I put my wineglass down. "Actually, I've been meaning to talk to you about that."

"About Jake?"

"About Jake *and* about my alter ego."

"Well? Let's hear it."

"Give me a little time, okay?"

Chapter Twenty-Three

The day finally came for my meeting at Smithers Publishing. I paired a dark green dress with my best silver link necklace and matching earrings, then pulled my hair back into a low, sleek ponytail and slipped on a pair of black boots. I stood in front of the full-length mirror in my bedroom and smiled. I felt professional, confident, and excited. In a way I was looking not just at my reflection, but at my future.

I put on my coat, then bent down to pick up the cardboard box that, thank God, had arrived in time.

An hour before the meeting, I stopped by the *Sun*. Eloise Zimmerman's secretary had left me a voicemail asking me to drop by her office at some point during the week. She hadn't specified a day or a time, so I figured I might as well go then. That way I would only have to get dressed up once.

I stopped first on the eighth floor to see if Nick was around. I found him working intently at his desk.

"Hey, stranger, how are you?" I said.

He turned around and smiled, then put a finger to his lips. You'd think I'd learn to stop interrupting him. I put the box down and turned on my heel toward the kitchen. On the way there I passed by Larry Bergman's office, still quiet, dark, and empty. The entire floor was subdued, with nearly as many vacant cubes as occupied ones. It all felt so stiff, so stale. *Are they ever going to refill those positions?* I was glad to have Eloise in my corner.

A few minutes later, I returned to Nick's cube holding a cup of coffee for each of us. This time he turned around and stood up.

"Bryson, how are you? It's been ages." He held his arms open to reveal a green T-shirt that said "WITTY SAYING" in white.

I laughed and placed both cups on his desk, then straightened up to give him a hug. "I brought you some caffeine. And I love the shirt."

"Of course you love it. It's amazing. Why are you so dressed up? You look hot."

I curtsied. "Why thank you. I've got a meeting with Eloise Zimmerman."

"You two still buddy-buddy?"

I smiled. "Actually, the column is going really well. The e-mails I've been getting from readers are mostly positive. Eloise said advertisers like my demographic."

"Sounds like you're cruising along splendidly."

The second I heard the word *cruising*, I yelled, "Oh my God!" then immediately covered my mouth with my hands. "Oh my God," I whispered. "I totally forgot to tell you. I figured out the deal with Ivy's boyfriend."

He raised his eyebrows, and I could see the hope in his eyes. "And?"

I shook my head. "Different guy."

His shoulders dropped a bit.

"And get this. It turns out that my friend Andie's guy *was* cheating on her, just not with another woman."

"You mean…?"

"Yes, I mean."

"For real? With a dude?"

"For real. With a dude."

He sat down in his chair. "Ouch."

"Tell Andie about it. She's pretty down. And she's never down about *anything.*"

He stroked his chin. "Hmm. Now *that* would make a sweet T-shirt."

"What would? You mean what happened to Andie?"

"Think about it. How amazing would it be to see me in a shirt that says, 'DON'T YOU WISH YOUR GIRLFRIEND WAS HOT LIKE ME?'"

I kicked him in the shin. "Hey now, Andie *is* hot. Any guy would be lucky to have her. Any straight guy, that is."

"Ouch." He leaned down to rub his leg. "That hurt."

I picked up the box. "The truth hurts, my dear. Now if you'll excuse me, I have a meeting."

* * *

"Eloise?" I leaned my head into her office. She was sitting at her desk in front of her computer. "Is now a good time?" I smiled at her.

She turned her severe profile toward me. "I prefer Mrs. Zimmerman."

"Oh, I'm sorry." I could feel my cheeks turn red.

"Please, have a seat." She slowly swiveled her chair to face me, and I sat down across from her and set the cardboard box on the floor. She was wearing an expensive beige pantsuit and pearls, her hair in her usual stiff beehive.

"I got a message that you wanted to see me?"

"Yes. Thank you for stopping by."

I shifted in my seat and smiled again. "I wanted to let you know that I've been having a lot of fun with the column, and the e-mails I've been getting from readers lately have been extremely positive—well mostly positive. In fact, just the other day I ran into—"

She held up her hand. "The reason I asked you to stop by is to inform you that we've decided to make some more editorial changes, one of which regards Honey on Your Mind."

I swallowed.

"We've decided go with Love, Wendy."

What?

"Love, Wendy? You mean Wendy Davenport's column?"

She rolled her pearls between her fingers. "Her popularity is growing quite rapidly, especially now that she has her own TV show."

"Oh."

What does that mean for me?

I bit my lip "So what does that mean for—"

She interrupted me again. "It's more economical for us to subscribe to a syndicated column than to pay for original content. Unfortunately, that means we no longer need your services, effective immediately."

My jaw dropped. Wendy Davenport, aka resident bottle blonde nightmare, had just taken *my* job? Effective immediately?

"Of course you can finish whatever you're currently working on, but that will be all." She swiveled her chair toward her computer, signaling that the meeting was over.

I sat there for a moment, not sure what to do.

"Did you need something else?" she said with her back to me.

I stood up slowly.

That's it? No parting words? No thanks for a job well done?

"Um, no, Mrs. Zimmerman."

I picked up the box and quietly left her office.

* * *

"Waverly, it's so nice to see you again."

"You too, Wyatt. Thanks for having me." We were in the Smithers conference room. I was still rattled from my meeting with Eloise, but I forced a smile as I stood up to shake his hand. Wyatt Clyndelle, for better or for worse, looked exactly like Clay Aiken. I really liked him.

"Can I get you a drink? Dean is on his way."

"Anything with caffeine and sugar would be great."

"I think I can manage that."

He left the room, and I sat back down and pulled a manila folder out of my bag. I glanced at the floor next to me, where I'd placed the cardboard box. I set the folder on the table.

You can do this. Forget about the Sun.

Wyatt and Dean Paxton entered a few minutes later with a tray of cappuccinos. I stood up again to greet Dean, whom I hadn't seen since the launch of my Honey Notes nearly a year before.

"Dean, hi, it's nice to see you." I extended my hand.

"Likewise." He took my hand and shook it. "Welcome back."

We settled into our seats and made light chitchat. After a few minutes Wyatt cleared his throat just slightly, enough to signal the start of the meeting.

"Waverly, to begin I must admit that we were both happy and a bit surprised to hear that you wanted to meet with us. We'd nearly given up on you."

"I'm glad to be here, and thanks for *not* giving up on me."

They both smiled politely.

I swallowed. "Well, like you just said, I know you've been waiting for me to come up with some more ideas for Honey Notes, which I've finally done. I'm sorry about the delay. I guess you could attribute it to a form of writer's block. Life-induced writer's block."

They laughed, and I opened the manila folder on the table and pulled out several sheets of new ideas for Honey Notes, then slid them across the table. "You'll see that this time I've gone with occasions: *birthday, Christmas, Hanukkah, Valentine's Day*, and *thank you.*"

They each took a page. Wyatt began to nod his head as he read. So did Dean.

"These are great, Waverly," Wyatt said. "Occasion-focused cards are exactly what we wanted." He handed his page, the one with birthday Honey Notes, to Dean. I'd put my two favorites at the top:

Front: Sick of seeing other women in your office get flowers on their birthday?
*Inside: Honey, they probably sent them to themselves. And if **they** didn't send them, whoever did is probably ugly anyway. Happy birthday!*

Front: Can't take another birthday without a boyfriend?
Inside: Honey, that's okay. Your girlfriends are here for you! And you know you hate wearing lace underwear anyway.

Dean laughed. "Not bad, Waverly."

I smiled. "Thanks."

"We'll definitely run these by the team," Wyatt said. "I'm sure they'll love them."

"I appreciate that. But that's not the only reason I wanted to meet with you today."

"It's not?" Wyatt said.

I shook my head. "I've come up with something else I'd like to share with you. That's another reason it's taken me so long to get in touch. I wanted to do something…more."

"More than the Honey Notes?" Dean said.

"Much more."

"Let's hear it," Wyatt said.

Then I told them my idea.

* * *

Fifteen minutes later, I sat with my hands interlaced on the table in front of me, waiting for one of them to say something. Wyatt was still reading the new papers I'd pulled from my manila folder.

Finally, Dean spoke. "I'm impressed, Waverly. That's definitely more than Honey Notes, and extremely creative as well."

I smiled. "Thanks."

"I agree," Wyatt said. "Well done, Waverly. We'll run this by the powers that be and see what they say. Give us a week or two to get back to you, okay?"

"Sure, that sounds good."

He pushed his chair back and stood up. "Thanks so much for coming in. I appreciate all the thought you put into this. So we'll be in touch?"

I nodded. "I look forward to it."

The three of us exited the conference room together. I thought it had gone well, but I wasn't sure what would happen next. After what had just happened to me at the *Sun*, I wasn't sure about anything.

Actually, that's not true.

I was one hundred percent sure that my dress had nothing sticking to it.

Chapter Twenty-Four

Later that week, I suffered through my first yoga class in months. I hadn't even made it back to my apartment when every muscle in my body started tightening up. What is it about yoga that uses muscles you didn't even know you had? And if you didn't even know you had them, why do you need them anyway?

On the way back up Fillmore, I stopped in front of the empty storefront Red had shown me. I peered inside, imagining what it would look like as something new.

I wondered when I'd hear from Wyatt and Dean. It hadn't even been a week yet, but I was anxious. For a moment I thought of McKenna and Andie, of Ivy, of Nick, of Jake, of Red, of everyone in my life who'd played a role in my new idea. I turned away from the store and continued up Fillmore. I crossed Sacramento, then ducked into Noah's Bagels to buy an Odwalla. When I got back to my street, I saw Red leaving our building.

"Red." I approached him with a smile. "How are you?"

He tipped his head. "Why hello there, Miss Waverly. I'm doing just fine. How are you?"

My eyes moved from his impeccable suit and hat to my long, hooded Cal Berkeley sweatshirt draped over my yoga pants. "I'm doing better than I look, I promise."

He laughed. "You're as lovely as ever, my dear."

"Thanks, Red. Where have you been? I haven't seen you in a while."

A shadow flickered across his eyes, and then it was gone. "I went back to Springfield for a bit, to attend to some personal business. I may be leaving here for good soon."

"Really? But it seems like you just got here." I was surprised by how much the thought of his leaving upset me.

"Time does fly. It's one of the wonders of life. How's that writing of yours going?"

I felt a chill in the air and crossed my arms in front of me. "Actually, in a roundabout way it's led me to something I'm really excited about. So I'm really...well...excited." I smiled at him.

"Why that's splendid, Miss Waverly. You see, sometimes it takes a while to put the pieces in place."

"I think you're right."

"And I love seeing that pretty smile of yours again."

"Thanks, Red. I like seeing it too."

"I tucked another letter under your door. Looks like it was delivered to my place when I was in Springfield."

"Another one? Our postman really needs to stop sniffing the glue on those envelopes."

He chuckled. "Well, you take care now, Miss Waverly. I'll be seeing you real soon."

"Bye, Red."

He tipped his head and ambled slowly toward Fillmore Street. I watched him for a moment as I fished my keys out of my pocket. When I opened my front door, I bent down to pick up the envelope he'd slid underneath. I was about to open it when I heard my phone ringing in my office. I hurried down the hall, tossing the envelope toward the coffee table as I passed by the living room. I checked the caller ID, but it was a private number.

"Hello?"

"Waverly, it's Wyatt Clyndelle."

I sucked in my breath. "Wyatt, hi. What's up?"

He paused for a moment, and I held my breath.

"I'm sorry, Waverly, but we're going to have to pass."

I frowned. "Really?"

"The thing is, we're a publishing company. And while it's a fun idea, we just don't see how it would fit into our product line. I'm sorry."

"Oh," I said softly.

"The good news is that everyone here loves the new Honey Notes you came up with. We'll definitely work those into our next product cycle."

"Okay."

"I'll keep you posted on their status, okay?"

"Okay, thanks Wyatt."

"Take care, Waverly."

I hung up the phone and sighed.

Fired by the *Sun*, then rejected by Smithers. Minor celebrity or not, how quickly I'd gone from up-and-coming columnist and aspiring entrepreneur to…unemployed.

Suddenly I wanted to go for a run. Even though I'd just come from yoga and was already pretty tired, I thought it might clear my head. I went into my room and changed into shorts and a long-sleeve shirt, then laced up my running shoes and headed out the door, unsure of which direction to go.

How appropriate.

I thought about it for a moment, then decided to retrace the steps of the walk McKenna and I used to take before work, back when she lived around the corner and I worked at KA Marketing. Maybe something familiar, something from the past, would help me feel less anxious about the future.

I'd never done the route as a run, if you could call my sluggish pace a run, and never without McKenna. This time I noticed several things I'd never paid any attention to before. A pretty house here, a postcard view there. It was all familiar, yet unfamiliar.

Beauty that had always been there, but which I'd never taken the time to notice.

When I reached the Lyon Street steps, the steepest part of the hill leading back to my neighborhood, I stopped to stretch my legs before putting them through the pain I knew was coming. I set my right foot on a bench and leaned forward. My body was sore, but the disappointment I felt hurt more.

Smithers had shot me down. Eloise Zimmerman had canceled my column. What was I supposed to do now?

I still had my Honey Notes, but they weren't enough.

* * *

When I got home, exhausted and vowing never to run the Lyon steps again, I kicked off my shoes and dragged myself to the kitchen for some water. I refilled it once more and plopped on the couch, too tired to take a shower just yet.

I lifted my head toward my still shaking legs. "Legs, please forgive me. I'm so sorry, but I really needed that."

Then I noticed the letter on the floor near the coffee table, which I'd totally forgotten. I leaned down to pick up the envelope and studied the neat red handwriting. *Who are these letters from?*

I removed the sheet of paper inside. Like the others, this one had a single word. But unlike the others, it didn't make any sense.

ve

"Ve? What is ve?"

I stood up and went to the bookcase, then ran my fingers across the spines until I stopped at a huge Webster's Dictionary. I pulled it down and sat back on the couch. I flipped to the

V section and ran my finger down the side of the page. *Vault, vaulting, vaunt, VD (yuck), veal, vector...*

I moved my finger to the top of the page and repeated the search.

"Ve" apparently meant...nothing.

What?

I tossed the letter on the coffee table and stood up to get some more water. Halfway to the kitchen, I froze.

Red's words from earlier rang in my ears.

Sometimes it takes a while to put the pieces in...place.

Suddenly my legs weren't so tired. I hurried to the coffee table, picked up the letter, and ran to my office. I opened the desk drawer and reached toward the back. I unfolded the other two anonymous letters I'd received and laid all three side by side.

be ... lie ... ve

believe

Believe?

I glanced at the floor, where the cardboard box I'd brought to Smithers was sitting. Then I stood up straight and looked at the mirror on the wall.

I smiled at my reflection.

All the pieces *were* there. They'd been there all along.

It was time for me to put them together.

"I *do* believe," I said to myself.

Chapter Twenty-Five

I checked the clock as I sliced the apples. It was nearly seven o'clock. *Ack.* I opened a box of water crackers and placed several on a platter with cheese and grapes, then ran into my room and stripped. I tossed my clothes in the hamper and opened my closet, pulling out a pair of jeans and a sleeveless black top. I slipped on some green flats and rushed into the bathroom to brush my hair.

At seven sharp, the doorbell rang. I ran to the bathroom mirror and dusted a blusher over my cheeks. *I hope it's just Andie,* I thought. I'd invited her, Red, Nick, and Ivy over, and while I couldn't care less what Andie thought of me or my apartment, I wanted to look nice for the other guests, especially Red. McKenna couldn't make it because she and Hunter were meeting with their realtor to make an offer on a house.

I trotted to the front door and pressed the intercom. "Hello?"

"It's me," Andie said.

"Cool." I buzzed her in and opened the door, then went back to the bathroom to put on some lipstick.

When I joined her in the kitchen a few minutes later, she had cracked open a bottle of wine and was munching on a cracker. "So what's the big news?"

"You'll see soon enough." I opened the cupboard and pulled down four more wineglasses. "Is this enough food? Do you think I should open a bag of chips?"

She nodded. "People will always eat chips."

I opened a bag of Ruffles and a can of mixed nuts, then poured them into bowls and set them on the table.

"You seem nervous," Andie said.

"I *am* nervous."

"Why?"

"I don't know, I just am." I turned toward the living room.

"I saw CJ yesterday."

I stopped in my tracks.

"No way."

"Way."

"What happened? Where did you see him?" After she'd spotted CJ kissing a guy, Andie had broken things off without telling him why. She didn't want to out him before he was ready to do it on his own.

"At Naked Fish on Chestnut. I was getting takeout, and I saw him there with some guy."

"The guy from the sighting?"

"I think so."

"And?"

"I went right up to their table to say hi, and CJ looked like he might jump right up to the ceiling and hang on with his fingernails."

"What did he say?"

She shrugged. "Nothing really, I mean, now that I *know*, it's sort of sad to watch. They were obviously together, but he was so clearly uncomfortable. It must be so hard to live like that."

"I can't imagine."

"So anyhow, I wanted to figure out a way to let him know that I'd be cool with knowing, even though I didn't want to come right out and let him know that I know, you know?"

I squinted at her. "What?"

"I wanted him to know he can be himself with me."

"Why didn't you just say that?"

"I just did. Anyhow, I gave him a hug and said I've loved knowing him, and that he's a wonderful guy, and then I whispered in his ear that maybe, when he's ready, we could go to a Ricky Martin concert together."

I laughed. "You did *not.*"

"I did."

"You think that was *subtle?*"

"Nebraska, Waverly, he's from Nebraska."

The doorbell rang. Still laughing, I walked over to answer it. "Hello?"

"It's Ivy and Casey."

Ivy *and* Casey? I buzzed them in, then sneaked a peek back at Andie, who was still in the kitchen. *Hmm.* At least this would put an end to the mystery once and for all.

A few moments later, Ivy bounded through the door. I gave her a hug, and she turned to the tall blond guy standing next to her.

"Waverly, this is Casey. I hope you don't mind that I brought him along, but…we just got engaged!" She held up her left hand, a diamond sparkling on the ring finger.

"Wow, congratulations." I gave her a hug. "That's wonderful!"

"It was a complete surprise, and it literally just happened, so I couldn't just leave him alone after that. But I couldn't bail on you either, so we're going to dinner after this. It's really okay?"

"Of course it is. This won't take that long. Come on in, have some wine. And Casey, it's great to finally meet you." I led them into the living room. Andie was now sitting on the couch. "Andie, this is Ivy and Casey. They just got engaged."

I watched for a reaction on her face, but there was none. She stood up and smiled. "It's nice to meet you both. Congratulations!"

"It's nice to meet *you,*" Ivy said. "Waverly's mentioned you many times. I hear our crazy mothers would get along fabulously."

Andie laughed. "I like you already."

"Andie, will you help me get them some wine?" I gestured toward the kitchen, then turned back to Ivy and Casey. "You two, please make yourselves comfortable."

When we got into the kitchen, I lowered my voice. "Don't you think he looks a lot like CJ?"

She gave me a strange look. "What?"

"Casey and CJ. Don't you think they look alike?"

She took a step back toward the living room to look at Casey, then shrugged. "A little, yeah, I can see that. But CJ's *way* shorter."

"He is? He looked so tall when I met him."

She laughed. "Waverly, I'm a hobbit. *Everyone* looks tall next to me."

I laughed too. All that stress for nothing. I would make a horrible eyewitness. We brought wine out to Ivy and Casey, and the doorbell rang. "That must be Nick." I walked to the front door to buzz him in, then waited so I could warn him that Casey was there.

A moment later, I saw him. He was wearing a button-down tan shirt with super thin blue stripes.

"Nick, you look great."

"Thanks, I wanted to look nice for, you know..." His voice trailed off, and my heart broke for him.

"Listen, Nick—"

"Is that Prodromou?" I heard Ivy's voice from the living room, and before I could say anything more, Nick had passed me. I turned around to see Ivy running up to hug him.

"Hey, stranger, it's so great to see you," she said.

"Of course it is. It's nice to see you too."

Then she turned to Casey, who was still seated on the couch. "Nick, this is Casey. We're getting married!"

I could see a brief flash of pain in Nick's eyes, but like a gentleman he hid it with a smile. "Wow, that's great news."

"Thanks." Ivy grabbed Casey's arm with both of hers and pulled him up. "Can you believe it?"

"Congratulations." Nick extended his hand to Casey. "She's a great girl."

Just then Andie returned from the bathroom. "Waverly, I love that new hand soap. It smells just like cranberry. Makes me crave a vodka cranberry. You got any vodka?"

Nick turned around.

"Hi," she said to him, suddenly shy. "I'm Andie."

"I'm Nick, and I love a good vodka cranberry."

I heard a knock on the door. "That's my upstairs neighbor. You guys are going to love this man." I ran to the front door and opened it.

"Hi, Red, thanks so much for coming over."

He removed his fedora and smiled. "Good evening, Miss Bryson. How can I be of help?"

I shook my head and motioned for him to enter. "You've already done *more* than enough. Now please, come meet my friends."

* * *

After everyone had been drinking and chatting for a few minutes, I stood up and tapped a fork against my wineglass.

"Thank you all for coming tonight, even though I didn't explain why I needed you here."

Andie held up her glass. "Free wine."

I smirked at her. "And Casey, I know you don't even know me, so thanks for dealing."

He held up his glass too. "Free wine." Ivy laughed and lightly hit him on the knee.

"Anyway, as the rest of you know, the past year or so has been about transition for me. Quitting my job, turning thirty, trying to figure out my next step in life, occasionally freaking out about it, et cetera."

They all nodded.

"Also, as you know, as part of this transition I launched a line of greeting cards for women called Honey Notes, and until quite recently I also was working as columnist for the *San Francisco Sun*."

"Acclaimed columnist," Nick said.

"Extremely talented," Andie said.

I laughed. "While the main purpose of the Honey on Your Mind column was to answer questions about relationships and dating, I received a lot of e-mails that didn't contain a single question."

"I miss those," Ivy said.

I shifted my weight from one leg to the other. "And some of the e-mails didn't really have anything to do with dating, either."

"I miss those too," Ivy said.

"The thing is, through all the e-mails people sent to Honey on Your Mind, I realized there are a lot of people out there who like to, well, share what's *on their mind*, so to speak."

I saw confusion on everyone's face except for Red's. He smiled as if he understood perfectly well.

"What I'm trying to say is that I think people could relate to what I was writing about, which made them want to share their own stories, even if they weren't actually asking for advice."

More confused faces.

"At first I didn't get it, but then I realized something. People were writing me, and reading the column, because…because they like knowing that they're not the only ones who don't have life all figured out. Does that make sense?"

Everyone was nodding, but I wasn't sure anyone was following.

I took a sip of my wine. "So I started thinking about combining the idea behind the Honey Notes with some inspiration from readers, as well as from my awesome *friends*, to create an entire line of Honey products." I swept my hand across the room to emphasize the word *friends*. "It took me a while to pull it all together, but that's what I came up with, and I'm excited about it."

Everyone raised their eyebrows. They were clearly lost. Everyone except Red, who smiled.

"I know I'm not explaining this very well, but what I'm trying to say is that instead of worrying about what to do next with my life, why not make *life itself* the focus of what I do next? The goal would be to make people point and nod and think, *Yes, that's totally true!* Whether the products are about dating...or just about...life."

"Life?" Andie said.

"Yes. I guess you could say this would be a line of products about...*life*."

"Why didn't you just say that in the first place? I think I fell asleep for a few minutes there."

I pointed at her. "Hey now, be nice."

"I'm just keeping it real." She leaned forward and refilled her wineglass.

"Anyhow, I was thinking about calling the line Waverly's Honey Shop."

"Waverly's Honey Shop?" Nick said.

"Yeah. What do you think?"

Andie looked at Ivy. "That's pretty catchy."

"I agree," Ivy said. "What would the products be?"

I leaned down to open the box on the floor next to me, then pulled out a few fitted shirts I'd mocked up. "Well first, I was thinking about Honey Tees. They'd be for women, at least to start. Some could be witty, others a bit more profound. Here are some I thought would be fun."

One by one I held the shirts up.

A pink one said, "E-MAIL BREAKUPS DON'T COUNT" on the front and "OR TEXT BREAKUPS" on the back.

A green one said, "STUFFED ANIMALS DO NOT BELONG IN CARS" on the front with "AND DOGS DO NOT BELONG IN PURSES" on the back.

A blue one said, "HAVING A PLAN DOESN'T MAKE YOU SMART."

A gray one said, "I KNOW NOTHING, BUT AT LEAST I KNOW THAT."

The last one, in black, said, "LIFE IS SCARY, NOW GET OVER IT."

Everyone laughed. "Those are great," Andie said.

Nick reached for one to get a closer look. "These definitely have the potential to be amazing. Of course, I like to think I'm somewhat of a role model for you."

I laughed. "Of *course* you are. You're awesome."

"What else do you have in that box?" Ivy said.

I leaned down and pulled out two neutral-colored tote bags and one black one. "I was also thinking about doing Honey Totes."

"Honey Totes?" Andie said.

"Yep." I held one up that said, "MAKE HAPPILY EVER AFTER HAPPEN" in bright blue. The second bag said "JUST SMILE" in pink.

I turned to Red. "These first two are all you."

"I'm honored, Miss Waverly."

Then I held up the black one. It said, "IS IT WORSE TO BE FAKE OR BITCHY?" on the front and "HONEY, JUST FACE IT—IF YOU'RE ASKING, YOU'RE PROBABLY BOTH" on the back.

I laid all three totes on the coffee table.

Ivy reached over and picked one up. "These are cute. I would totally use them."

"Me too," Andie said. "Especially if you made one with that stuffed animals line on it. I can't *stand it* when people have a million stuffed animals in their cars."

"Anything else in that bag of tricks?" Nick said.

I set my glass on a bookshelf, then reached into the box and pulled out a wine bottle sack and six matching coasters that each said, "Girlfriends + Wine + Laughter = Fountain of Youth" in burgundy font.

Andie examined a tote bag while Ivy ran her fingers over a coaster. "Oh my God, I love these," Andie said.

"So cute," Ivy said.

Then I reached into my bag and pulled out a small box covered in blue and white striped fabric that said, "Stuff I'll Never Use" in bright green lettering, as well as a small blue pillow that said "Dream" in white lettering.

"Ideally these will be bigger. These are just miniature prototypes."

"Adorable," Ivy said.

"You have anything in that box that's *not* for chicks?" Nick said. "I mean, I love chicks, but I don't want to be one."

I walked in place. "Baby steps, my friend, baby steps." I reached down and pulled out an eye mask for sleeping. It was light blue and said, "Tomorrow Will Be Better" in white font.

"This one's also for you," I said to Red.

He winked.

Ivy put the mask on. "How do I look?" Casey messed up her hair and kissed her forehead.

"Waverly, these are all great," Andie said. "I'm really impressed."

"Thanks, I have a bunch more ideas, but I haven't had samples made yet." I took a sheet of paper from my manila folder in the box and held it up. "Here's a list of the other products. I was thinking I could use the tagline 'Sometimes We All Need a Spoonful of Honey,' just like on the back side of the Honey Notes."

Everyone huddled together to read. In addition to everything I'd shown them, the list included compacts, cocktail napkins, sticky notes, toiletry bags, and oversize coffee mugs. Each came with a suggested saying, but the product line and colors would be mix and match.

"This is fantastic," Ivy said.

"I agree," Nick said. "Really, Waverly, these are cool ideas."

"You think so?"

"Definitely. And you know I'm in touch with my feminine side."

"Just one of the many things that make you amazing." I interlaced my hands in front of me and made eye contact with everyone in the room. "Last week I had a meeting about this idea with Smithers Publishing, the company that makes my Honey Notes."

They all nodded.

"I was hoping they'd want to invest in the product line, maybe even help me open a store. There's an open spot on Fillmore that would be perfect." I glanced at Red, and he smiled.

"Waverly's Honey Shop," Ivy said softly, nodding slowly.

"And?" Andie said. "What happened?"

I frowned. "And they shot me down."

"What?" Nick said.

"They shot me down."

"They suck," Andie said. "I hate them."

"Why did they say no?" Ivy asked.

"They said it wouldn't fit it into their product line."

"Weak," Nick said. "Very not amazing."

Andie stood and held up an empty bottle. "I'm getting some more wine. Anyone else want some?"

Everyone raised a hand. Everyone but Red, who was drinking water.

"I'll help you." Nick stood up and followed her. A few moments later they returned with two bottles and filled everyone's glasses. I cleared my throat to regain their attention.

"When the people at Smithers said no, I thought that would be the end of it. But after briefly wallowing in self-pity, I realized how much I believe in this idea, how excited I am about it."

"It *is* a good idea," Andie said.

"You *should* be excited about it," Nick said. "Hell, *I'm* excited about it."

"So…I've decided to do it on my own. *Here.*" I pointed to the floor. "My dear friends, you are looking at the future worldwide headquarters of Waverly's Honey Shop."

"Nice digs," Nick said. "Does it have a gym?"

I laughed. "I've decided to launch the company on my own, at least online. But to do that, I'm going to need some help, which is why I've asked you here tonight."

I looked at Nick, who at the moment was staring at Andie.

"Nick, will you help me build a website? Nothing fancy?"

"Piece of cake."

Then I turned to Ivy. "Could you help with product shots, to make the selection look beautiful?"

She smiled. "I'd love to."

"And Andie, the finance wiz. I was hoping maybe you could help me with the numbers side of things? Just until I figure that out on my own?"

"Why of course. I could do that in my sleep."

"And one last thing," I said, looking over at Red. "To make life a little bit easier for those who could use some help, I'm going to donate a portion of every sale to charity, ideally one for kids. Maybe you could facilitate some introductions?"

He tipped his head and smiled. "I'd be honored, Miss Waverly."

I put my palms up and faced the rest of the group. "So you're all in?"

Nick raised his glass. "One team, one dream."

"Oh, and since the *Sun* canceled my column, I thought I could revive Honey on Your Mind as part of the site to—"

Ivy interrupted. "YES! I love that column!"

Andie raised her glass to her. "Now I know why Waverly likes you so much."

"I could say the same about you," Nick said under his breath.

I laughed. "As I was *saying*, adding the column could also help get the word out." I bent down to pull a manila folder from the box, then opened it and removed a sheet of paper with a rough timeline. "I think if I power on this, with all your help, I should be able to launch the site in…about three months."

They all nodded.

"Sounds reasonable," Nick said.

I took a deep breath. "Great. Now before we get started, there's just one more thing I have to do."

Chapter Twenty-Six

"Passport?" Andie said.

"Check."

"Credit card?" McKenna said.

"Check."

"Okay, you're good. That's all you really need," Andie said. We were standing outside McKenna's black Land Rover at the international departures terminal at SFO.

"I can't believe you're going to Argentina," McKenna said.

I held my palms up. "*Third time's a charm*, right?"

Andie blew a bubble and popped it. "I thought it was *three strikes and you're out.*"

McKenna elbowed her. "Filter."

"Ouch," Andie said.

I hugged them both. "I'll e-mail you." I reached for the handle of my suitcase and turned to go.

"*Vino* and *cerveza*," Andie said.

"What?"

"That's wine and beer, in Spanish. Make sure you remember how to say those two words, because you might need them if things don't go so well."

McKenna grabbed her arm and pulled her toward the car. "You need a time out."

Andie laughed as McKenna dragged her away. "We love you!"

"I love you too!" I blew them a kiss and entered the airport.

* * *

Nearly twenty hours later, I was in Buenos Aires. It was barely eight in the morning when we landed, which was unfortunate given that the only thing in the world that I wanted to do at the moment was lie down and SLEEP.

Feeling like something the cat dragged in, I jumped in a cab and handed the driver the address of my hotel. It was located in the Recoleta neighborhood, which I sort of remembered from my previous trip way back when. I had a full day to get used to the time change and wander around the city before Jake's team played the following evening. I also needed to figure out what in the world to say to him.

I squeezed the handle of the "Just Smile" Honey Tote I'd brought with me.

I could do this.

* * *

The first thing I did after I checked into my hotel was...pass out. I'd planned to go for a nice long run to wake myself up and explore the area, but who was I kidding?

When I woke up, it was nearly two o'clock, and for a moment I had no idea where I was. Then slowly it dawned on me. *I'm in Buenos Aires. Holy crap.* I dragged myself out of bed and took a shower, then got dressed and headed downstairs to check out the neighborhood.

Recoleta was quite charming, the tall, European-style apartment buildings adorned with flower-lined balconies. After a couple blocks I stumbled upon the center of the district, which was filled with cafés and bars and people. I spotted an empty bench near a patch of flowers and sat down. The air smelled like freshly cut grass. I inhaled deeply, closing my eyes to enjoy it. Then I heard music and opened my eyes. A girl was playing the accordion about fifteen feet away from me, her instrument case laid open on the cement in front of her to collect tips. She was young but obviously very talented, and the gentle music floated through the air over the chatter of the people strolling by or sitting in one of the many cafés lining the main walkway. From what I could tell, everyone was drinking coffee, beer, or red wine. And no one seemed in a hurry.

I sat there for several minutes, people-watching and enjoying the beautiful music. Just sitting. And listening.

After a while I decided to call it a day. On the way back to my hotel I spotted an Internet café. I ducked inside to e-mail Andie and McKenna that I was safely on South American soil.

Then I saw a new e-mail in my inbox.

It was from Paul Bryson.

Dad?

My dad had never e-mailed me before.

I clicked to open the message.

To: Waverly Bryson
From: Paul Bryson
Subject: I GOT THE INTERNET

HI WAVERLY, I AM ONLINE. BETTY GOT ME AN ACCOUNT.

LOVE,
DAD

Ah, Dad.
Gotta love the ALL CAPS.
Gotta love Betty, too.

* * *

I woke up the next morning at the crack of...eleven. I took a hot shower, then did a time check to plan the day. Jake's game was at seven, just a few hours away. I hoped I wasn't about to humiliate myself in front of him...again. I'd had enough Waverly moments around this one guy to qualify for lifetime elite status in emotional faceplanting.

Around noon I left the hotel, ready to explore the Boca district. The famous part of the neighborhood is called El Caminito, which means "the little street." True to its name, it's just a few blocks long in each direction. The area is beautiful in a wonderfully unique way. All the buildings, most of them about two stories high, are painted a mix of bright colors, some with yellow doors and blue shutters, others topped by red roofs and sporting green windowsills and hot pink trim. Arts and crafts and handmade jewelry stands fill the cobblestone streets, most of which are off-limits to cars and lined by cafés, clothing and souvenir shops that sell everything from postcards and full-length leather coats to bottle openers in the shape of Eva Peron and Diego Maradona.

Adding an extra layer to the energy of El Caminito was the distinctive sound of tango. As I began my walk along the pathway, I heard music emanating from a tiny restaurant. I poked my head inside. Two professional dancers regaled the patrons, who cheered and clapped over bottles of wine and big baskets of bread that covered their long wooden tables. The interior had high ceilings and was much larger than I'd expected. Even though everyone was sitting close to each other, the place didn't seem overcrowded, the dexterous waiters seamlessly darting in and out of the joyful crowd and looking like they were having as much fun as the tourists.

I watched the couple dance in perfect unison to the music, fascinated as much by their precision and physical beauty as by the woman's ability not to trip in her stiletto heels. After a few minutes they took a break, so I kept moving and continued to explore the area, wandering in and out of shops and eventually arriving back to where I'd begun.

With a tinge of disappointment, I realized I'd finished walking the Caminito loop. I'd enjoyed the mental break from stressing about the real reason I was there, but I knew it was time to head back to the hotel.

What in the world am I going to say to him?

* * *

At six o'clock I left my hotel again, this time in a taxi for the basketball arena. I was so nervous that my hand was shaking as I handed the driver the piece of paper with the address. I was either the most romantic person alive or completely insane, and I wasn't sure I wanted to know which.

We drove past the Obelisco, the most famous landmark in Buenos Aires, which looks *exactly* like the Washington Monument. I remember reading somewhere that once a year the Obelisco is covered in a huge condom to promote safe sex. I can only imagine the right-wing outrage if Planned Parenthood tried a stunt like that in DC.

As we rolled along, I played with my earring, mentally rehearsing what I'd decided to say to Jake. It had been weeks since we'd had any contact at all. I'd thought a hundred times about e-mailing him, but given how complicated and messed up everything had become, it just didn't seem…appropriate. I pressed my palm against my forehead. *Like flying halfway around the world— uninvited—is appropriate?*

The cab stopped, jolting me out of my thoughts. I blinked and realized we had arrived. I paid the driver, then stepped outside to find the ticket line. I had no concrete plan for reaching Jake after the game was over, but I figured if I'd come this far, I'd find a way.

* * *

A little more than two hours later, the final buzzer buzzed, and the game was over. Jake's team, Deportivo Libertad, had beaten its rival, Boca Juniors, by just two points, and the fans were going nuts. I was sitting in the home team section, so all around me people were hugging and crying. In the nearby Boca Juniors section, people were also crying, but they certainly weren't tears of joy. Apparently people in Argentina take their sports seriously.

I kept my eyes peeled to the side of the court, where I'd spotted Jake late in the first half. He'd attended to several players throughout the action, most notably an enormous man who had apparently suffered an ankle sprain. He returned to the court after Jake quickly taped him up, so I guess Jake had done his job.

As the crowd thinned, I casually made my way toward the court. The security guards were focused on herding everyone through the exits, so I managed to blend in with a bunch of official-looking people moving toward the private hallway that led to the offices and locker rooms. I followed along and put my head down, hoping no one would actually *speak* to me. Then the jig would be, as they say, up. And I'd be, as they say, on the street.

The group began to shrink as people disappeared through various doors, and it was only a matter of time before someone noticed that I didn't belong. In a moment of panic, I ducked into a ladies' room and hid in a stall.

Nice. I'm hiding in a restroom stall.

When I emerged about ten minutes later, all was quiet.

I glanced up and down the hallway.

I was alone.

Slowly I started walking, peering carefully at the closed doors. Several had the word OFICINA on them, along with someone's name. I kept moving, and soon I came across a placard that said VESTUARIO DE VISITANTES. I could hear loud voices inside.

"Visitor locker room," I whispered to myself. I'd looked up the translation for "locker room" ahead of time.

I continued walking, and then I saw it.

VESTUARIO: DEPORTIVO LIBERTAD.

I could hear the sound of voices behind this door, too.

This had to be it. I took a deep breath, then slowly pushed the door open.

Chapter Twenty-Seven

I poked my head inside and scanned the room. To the left was a long corridor lined by a row of lockers, followed by the entrance to a shower area. I could hear water running, loud voices, and even some singing. To the right was another hallway. Straight ahead of me was a sitting area with a few chairs and couches. The back wall was covered with posters and announcements in Spanish.

I didn't want to go near the showers, and I didn't want to wander into someone's office, so I walked to the back of the room and examined the posters, which were mostly of individual players. One showed the whole squad, including the coaches and support staff. I spotted Jake in the back row, his blue eyes smiling at the camera.

"Hola, Jake," I whispered.

Just then I heard a noise.

I froze.

Very slowly, I took a few steps backward and peered down the hall to the left. I saw a very tall man wearing nothing but a towel. Before he could see me, I slipped toward the couches, away from his line of sight.

The sound of voices grew louder as more men exited from the showers and headed to their lockers. I wondered if the door I'd come through was the one they'd use to leave. Was I trapped? I sat down on a couch to think.

What am I doing here?

A moment later I heard the click of the door opening.

A man in a coat and tie stood in the entrance, a clipboard in his hand and a confused look on his face.

"*Te ayudo?*" he said. I think that meant, *Can I help you?*

"Um, Jake McIntyre?" I stood up and pointed to the poster of the team behind me.

He took a few steps toward me. "Are you American?" he said in English.

"You speak English?"

He smiled. "Little bit. You are looking for Jake?"

I bit my lip. "Is he here?"

"*Un momento.*" He held up a finger and disappeared down the hall toward the lockers.

I stood there, not sure what to do. I could hear more players making their way from the showers to the lockers, some of them still singing in Spanish. Without moving my feet, I turned my head and studied the posters again.

After a minute or so, I heard the sound of footsteps.

"*Senorita?*"

Clipboard Guy was back, gesturing for me to follow him. I smiled nervously and complied. He led me down the long hallway past the lockers and stopped in front of a closed door. Then he winked and walked away.

"*Gracias,*" I said softly.

I stared at the door for a moment.

Then I knocked.

Nothing.

I waited.

Still nothing.

I knocked again, this time louder. Then I heard footsteps.

I held my breath, and a moment later the door opened.

There he was.

I think my heart may have momentarily stopped beating.

"Waverly? What are you doing here?"

I smiled awkwardly. "Um, surprise?"

"What are you doing here?" he said more quietly.

"I...I came to see you." I kept smiling and held onto my "JUST SMILE" tote bag for dear life.

He didn't smile back, and in that instant, I knew I'd made a mistake.

A horrible mistake.

Oh my God.

What have I done?

"Waverly—" He opened his mouth to speak, but I reached up and covered it with my hand, my tote bag dropping to the ground. After coming so far, physically and emotionally, I couldn't let him turn me away again. I just couldn't, not without telling him how I felt.

"Please, before you say anything, please just let me speak."

"Waverly—" he said through my hand.

"I know that it's crazy for me to be here, but I need to talk to you."

"Wav—"

"Please, Jake, please just let me say this, before I lose my nerve." I kept my hand on his mouth and used the other one to wipe away a tear from my cheek. "I know I screwed up. I know I blew it. And you were right, I wasn't ready before."

"Please, don't—"

I kept my hand on his mouth. "But I'm ready now, Jake. I promise you I am. *Please* let me show you that I am." I blurted it out, my voice rising. "I know I've been afraid, but I can't let you go just because, just because I'm scared of getting hurt again..."

"Waverly, I—"

I could feel the tears streaming down my cheeks. "I want to make it work. I don't care about distance...I don't care about your ex-girlfriend...I don't care about anything else. You...you bring out something special in me, Jake...you make me believe in myself."

"Wav—"

I kept pushing my hand against his mouth. "I know you think I'm nuts to come all this way, but I did it because...because... because I love you, Jake McIntyre. I...I...love you."

I finally removed my hand from his mouth.

"There, I said it." I raised my palms and smiled weakly at him. "Okay? I said it. I love you, Jake. I need you. I want to be with you. I'm ready to be with you. And I'm not just saying that. I *believe* it."

He sighed but didn't say anything.

My voice began to crack. "I just hope...I just hope it's not too late for you to believe it too."

He still didn't say anything, and I could feel my heart starting to break. I looked at the floor.

"Now you can say whatever you have to say. Go ahead." I was exhausted.

He took a step backward, then opened the door the rest of the way.

I looked up, and my jaw dropped.

Behind him were about a dozen extremely tall men in various states of undress, plus about six men in suits and a few others wearing white polo shirts and khaki pants, some of them holding clipboards.

Every single one of them was staring at me.

Jake held out his arm. "Waverly, I'd like to introduce you to the Deportivo Libertad squad, plus the entire coaching staff, and two assistant trainers."

"Oh my God." I covered my face with my hands.

All the men started laughing, then clapping, then cheering. "*Amor!*" one of them yelled, taking off his towel and waving it above his head. Yes, that left him naked.

Jake leaned down and whispered in my ear. "Can you give me a few minutes?"

* * *

"I can't believe I poured my heart out in front of a roomful of half-naked men. I'll never forget that fully naked guy at the end."

"Hey now, I tried to stop you, *several times*, I might add." Jake laughed and refilled my wineglass. It was about an hour later, and we were seated at an upstairs table at Las Chulitas, a trendy, intimate restaurant just a few blocks from my hotel.

"You could have tried a little harder."

"You've got quite a death grip, Miss Bryson." He put a hand on his jaw, then leaned over the table and tucked a loose strand of hair behind my ear. When he touched my skin, I felt a current of heat run all the way down the side of my body.

"I've missed you," he said softly.

I smiled. "I've missed you too. *Obviously.*"

He leaned back in his chair and scratched his eyebrow. "I still can't believe you flew all the way here. You're kind of crazy, you know that?"

I nodded. "I've come to accept that about myself."

"It suits you."

"Hey, speaking of crazy, I have a joke for you."

"Okay, lay it on me."

I sat up straight in my chair. "Okay, so these two psychologists share an office, and the Monday after Thanksgiving they're chatting about their respective weekends with their families."

He nodded.

"So they're chatting, and the first guy asks the other how his Thanksgiving went. And the second guy says, 'Actually, it didn't go so well.' So the first guy says, 'What happened?' And the second guy says, 'Well, everything was okay until we sat down for dinner.

I was sitting directly across from my mother…and I wanted a hot buttered roll. So what I meant to say was, *Will you please pass me the hot buttered rolls*. But what came out was, *You bitch! You ruined my life!*"

Jake laughed out loud.

"You like?" I grinned.

"Not bad. Not bad at all."

"Thanks." I took a tiny bow.

"That was *much* better than your peanut joke."

I pointed at him. "Hey now, I love my peanut joke."

He put his hands up. "Okay, I'm backing off. I know how fired up you can get about these things."

I laughed. "Oh my God, that reminds me, I totally forgot to show you something." Over dinner I'd told him all about my idea for Waverly's Honey Shop, but I'd left out my favorite part.

"You forgot to show me what?"

"Check this out. A Honey Tee about something else that fires me up."

I unzipped the hoodie I'd been wearing and held it open to reveal a black tank top that said, "Do Not Post What You Ate for Breakfast on Facebook."

He laughed and nodded. "Not bad."

"Thanks." I zipped the hoodie back up. "It's my way of trying to stop the madness."

"You look really pretty tonight, by the way."

"I do?"

"You do. Very pretty."

I blushed. "I'm glad you think so."

"While we're on the topic of breakfast, want to hear what else I think?" He leaned toward me and lowered his voice.

I felt my neck get hot.

"I think I'd like to have it with you tomorrow…in bed," he said quietly.

I swallowed. "You would?"

He smiled. "I would. What do you think?"

I gazed into his blue eyes and got lost for a moment. Then I smiled back.

"I think…I think that can be arranged."

* * *

We crossed the hotel lobby in silence, holding hands and savoring the anticipation of what was about to happen. When we reached the elevator, I stood in front of him and leaned my forehead against his chest. Once again I was intoxicated by his scent.

I looked up to see what floor the elevator was on. *Hurry up!* I wanted to shout.

Finally it arrived, and we stepped inside. I pushed the button for the sixth floor. Just as the doors were about to shut, a man in a suit jumped inside and hit the button for the third floor. We took a step backward, and Jake put a hand on my neck and slowly began to caress my ear. I sighed and closed my eyes.

When we reached the third floor, the man tipped his head politely before exiting. As soon as the doors closed, Jake leaned down to kiss me.

"You're beautiful," he whispered.

We didn't stop kissing until the elevator stopped again. The doors opened, and I took his hand and led him down the hallway toward my room. I fumbled for the card key as he put his arms around me from behind, distracting me so much that I nearly dropped my wallet. Finally I fished out the key and slid it in into the lock.

It didn't work.

I pulled it out and tried again.

It didn't work.

I tried a third time.

Nothing.

"Are you *kidding* me?"

Jake laughed and gestured for the key. "Let me try." As I handed it to him, he kissed me gently on the lips. Then he turned to face the door and slowly inserted the card into the lock. The green light lit up.

"You can thank me later."

I pressed a finger against his chest. "Don't get an attitude, now."

I pushed the door open, and he followed me inside. As soon as the door closed behind us, I turned to face him in the darkness.

"I want to see you," he said.

I turned on a small lamp near the bed, then tossed my tote bag and the card key on the nightstand.

I held my palms up. "Here I am."

He smiled and leaned down to nuzzle my neck. Then he gently removed my hoodie and set it on a chair. He reached for my left hand and began kissing it, slowly working his way up to my elbow, then to my shoulder and neck.

"You smell good," he whispered.

"You do too," I whispered back.

He pulled my tank over my head and laid it over the back of the chair. Then he put his warm hands on my bare waist and leaned down to kiss my collarbone.

"Your skin is so soft."

He caressed my neck with his lips while slowly running his hands over my shoulders, then down the sides of my waist to my stomach. He slid a finger under the top of my jeans, which I suddenly wished I wasn't wearing.

"You okay?"

"Mm, you have no idea."

He unbuttoned the jeans and helped me step out of them, kicking them away from us as he pulled off his shirt. I moved my eyes slowly from his sculptured chest up to his blue eyes.

"Have you ever noticed that you have a ridiculous body?" I whispered.

He smiled but didn't say anything. Instead he took my hand and led it to the button of his own jeans, which I slowly unzipped. He stepped out of them and moved toward me, pulling our bodies together. He kissed me on the mouth, gently touching my tongue with his. My whole body heated up, and I felt like I was…floating.

Finally, we broke apart. My heart was beating fast, my breath heavy.

"Waverly?" He smoothed my hair with his hand.

"Mm?"

"Thank you for finding me," he whispered.

"Thank you for helping me find myself," I whispered back.

Chapter Twenty-Eight

"A Ralph Lauren swimsuit! It's adorable! Thank you so much, Shannon." McKenna, about to pop, was graciously opening a huge stack of gifts for her daughter, who at the age of negative two weeks was already sporting a wardrobe way more stylish than mine.

Andie leaned toward me and lowered her voice. "Want to bet on how many Diaper Genies she gets? You know there's going to be at least one in that stack. There's always at least one."

I laughed. At every baby shower I'd ever been to there was a discussion about the wonders of the Diaper Genie. Sad, but true. Guys don't know this stuff. At least there were no games at this shower. That's because Andie and I were hosting it, and we hated shower games. We hated showers too, but we loved McKenna more than we hated showers.

I stood up to refill my punch glass. Neither my place nor Andie's was big enough to host a proper baby shower, so we were throwing tradition out the window and having it at McKenna and Hunter's new house up in Mill Valley. It was a two-story Victorian with hardwood floors and high ceilings. Pale pastel walls subtly changed shades with each room, and the matching furnishings made the whole place look like something straight out of a Pottery Barn catalogue. It was gorgeous and perfect, but also warm and inviting, with enough framed pictures and flea market antiques to make it look like a real home and not a generic showroom. The Kimball family was well on its way to suburban bliss.

"Is there alcohol in that?"

I turned around to see that Andie had followed me into the kitchen. "I need a drink. I love McKenna, but kill me now."

I pointed at her. "Be good."

"I know, I know, I'm trying." She leaned her hip against the counter. "I just hate showers. Bridal showers, baby showers, I hate them all. Why don't guys have to go through this hell? It isn't fair."

"Now that is a question without an answer, sort of like, *Why don't the heat lamps at outdoor restaurants in San Francisco ever work?*"

She laughed. "That is SO true. You should totally put that on a Honey Tee."

I laughed too. "It's always the same story. *Oh, we JUST ran out of propane. We're so sorry for the inconvenience.* Yeah, SURE you did. Can you lend me a blanket please?"

Andie refilled her punch. "I just want to get back to the city. Nick's taking me to see Wilco at the Fillmore tonight." Nick and Andie had been dating since about a day after they'd met at my apartment. I don't know why it had never occurred to me to set them up, but that was probably a good thing, because I was done with meddling in other people's social lives. At least those of my friends, that is. I was still excited about reviving the Honey on Your Mind column on my soon-to-be launched website for Waverly's Honey Shop, which was coming together nicely. Scotty even thought it might be a good fit for a future *Today Show* feature. If that happened, things could really take off.

"Waverly? Hello?" Andie waved her hands in front of my face.

I blinked.

"I'm sorry, did you say something?"

"What time does Jake get in?"

I blushed at the sound of his name. "Not until eight."

"Are you totally dying?"

I smiled. "You have no idea." I hadn't seen him since my trip to Buenos Aires nearly two months earlier, but we'd Skyped nearly every other day. His stint with Deportivo Libertad had finally ended, and he'd gone home to Atlanta for a few days before packing up again to come to San Francisco. He was planning to stay for a whole week, and I couldn't wait to see him.

"Everything seems to be falling into place, doesn't it? McKenna with her new house and the baby, you with your new business and Jake. Even me, dating a completely normal guy. I never thought *that* would happen."

I took a sip of my punch. "It's sort of fun, isn't it? Feeling a bit more grown up? Makes me wonder why I was so scared of it."

"Hey now, don't you go getting married and pregnant too. I mean, I'm all for your newfound love of change, but let's not get crazy or anything."

"Ha. I don't think you have anything to worry about. I think my life is going just fine as it is."

"I'll drink to that, even if it's not spiked." She held her glass up to mine.

We took our punch back into the living room, and after McKenna had opened five hundred more outfits her daughter would probably never wear, the shower was finally over.

She got three Diaper Genies.

* * *

"Thanks so much for everything. You two are the best." McKenna hugged me and Andie close. We'd cleaned up and bid farewell to the guests, and now we were saying our own goodbyes before driving back over the Golden Gate Bridge to the city.

"We'd do anything for you," I said. "Look at Andie here, spending the Saturday of the Union Street Fair at a baby shower in Marin. That's like, her biggest nightmare."

Andie nodded. "I should really be in a beer tent on Union Street right now."

McKenna laughed. "I hope you realize how much I appreciate that you're not."

"I do," Andie said with a nod as she walked down the driveway toward my car.

McKenna grabbed my arm and lowered her voice. "I want to tell you something."

Andie was already pulling out her phone, probably to call Nick. "Hey, Andie, I'll be right back, okay?" She gave me a thumbs-up, and I followed McKenna back into the house.

"What's up?"

She took my hands in hers and squeezed. "I know I haven't been around much lately, but it's not because I don't love you. You know that, right?"

"Of course I do."

"You're like a sister to me, and I feel terrible that I haven't been there for you because of, well, *her.*" She put her hand on her enormous belly. "And *this.*" She looked around her new house.

"It's okay, Mackie, really. I've grown up a lot in the last year, and maybe that wouldn't have happened otherwise. I think it was good to have to figure things out on my own for once."

She leaned forward and hugged me. "I love you, Waverly."

I hugged her back. "I love you too."

She wiped a tear from her cheek. "I have some news."

"News?"

She nodded. "Hunter and I…we're going to name the baby Elizabeth…Elizabeth Waverly Kimball."

My eyes opened wide. "You are?"

She smiled. "Are you okay with that?"

"Are you kidding? I'm more than okay with that." I leaned toward her belly and whispered. "Elizabeth Waverly Kimball, I can't wait to meet you." Then I stood up and pointed at her. "No frilly headbands, right? You promised."

"I promise. Can you believe I'm going to be a mom?"

"I believe a lot of things now." I hugged her goodbye. "But I will never, *ever*, believe that anyone looks good in skinny jeans."

She laughed. "Bye, Waverly."

"Bye, Mackie."

* * *

It was nearly five by the time I dropped Andie off at her apartment. I was looking forward to taking a quick nap on the couch before getting ready for Jake's arrival. I found a parking spot on Clay Street right by Fillmore, then popped into the corner store to buy a small carton of chocolate milk, which for some reason I'd been craving all afternoon.

I poked a straw into the carton and headed down Fillmore, then took a right on Sacramento and smiled to myself. I couldn't believe in a few hours I was finally going to see him again.

Then I stopped walking.

I already *was* seeing him again.

I squinted, and yes, there he was.

Jake McIntyre, sitting on my doorstep.

Suddenly I got nervous and flustered and excited all at the same time. I also started walking faster. *What is he doing here? Do I look okay? Can you see the punch I spilled on my dress?*

When I got about twenty feet away from him, I stopped.

"Mr. McIntyre? Is that you?"

He looked up and smiled.

"Miss Bryson, yes it's me." He stood up and held his arms out, and I practically jumped into them, nearly spilling my chocolate milk all over the sidewalk. He wrapped his arms around me.

"I thought you weren't getting in until later. I was all ready to pick you up at the airport."

He stepped back from me and turned toward my building, then leaned down to pick up a large paper bag on the front step.

"I wasn't, but then I remembered something you once said."

I tilted my head to one side and looked at him. "I say a lot of things. Can you help me out here?"

"You said that you'd always dreamed about coming home one day and having a guy sitting on your doorstep, waiting for you, with flowers." He reached into the bag...and pulled out a bouquet of hyacinths.

My eyes immediately filled with tears. "I told you that?"

"Well, not to me directly, but you mentioned it once in your column." He handed me the hyacinths and set the bag down.

"You've been...reading my column?"

He nodded. "Always. So I changed my flight, and these, Miss Bryson, are for you."

I set my chocolate milk on the ground and took the bouquet. I held them close and inhaled, staring at them for a moment before lifting my gaze to meet his.

"They're beautiful, but hyacinths? Are you trying to...apologize for something?" I would never forget the hyacinths in my debacle of a trip to Atlanta. *Ugh.*

He nodded again.

"But what do you have to apologize for? You haven't done anything wrong."

"Actually, yes, I have."

He leaned down and reached his hand into the bag again. This time he pulled out a bouquet of roses, *red roses*, and handed them to me.

"Oh Jake, they're gorgeous." I leaned my face into them and closed my eyes. They smelled fresh and sweet and…wonderful.

After a few moments I opened my eyes, and as I did so he took a step closer. He put his arms around my lower back, which immediately overheated. He leaned down and lowered his voice. "I'm apologizing because I forgot to tell you something in Argentina…something important."

"You did?"

"Yes, I did, so I brought these roses along to help me say it, because I speak a little flower too, you know."

I raised my eyebrows and smiled. "You do?"

"I do." His blue eyes stared intently at me, suddenly turning from playful to…serious.

I swallowed, feeling a little wobbly.

"What are they…what are they saying?"

He held me close, then whispered into my ear.

"They're saying…I love you."

They're saying he loves me?

"They are?"

"They are."

My voice cracked. "You…love me?"

"Yes, I do. I love you, *Waberly* Bryson."

I laughed and hugged him.

"I love you too, Jake McIntyre…so *muck*."

Somewhere, far, far away, a radio had to be playing "Don't Stop Believing" by Journey.

Epilogue

Late the next morning, Jake and I left my apartment hand in hand. I planned to spend the day showing him around San Francisco. I wanted to share with him what life was like there, what *my life* was like there.

I smiled to myself as I realized that I was no longer afraid to let him in.

We were nearly to the front door of the building when I stopped. "You know what? There's someone I want you to meet."

He raised his eyebrows. "Papa Bryson?"

I pushed him in the shoulder. "Not my dad, although now that I think of it..."

"I'd love to meet your dad. Show him how I can beat you in Scrabble."

"I'll send him an e-mail about it. Or maybe I'll write on his wall. It's only a matter of time before he's on Facebook and tweeting too."

Jake laughed, then pulled me toward him and kissed the top of my head. "So who do you want me to meet?"

I nodded toward the stairs. "Mr. Springfield...I mean Red... he lives on the second floor. He's the nicest man. I don't know how he does it, but he always seems to say exactly the right words, exactly when I need to hear them. I think you'd really enjoy meeting him. And I know he'd love to meet you."

"You want to see if he's home?"

"Sure."

I'd never been to Red's apartment. Actually, I'd never been to any apartment in my building besides mine. At the top of the stairs I pointed to 2A. "There it is. You think it's too early?"

"It's eleven thirty, Waverly."

"Touché." I stepped toward the door, then realized it was already open. Not just unlocked, but *open*, like twelve inches open.

I looked at Jake and raised my eyebrows. He did the same to me.

I knocked lightly.

"Red?"

No response.

"Red? Are you there? It's me, Waverly."

Still no response.

Slowly, I pushed the door fully open.

The apartment was in disarray. Part furnished, part boxes, part…empty.

"What the…" My voice trailed off. I stepped inside and raised my palms. "What's going on?"

For a few moments we scanned the room in silence. Then we heard a voice.

"May I help you?"

We both turned around. In the front doorway stood a thin woman wearing a plain white shirt and jeans with her black hair pulled into a low bun. She was holding an empty cardboard box.

"Hi, um, do you know where Red is?"

"He's gone," she said quietly.

"Gone? Gone back to Missouri?"

She shook her head. "He passed away."

I gasped. "What? When?"

"Last week."

I put my hands over my mouth. "What happened?"

She sighed. "He went in his sleep. It was just his time."

I held out my hand. "I'm Waverly Bryson. I live downstairs. This is my boyfriend, Jake McIntyre."

She took my hand and smiled gently at both of us. "I'm Loretta Springfield. It's nice to meet you both."

"Are you his…"

"Niece. He was my mom's brother."

I put my hands across my heart. "I'm so sorry."

"Thanks."

"Did you just come in from Springfield?"

She shook her head. "I live here. My sister still lives in Springfield. She's seven months along. He was so excited to have another baby in the family. Family was really important to him."

"He mentioned that."

She smiled at an unfinished puzzle on the kitchen table. "Oh, Uncle Red. Always with the puzzles."

"Puzzles?"

"Oh yes. He *loved* puzzles. And word games. And lists. If he wasn't working on a puzzle or a word game, he was making a list of things he wanted to see, things he wanted to do."

I thought of how Red always had a crossword puzzle with him, about his clever way with words. My eyes followed hers to the kitchen table. Next to the puzzle sat a notepad with what appeared to be a to-do list.

In red pen.

Slowly, I stepped toward the table, Jake following. I stared at the paper.

Walk over the Golden Gate Bridge
Visit the Rose Garden
Buy flowers for Loretta

The words were in clear, neat handwriting…exactly like the mystery letters I'd received.

I blinked.

"This is his handwriting?"

Loretta smiled. "And he always used a red pen. That's why they called him *Red*."

"That's why?"

She nodded. "It started when he first became an English teacher, back when my sister and I were just little kids. The principal started calling him that one day, and it stuck. Words and a red pen. That was Uncle Red for you."

I looked up her, dazed. "He always had the perfect words to help me see life more clearly. From the first day I met him, it was like he already knew me. I could never figure out how."

"Oh yes, he was always keeping an eye out for others. He had a really bright future ahead of him, but when our dad died, he gave up everything so my mom wouldn't have to raise us alone."

"You mean he gave up teaching for you?"

She shook her head. "Baseball. He played in the minor leagues for a few years, the San Jose Giants, but then he took the teaching job so he could be closer to us."

The hair on the back of my neck stood up.

The San Jose Giants?

I reached for Jake's hand.

"Are you okay?" he whispered.

My mind began to race. My dad's place...his team photo on the wall...the familiar eyes...my dad's comment about his teammate's love of word games...how they always looked out for each other...how they still kept in touch...

Red had been looking out for me this whole time.

My eyes filled with tears. I smiled at Loretta and tried not to cry. "Your uncle was a wonderful man," I whispered. "I'm so sorry for your loss."

I'm so sorry for my loss too.

"Waverly? Are you okay?" Jake said.

I nodded slowly.

"Are you sure?"

I squeezed his hand and nodded again. "It's a beautiful world outside. Let's go enjoy it."

The End

If you enjoyed *It's a Waverly Life* by Maria Murnane, the (mis) adventures never end for Waverly Bryson.

Turn the page for the first two chapters in Waverly's latest story:

Honey on Your Mind by Maria Murnane
(available July 2012!)

Honey on Your Mind
Waverly Bryson Takes New York

Chapter One

"I can't believe you're giving up this great apartment," Andie said. "Do you know how many people would kill to live here for so cheap?"

I squinted at her. "You can't believe I'm giving up this *apartment*?"

She laughed and took a sip of Diet Coke. "I mean, I can't believe you're *moving*. You know I'm totally going to miss you."

"Thank you. That's much better."

She rolled her eyes. "Please, we've been over this like a thousand times. You know I hate you for leaving me."

"I know, I know. I sort of hate myself right now." I looked around the nearly empty living room, the families of tiny dust bunnies skittering across the hardwood floors. The whole place looked much smaller now than in my memory of when I first saw it. Had it already been ten years since college? Part of me could still remember what it felt like to move in...my first real apartment...my first real job...my first taste of real life.

My thoughts drifted from the past to what lay ahead and the woman who, albeit inadvertently, had made it all happen.

Wendy Davenport, ugh.

Several months earlier, my good friend Scotty Ryan, a features reporter for the *Today* show, had invited me to appear on a Valentine's Day segment about love and dating. At the time, I was writing a newspaper column on those topics, so it was a good fit, not to mention great exposure. Overall, the appearance had gone well, despite the fact that I was unexpectedly ambushed by Wendy, who also had been invited to appear. I hadn't known it at the time, but Wendy had been jockeying for a position as a TV talk show host. She showed me up on stage by asking some pointed questions about my *personal* love life that I wasn't prepared to answer at all, much less before millions of people.

Since then her syndicated advice column, *Love, Wendy*, had been turned into a full-blown TV talk show on NBC, and they'd made Scotty the executive producer. Shrugging off our rocky introduction, Scotty thought I would make a good addition to her show, and he was higher up in the decision-making food chain than she was.

Then came the phone call that changed my life.

It was a part-time gig, but part-time in TV pays the rent. It would also give me a financial boost to get my online project, Waverly's Honey Shop, off the ground. In a moment of inspiration, I'd recently launched a small line of T-shirts, tote bags, and other products with fun slogans about trying to figure life out (my personal favorite was I KNOW NOTHING, BUT AT LEAST I KNOW THAT), but it was stalled until I could improve my cash-flow situation.

"Waverly? You still there?"

I blinked. "Sorry, yep, still here. What did you say?"

"I asked when you're going to meet up with Paige."

I closed my eyes and scratched my forehead. "Um, I know the answer to that. I really do."

"So it's on your calendar?"

I opened my eyes and nodded. "It most certainly is. It's just that my calendar is currently located in a box somewhere, a box whose location is currently uncertain."

"You'll love her. She's by far the nicest person in my family. In fact, she's too nice."

I raised my eyebrows. "Nicer than you?"

She coughed and took another sip of her drink. "Yeah, right. Like you or anyone I've ever met would use the word *nice* to describe me."

I laughed and reached for a broom propped against a wall. "Good point. I'm really looking forward to meeting her."

"You know, now that I think about it, she might give you a run for your money in the 'bad date' department."

I turned around. "*Excuse* me?" I'd yet to meet anyone who could match my repertoire of dating horror stories.

"You'll see. I told you, she's a bit too nice for her own good." She pointed at me. "And as *you* know all too well, missy, nice girls get dumped on a lot."

I opened my mouth to protest, but we both knew she was right. I considered myself a nice person, and though I had a boyfriend now, my romantic history was, shall we say, *checkered*.

As I stood there holding the broom in silence, Andie finished her drink and took another look around. "So are you all packed? The taxi's coming at the crack of dawn, right?"

My eyes wandered across the room until they came to rest on a tangle of black cables sticking out of the wall. I still didn't know what half of them were for. I nodded. "I'm actually not bringing all that much with me. I realized once I started going through my clothes how I never wear most of what I own anyway. So I'm pretty much going to start over after I'm settled. It's a good excuse to go shopping in New York, don't you think?"

"Definitely. Did you end up sending all your furniture with the movers?"

I began to sweep. "Most of it. I sold some stuff on craigslist and gave some to Goodwill. I figured it would be fun to do a bit of decorating when I get there. Maybe hit some antique shows, flea markets, that sort of thing."

She put a hand on her hip. "Look at you, all Brooklyn hipster already. I'm impressed."

I laughed. "Brooklyn Heights is *hardly* the hipster part of Brooklyn. It's basically cute brownstones surrounded by cute coffee shops. And guess what? I got my new landlord to paint the walls in—"

She interrupted me. "Don't tell me. Various shades of green and blue?"

I narrowed my eyes. "How did you know that?"

"Hello? You've only been saying for years that you wanted to paint your walls various shades of green and blue."

"I have?"

"OK then, someone clearly hasn't been listening to herself. Anyhow, part of me is a little jealous of this big adventure of yours. I've always wanted to live in New York."

"Really? I didn't know that."

"Yeah, Paris, London, and New York. I've always thought they would be fun places to live at some point. I mean, look at all the action in my life right here, and San Francisco is a *fraction* of their size. Can you imagine how much trouble I could get into if I left here?"

"I'm afraid to even think about that."

She nodded. "Oh, you'll be thinking about it soon enough. Believe me, my dear, now that I have a couch to crash on, I'll be coming to visit you on a regular basis."

"You'd better."

She rubbed her hands together. "Oh, I will. Now let's go to Dino's. McKenna's probably arriving soon, and I'm starving."

I leaned the broom against the wall and picked up my purse from the floor. "Sounds good. I think this place is clean enough that I should get my security deposit back."

As we left the nearly empty apartment, I tried not to look back.

* * *

"The usual?" Andie barely glanced at me as she flagged down the waiter. We always ordered the same thing, so I just nodded in agreement. Within seconds, a frosty pitcher of Bud Light appeared on the table between us. They knew us well at Dino's.

I picked up the pitcher and poured us each a glass, then slowly looked around the restaurant. "I'm really going to miss this place, Andie."

"And this place is really going to miss you. But *you*, my friend, are on to bigger and better things, so let's be adults and deal with it." She raised her beer for a toast.

I sighed as I clinked my mug against hers. "Believe me, I'm doing my best."

"So Jake's meeting you there?"

I nodded with a smile at the thought of seeing Jake again, especially of seeing his blue eyes again. "He's going to help me unpack and get settled. He flies in Friday afternoon, and the movers arrive Saturday morning."

She covered her heart with both hands. "So romantic. At least you'll be living on the same side of the country now."

"Yeah, that should make things a lot easier. Not that I don't like Atlanta, but I'm getting sick of those long flights, not to mention the airplane hair." Jake and I had officially been a couple for six months, but it had been nearly a year since we first kissed and almost two since I'd met him. He'd been living in Atlanta that whole time—which meant an awful lot of bad in-flight movies... and flat airplane hair.

"Totally understandable. Airplane hair blows, especially when a hottie like Jake's waiting for you on the other side of security. She took a sip of her beer, and then gestured toward the entrance. "Hey, there she is."

I turned around to see an uncharacteristically disheveled McKenna approach our table. I stood up to give her a hug, but she stiff-armed me.

"I have fresh baby puke on me. You'd be wise to keep your distance." She looked exhausted.

I laughed and sat back down. "It's nice to see you too."

McKenna plopped into a seat next to Andie, whose eyes bulged at the post-baby boobs. "Holy hell, woman. Have you registered your cannonballs with the police department? You could do some serious damage with those things."

McKenna hung her purse on the back of her chair. "Always a comedian. I'm sorry for being late. Hunter was stuck in surgery, Elizabeth was having a fit trying to latch on, and I just couldn't get out of there. Then, of course, I hit traffic on the bridge. You know how it goes."

Andie picked up her beer and smiled. "Actually, I don't know how it goes, because I, as you know, am blissfully childless and live right here in the city. Did I mention I took a nap this afternoon?" She yawned and stretched her tiny arms over her head.

McKenna laughed. "Suck it."

"I'll leave that to your daughter," Andie said.

McKenna laughed again. "I hate you right now. I'm laughing, but I'm hating."

Andie took a sip of her beer. "Hey now, *you're* the one who got married and pregnant. It's not my fault that I'm well rested and having regular sex."

"Still hating you," McKenna said.

"So Elizabeth's not sleeping through the night yet?" I asked.

McKenna shook her head. "It's brutal. I adore the munchkin, I really do, but I've never been so sleep-deprived. Even in my early days of investment banking, it wasn't this bad. Who would have thought such a small person could wreak so much havoc?"

"She's not that small," Andie said. "She's sort of a chunk, if you ask me."

McKenna put her hand over Andie's mouth. "Seriously, could you shut it? I don't want to do something that will get me arrested."

I tried not to laugh. "Thanks for making the effort to come into the city, Mackie. It means so much to me that you're here on my last night."

Her face went soft. "Oh gosh, Wave, are you kidding? I wouldn't have missed it for the world. I still can't believe you're going to become a New Yorker."

"You and me both. But I just felt like I couldn't turn this opportunity down, no matter how scary it is."

She nodded. "Definitely, there's no way you could have said no. I'm going to miss you to death, but I'm so excited for you."

I interlaced my fingers in front of me. "I'm terrified, but I agree."

"I feel like I'm about to start the next chapter in The Book of Waverly—if I ever had the time to read anything besides the side of a diaper box, that is."

"Hello? I'm trying to eat here," Andie said.

McKenna ignored her and put her hand on my shoulder. "I'm so proud of you, Wave, I know how hard change is for you, but I think this will turn out to be the best thing you've done for yourself in years."

I raised my eyebrows. "Better than when I finally grew out my bangs?"

Andie sipped her beer. "And thank God you did. No one with a cowlick should *ever* have bangs. Those things were totally crooked."

"Thanks for the reminder," I said.

"My pleasure." She reached for a fresh slice of pizza. "So tell us more about the new job. When do you start?"

"In two weeks."

"I can't believe you're going to work for that woman after the way she treated you," Andie said. "Talk about a bitch."

I sighed. "I know, but I don't think I'll be working *with* her all that much, to be honest. I'll just be taping a segment for two shows a week, three if it goes well. If I'm lucky, maybe I won't have to interact with her at all."

"A control freak like that? I doubt it," Andie said.

"So the rest of the time you'll be dealing with getting your honey products off the ground?" McKenna asked.

"Yep."

Andie pushed her hair behind her ears. "That and learning how to act normal on TV. We know how well that went last time."

I winced at the memory of my one previous television appearance. Not a *complete* disaster, but hardly a smashing success. "This is true, and I promise to get better. As for the honey products, Waverly's Honey Shop may be a breakout phenomenon in our little world of three, but if I want to kick it up a notch, I really need to, well, kick it up a notch. I'm so glad Andie's cousin is going to help me with that."

"At least the TV job will help you pay for it," McKenna said.

I nodded. "Thank God. Bootstrapping my little business is turning out to be a lot more expensive than I thought it would be."

"I can't believe everything worked out this way," McKenna said. "It's almost like it was meant to be."

"I know, talk about perfect timing," Andie said.

I picked up a piece of pizza and thought about the rent-controlled apartment I'd just given up. "I hope you're right, my friends, because otherwise I just made a huge mistake."

Chapter Two

At dawn the next day, in a surreal haze of excitement, disbelief, and denial, I said good-bye to San Francisco. I locked up my apartment for the last time and hesitated before slipping the keys under the door. I couldn't help but wonder if I was making a mistake, but I knew it was too late to turn back now. I ran my fingers over the number that had marked my address for years.

Am I really doing this?

I turned and walked slowly toward the lobby. I could see the taxi waiting outside.

After standing by the front door for a few moments, I finally decided it was time to let it go.

As the cab slipped away in the early morning sunlight, I waved silently at the building I'd called home for so long. Then I turned to face forward, trying to shift my focus to the adventure ahead.

* * *

"It's beautiful, Waverly, I'm really impressed." Jake ran his hand along the crown moldings in the living room and looked up at the high ceilings.

"Isn't it great?" I walked around and began to point. "I thought I could put the couch here, the TV here, my bookcase here, and my desk here. What do you think?" I'd downsized to a one-bedroom apartment, so my living room was now going to double as an office, as well as a temporary warehouse for all my Honey products. To date, I'd been fulfilling the few orders I got with sporadic trips to the post office, but I hoped all that would change once I met with Andie's cousin, Paige.

He nodded and put his hand on the wall. "That'll work. By the way, I really like the colors you chose."

"I know, aren't they great? Isn't it all great? I've always wanted to live in an apartment with walls in various shades of green and blue. I can't believe I—"

I stopped talking and put my hands over my mouth.

"Oh my God, wait, that reminds me. I have a joke to tell you."

He laughed. "Do you *really* have to?"

I pointed at him. "You be nice. Wanna hear it?"

"Is that a rhetorical question?"

"Maybe."

He walked toward his suitcase. "I'll let you tell your joke if you let me give you something first, OK?"

My eyes brightened. "Give me something?"

"It's nothing big, just a little housewarming gift." Next to his suitcase was a medium-sized shopping bag. He picked it up and handed it to me.

"For me?"

"For you."

I opened the bag and looked inside.

It was a plant.

A plastic one.

I laughed and pulled it out. "Are you trying to tell me something?"

He put a hand on my shoulder. "Just trying to stop the carnage. I've seen what you can do."

I squeezed his hand and set the plant down. "Thanks for the vote of confidence. So are you ready for my new joke?"

"Do I have a choice?"

"Of course not. So there are these two green olives just hanging out on an olive tree, chatting about their day, when all of a sudden one of them plummets to the ground." I pretended to be an olive plummeting downward.

Jake nodded.

"So the one on the ground is just lying there on its back, stunned, and the one still safely attached to the tree yells down to it, 'Are you OK?'"

Jake nodded again.

"And the one on the ground yells up at him, 'OLIVE, OLIVE!'" Jake didn't say anything.

I held my palms up. "You get it? *O-live, I'll live*?"

He smiled. "Oh, I got it. I'm tempted to jump out the window and plummet to the ground myself, but I got it."

"Hey now, you *know* that was funny." I pushed his shoulder.

"Don't quit your day job, Miss Bryson. So what were you saying about your walls?"

I was about to reply, but when I looked into his eyes, I momentarily forgot what I was going to say. Jake's eyes, an intense blue that put my walls to shame for even trying to associate themselves with the same color family, had a way of doing that to me. I needed to come up with a new color to describe them. Plain old *blue* just didn't seem sufficient. *Hot-guy blue? Babe-ilicious blue?* Nothing seemed appropriate.

"Waverly, you there?"

I blinked. "Sorry, spaced out for a second. Um, so anyhow, I was about to say that I can't believe I found a neighborhood *and* an apartment I love as much as what I had back home. I swear I'm never moving again though. Moving *sucks*."

Jake looked at me as if he were going to speak, but instead he turned to check out the walls again. The landlord had done right by me, and the colors gave the place a fun personality that shouted *Look at me! I'm a super-cute New York apartment!* I adored it.

I'd chosen to live in Brooklyn not just because it was cheaper than Manhattan, but also because, to be honest, I was a little afraid of Manhattan. I'd been there several times over the years, and while I liked to think of myself as reasonably sophisticated, I secretly felt overwhelmed by the crowds, the shrieking of ambulances, and the constant chaos in general. Brooklyn Heights was neither scary *nor* sleepy. In fact, it was charming and clean, with tidy rows of brownstones and a village-like coziness that made me feel instantly at home. During the weekend I'd spent there looking for an apartment, I was pleasantly surprised to see that the main street teemed with more foot traffic than most neighborhoods in San Francisco. And it was right on the other side of the iconic Brooklyn Bridge, just one subway stop away from the infamous corridors of Wall Street in Lower Manhattan.

"So how'd you sleep on that thing?" Jake pointed to the blow-up mattress in my empty bedroom, where I'd just spent two uncomfortable nights.

I put my hands on my lower back and grimaced. "Let's just say I've aged a bit since Wednesday. An air mattress may feel like a normal bed at the beginning of the night, but at some point you inevitably wake up lying on the ground, surrounded by mattress."

He laughed and slid his arms around my waist. "Want to give it another try?"

I looked up at him and raised my eyebrows. "You mean *now*?"

"I mean *now*. What do you think?"

I glanced at the mattress, then back at him. My cheeks flushed. "I think…I think I could be convinced."

He smiled. "Well then, let me convince you."

He took a step toward me and gently placed one hand on the back of my neck. I lifted my head as he leaned down to kiss me, his lips warm and soft. I wrapped my arms around him and kissed him back.

"You smell so good," I whispered, suddenly feeling a little tipsy.

He briefly nuzzled my neck before straightening up and taking a step backward. He stared at me for a moment, the look in his eyes speaking for him, then pulled his T-shirt over his head and tossed it onto the hardwood floor. I admired his strong chest and abdomen. He was nearly thirty-six years old, but he looked like he could still be playing college basketball.

"Come here," he said softly.

I inched toward him. He gently pulled on the spaghetti straps of my tank top, then slowly removed it and lobbed it in the general direction of his T-shirt. He put his hands on the small of my back and pulled me toward him. We began kissing again, and I reached for the top of his jeans. I unbuttoned them and began to slide them over his hips with both hands.

Then I stopped.

"Are you going commando?"

He nodded.

I laughed. "Is this new? I've never seen you like this."

He shrugged. "It's fun once in a while. Sort of liberating. Plus, I like to keep you on your toes." As he said this, his jeans fell to the ground, and he quickly kicked them away, along with his flip-flops. I was wearing a jersey skirt, which took approximately one second for him to remove. I pushed it with my bare foot toward the growing pile of discarded clothes.

"This is sexy," he said softly as he kissed my shoulder.

"Mmm."

"*You're* sexy," he whispered, nuzzling my neck.

"Mmm."

We kissed some more, and as the heat began to spread through my entire body, I couldn't think about anything other than how attracted I was to him. We both started breathing harder, but we didn't stop kissing.

He unhooked my bra and lightly threw it on top of the clothes pile. The look in his eyes, which were locked onto mine, made it clear that neither of us wanted to be standing up anymore. He pressed his body against mine and began to move us toward the mattress.

When my foot touched the bed, I reached down with one hand and eased myself onto my back. I looked up at him, standing over me, his wavy brown hair falling into his beautiful eyes.

I reached my arms up to him.

"Now it's your turn to come here," I said softly.

He smiled and nodded.

Then he kneeled on the mattress.

He slowly began to lower himself on top of me.

Then his weight blew a huge hole in the mattress, and together we sank to the floor.

He collapsed on top of me, totally cracking up.

"Nice," he said, still laughing.

I started cracking up too. "How...ro...man...tic...but...I...can't...breathe."

* * *

The movers arrived early the next morning, and Jake and I spent the weekend getting everything unpacked and sorted. By the time Sunday night came around, we were exhausted. But at least we had my sturdy queen-sized bed on which to collapse. After the air mattress experiment had literally exploded in our faces, we'd spent Friday at a boutique hotel down the street. Jake insisted on paying. He always did.

"So tell me more about the job." He played with my fingers as we lay side by side on our backs, gazing up at the old-fashioned ceiling fan in my bedroom.

"To be honest, I'm pretty much going to be drinking from a fire hose. I don't know *anything* about how a TV show works, but Scotty said it's a lot easier than it looks, and that I'll learn as I go."

"Just don't plan on telling any of your jokes on the air."

I lightly pushed his arm. "Shut up. You know you love my jokes. Scotty's convinced that the viewers will respond to what I have to say, so he's excited to get me out there, even though I'm a total rookie."

"And what *do* you have to say, exactly?"

I laughed. "Honestly? I have no idea. *Honey on Your Mind* was always such a hodgepodge, you know? An entertaining hodgepodge based on hilarious reader e-mails, but a hodgepodge nonetheless. So I guess I'll be free to report on whatever's *on my mind*, so to speak."

He laughed. "So they really haven't given you any direction?"

"Not yet."

"Not even a list of topics to cover?"

"Nope."

"So what exactly are you supposed to *do*?"

I put my finger on his chin. "You ask a good question."

He laughed. "You really up and moved across the country without a formal job description?"

"Apparently I did. I guess I'm just trusting that Scotty will take care of me."

"You *do* realize that's a little crazy, right?"

"Good point. But we've already established that you think I'm crazy, so are you all that surprised?"

"Actually, I am. I guess your craziness never ceases to surprise me."

I pushed his shoulder again. "Be nice."

"But seriously, what's the plan?"

I shrugged. "I guess we'll see what happens at that first meeting. It should be illuminating, to say the least. I'm sure Scotty will point me in the right direction. After all, he convinced the higher-ups at NBC that I'm worth a paycheck, right? He must have *some* ideas floating around in that pretty head of his."

"Did I ever tell you that I've seen the show?"

"You've seen *Love, Wendy*?"

He nodded. "Just once, after you got offered the job. I stumbled across it on a road trip. I was ironing my shirt before a pregame meeting and turned on the TV." Jake was the head trainer and physical therapist for the NBA's Atlanta Hawks.

I propped myself up on my elbow and looked at him. "So what did you think? Was it cheesy? I'm not sure what to make of Wendy's style, especially given all that hairspray holding her blonde helmet in place. If she's not careful, she could easily catch on fire around an open flame."

"It's actually not bad. I was surprised, given how you'd described her to me. I expected her to be wearing a tiara or something."

I raised my eyebrows. "Really? You didn't think it was that bad? In the only episode I saw, she was talking about all the beauty pageants she used to compete in. After that I couldn't bring myself to watch again."

He laughed and messed up my hair. "It was fine, really. Maybe she's not as bad as you think."

"I hope you're right. If nothing else, it means so long, erratic print column and near poverty; hello, TV version and regular paycheck."

"Nothing wrong with a steady paycheck. So tell me, what's on your mind right *now*?"

I nuzzled my head against his chest. "You mean besides the fact that I'm never moving again?"

"Yes." He gently caressed my cheek.

"To be honest, it's not suitable for family-oriented programming."

"I like the sound of that." He lifted my face to his, and I immediately forgot all about Wendy Davenport.

Thank You!

My amazing sisters Monica and Michele were the first to read the initial early pages of *It's a Waverly Life*, and I can't thank them enough for gently (but firmly) suggesting I hit delete and start over. On the second try I also received much-needed enthusiasm and suggestions from trusted friends Alison Marquiss, Alberto Ferrer, Sarita Bhargava, Alexandra Kustow, Terri Sharkey, and Rob Sullivan, as well as my agents, Mary Alice Kier and Anna Cottle, none of whom were afraid to point out where the story needed work. When I finally had a finished draft, I was then awed by my editor, Christina Henry de Tessan, whose feedback and guidance helped me turn it into a novel of which I'm truly proud to be the author. She is legit, and her belief in my talent has me excited to continue the series.

Then of course there is my Mommy Dearest (yay Flo!), who has probably read this thing more times than I have. I hope she knows how much I appreciate her eagle eye for typos, not to mention all those marathon editing sessions we had over the phone. And Dad, thanks for just being there.

Despite the rocky start, writing *It's a Waverly Life* turned out to be a much smoother process than writing *Perfect on Paper*. I realize that a major reason for that was because I had absolutely no idea what I was doing the first time around, so I learned a ton along the way. However, *It's a Waverly Life* was also easier because

I looked to friends and fans for inspiration, and they didn't disappoint. Some of my favorite moments in this book happened in real life, and I'm so grateful to those who shared their hilarious stories with me. Others helped by offering their expertise, from clothing tips for men to sightseeing suggestions for a weekend in Atlanta. For all of it I offer a huge thank you to loyal readers Jendy Avens, Nicole Carpenter, Kara Dyko, Christine Le, Ciara O'Connell, Michelle Potthoff, and Kathleen Riley, and to friends Lindsay Barnett, Lauren Battle, Billy Burkoth, Geno Calixto, Donnalynn Civello, Christina Cox, Liz Doogan, Annie Flaig, Lauren Grant, Dave "Davio" Irving, Siobhan Jones, Bill Kimball, Steph Loehr, Sean Lynden, Kara Mele, Greg Miliotes, Dustin Moore, Luke Morey, Nate Prodromou, Gerun Riley, Meg Russell, Bridget Serchak, Amy Shapiro, Jessica Silverstein, James Snavely, Kristin "Lombo" Sperling, Ithti Toy Ulit, Martha West, and Chris Zaharias. You've all made me laugh out loud at one point or another, and I hope to return the favor in this book.

One last thing: Words can't express how grateful I am to Alex Carr at Amazon for making all of this happen. Waverly Bryson may have Red Springfield looking out for her, but I have Alex, and I feel just as lucky!

About the Author

Maria Murnane abandoned a successful career as a public-relations executive to pursue a more fulfilling life as a novelist and inspirational speaker. Her own "story behind the story" is an entertaining tale of the courage, passion, and perseverance required to get her first novel, *Perfect on Paper*, published. She graduated with high honors in English and Spanish from the University of California-Berkeley, where she was a Regents' and Chancellor's Scholar. She also holds a master's degree in integrated marketing communications from Northwestern University. She lives today in New York City. For more information about her books, her speaking engagements, and her consulting services, please visit www.mariamurnane.com.

27581992R00173

Made in the USA
Lexington, KY
15 November 2013